BLACK
MOUNTAIN

Gerry Adams is a former President of Sinn Féin and a former Teachta Dála (TD) for Louth and East Meath, and before that the MP and MLA for West Belfast. He has been an activist since his mid-teens and remains active in Sinn Féin and in his local community. He is a former political prisoner. In 2020, the British Supreme Court ruled that his imprisonment in the 1970s was unlawful. An internationalist, he has travelled widely – from the USA, Cuba and Palestine to the Basque Country and South Africa, he has supported progressive causes. He was one of the key figures in the Irish peace process and is now a key advocate of Irish Unity as set out in the Good Friday Agreement, which he helped to negotiate.

He is the author of eighteen books, including *Falls Memories* (1982); *The Politics of Irish Freedom* (1986), a statement of his political beliefs revised and expanded as *Free Ireland: Towards a Lasting Peace* (1995); *An Irish Journal* (2001); *Hope and History* (2003); *The New Ireland* (2005); *An Irish Eye* (2007); and *My Little Book of Tweets* (2016). *Black Mountain* is his second collection of short stories.

GERRY ADAMS

BLACK MOUNTAIN

BRANDON

First published 2021 by Brandon
An imprint of The O'Brien Press Ltd.
12 Terenure Road East, Rathgar, Dublin 6, D06 HD27, Ireland.
Tel: +353 1 4923333 Fax: +353 1 4922777
Email: books@obrien.ie
Website: www.obrien.ie
The O'Brien Press is a member of Publishing Ireland.

ISBN 978-1-84717-630-1

'A Good Confession' and 'The Mountains of Mourne' were first published
in *The Street and Other Stories*. 'Dear John' was first published in *Cage Eleven*.
'The Sniper' and 'First Confession' are extracts from *Before the Dawn*.

Cover image: Sunrise over the Trignonometry Point on the summit of
Black Mountain by Mal McCann.

10 9 8 7 6 5 4 3 2 1
25 24 23 22 21

Printed and bound by ScandBook UAB, Lithuania.
The paper in this book is produced using pulp from managed forests.

Published in:
DUBLIN
UNESCO
City of Literature

For Richard

CONTENTS

FOREWORD

I first met Gerry Adams in 1982. I was in West Belfast to talk about a book of mine, staying in what might be called a political house. One mid-morning he passed into its living room – familiar from media images, professorial in sweater and with pipe, a touch shy, perhaps, but carrying an authority I had only very rarely seen – and then passed silently out. I hadn't expected it. He seemed an apparition. But a little later someone asked on his behalf if he might be given a copy of my book. Funds were short. I said I'd trade one for his *Falls Memories*, his first.

And so we started exchanging books by post or by hand over three decades, but though writing is all I professionally do, and though he was leading a movement through war, peace negotiations and the implementation of the eventual agreement, he soon outpaced me. I am currently at seven, this is his eighteenth, and the number does not include seven biographical pamphlets commemorating people he admires and a small book of poems in Irish and English. Many, as might be expected, are acts of persuasion. Others, perhaps less expected, are acts of the imagination, like the one you are holding.

One of the poems, 'The Second Chance', addressed to his wife, speaks to the interface of the personal and the political:

Our eldest lad Gearóid
Was four and a half
Before we first walked together
Through the Royal hills of Meath.
Miles away from the barbed wire
And the Visiting Boxes of Long Kesh.
Hunting monsters in Aughyneill.

Over forty years later Gearóid and
Róisín's oldest lad Ruadan arrived
In the foot steps of his three sisters.
To give me back the four and a half years
That his Daddy and I never had.
Without the barbed wire
And the Visiting Boxes of Long Kesh.

His first short pieces were about life within that barbed wire when he was an internee. They were smuggled out and published under the name 'Brownie' in *Republican News* and later collected in *Cage Eleven* (1990). 'The Five Sorrowful Mysteries weeps quietly in the toilet,' he writes of his comrades.

Crazy Joe, in the depths of a big D since Scobie left him, stares dejectedly at the blank TV screen and worries about his nose. The Hurdy Gurdy Man polishes his boots, again. Cleaky polishes the top of his head, again ... Surely-to-God is making his nineteenth miniature piano ... Guts Donnelly writes to his wife. On the next bed Twinkle Higgins writes to somebody else's wife ... Che O'Hara writes to Downing Street demanding his release and a British withdrawal from Ireland. It is Christmas week in the middle hut.

There are archivable, consonant-rich Belfast words such as glyp, latchico, sleekily, stumer and skite. The pieces are warm, witty, self-effacing, quick to bring a character to life, and written with a natural ease any writer might covet.

It was his fifth book. Six years later came his ninth, an autobiography, *Before the Dawn*. I was living in London at the time, just thirty metres from the pied-à-terre of former Northern Ireland Secretary Douglas Hurd. He had a twenty-four-hour two-man police guard when in residence. One hot summer afternoon while I was disassembling a bench in front of my house one of the policemen walked over. Perhaps he was bored. He offered some advice about the bench. He asked me what I did. It turned out he'd read something of mine in a magazine. He asked then if he could use my bathroom. He was gone a long time. I went on with the bench. He tipped his hat as he walked past me on his way back to his post. When I later went upstairs I saw that I'd left

Before the Dawn, face up, a large photograph of the author on the cover and signed on the title page 'Do Timothy, le buíochas, Gerry Adams, London, September '96', on a little table beside the toilet on which the policeman had been sitting. Perhaps a new file was opened somewhere, or an old one added to, as a result of the exchanging of books.

Writers often speak of *having* to do it. They *are* it, their identity depends on it. Ideas take them, seem necessary to them and, they hope, to the universe. They marinate them, go for walks with them, stare at walls thinking of them, wake in the night, feed them as birds do their young. These are not options open to him. Some time when he was a teenaged barman in the Shankill Road and the demand for civil rights was rising, he took a step away from his personal life and into history, along with thousands of others of his generation. He wrote, and writes, on the run, even if no longer from soldiers, in cars or planes or short slots in evenings after a long day. No time to marinate. Yet it calls him, and has done throughout his adult life. When I asked him what it meant to him he said he found it therapeutic. Some of the writers described above might wonder how an activity which has driven practitioners beyond neurosis could in itself be calming or curative, but for him it is, perhaps, the time alone, the relief for the intellect from strategising, the fleeting connection with subtle human feeling instead of the grind of political combat.

But it may too be a matter of the times he was in. Oppression and the struggle against it often convert into paint on walls or canvas, ink on paper, whether in Cuba, Vietnam, Spain, South Africa, Nicaragua or Ireland. A long dormancy of compliance stirs into resistance. There is a feeling of awakening, of self-discovery. The ordinary is elevated to the mythic. Confidence and, in turn, expression grow. If you watched it on television you would think that West Belfast was a place of glass-strewn wastelands, lurking shadows, women on Valium, catatonic children, masked men, medieval fanaticisms, rubble, craters and coffins. If you went there you would find improvised theatres with people sitting on one another's laps, Irish-speaking children, murals of the Sioux, Bob Marley and Cúchulainn, debates, festivals, transformative housing initiatives. The Armalite eventually left, leaving ballot box, rights campaigns, paint and pen. Thousands participated, among them Gerry Adams.

You have here a book of stories written by someone better known for things other than writing stories. Not all approve of his choices. He tends to be popular with the populace but to draw the ire of the powerful and the influential, in Britain but most particularly in Ireland. Great effort is put into delegitimising him, to denying him rights to be heard that they themselves enjoy, to placing him in permanent quarantine. When in 1993 President Mary Robinson made it known she intended to visit a community event in West Belfast and while there to shake Gerry Adams's hand, news organisations condemned, John Major called Albert Reynolds in alarm, the British ambassador made an official complaint, security protection was withheld and Dick Spring, leader of the Labour Party, spent days imploring her not to do it. She came, she talked, she listened to the McPeakes play reels and shook Gerry Adams's hand. Afterwards her approval rating stood at seventy-seven per cent. That same year, RTÉ went all the way to the Dublin High Court to defend its refusal to carry a twenty-second ad for this book's antecedent, a collection of stories called *The Street*.

But neither the stories of *The Street* nor these are anthems. They do not intend to convince. There is no party line. In one of those formulations critics make to categorise fiction, it is said that there are two kinds of storyteller – the one who leaves the village, sees the world and returns to describe what he or she has experienced; the other stays home, observes and then describes to the villagers how their life looks. The stories here are definitely of the parish. They venture out briefly to the rural north and to Galway and Dublin, but are otherwise planted in West Belfast, below the Black Mountain. Many from there will recognise themselves, or will think they do. The stories are ironic or funny or poignant or telling, but the most extended and substantial among them are gestures of compassion towards the wounded and marginal, told by someone with a good ear, a responsive heart and access to the kinds of stories often heard only by priests, doctors or, in this case, a community activist and one-time MP. They are sketches or wrought in detail with a fine brush, according to subject and the availability of time. They bear witness, they seek to understand and to advocate for understanding, whether the subject is child, elderly nun, sniper, thief, migrant or a pair of old boys from the Murph looking to scam and with habits as fixed as railroad tracks. The understanding is often surprising, particular and revealing.

In May 2020 I learned he was up against a deadline to finally deliver the collection of stories he'd long been promising The O'Brien Press. I asked him if he'd like me to go over them with him. He took me up on it. It was pandemic time and we went back and forth by email and phone over the summer, usually in the evenings after he'd been all day in meetings about uniting the island, before or after his dinner, before or after he had to write a position paper or funeral oration, sometimes when he was in his garden shed, rainwater dripping from the roof, blackbirds singing, a grandchild calling out, and once during a break he took in Donegal, the sun going down splendidly, he said, over the Bloody Foreland and with Van Morrison's *Veedon Fleece* and a glass of wine for company – snatched time in an activist's life, just as it was during the writing of these stories.

Timothy O'Grady

INTRODUCTION

I like short stories. Ever since my Granny Adams brought me to the Falls Road Library when I was a school boy in the 1950s. Until then the *Beano*, the *Topper* and the *Dandy* were my reading material. But the Falls Library introduced me to books. Granted it was Enid Blyton and Richmal Crompton. They soon gave way to Biggles and Tarzan of the Apes and then Zane Grey. Hardly any connection with my life in Belfast. Frank O'Connor and Liam O'Flaherty and Seán Ó Faoláin, Edna O'Brien and Michael McLaverty followed in their own time, along with Charles Dickens, Brendan Behan, John Steinbeck, Ernest Hemingway and Walter Macken. Seamus Heaney was special. And Patrick Kavanagh. Then eventually Gabriel García Márquez, Toni Morrison and Alice Walker, and many, many more who wrote about my kind of people. The working poor. The rebels. The stoic long-suffering mothers. The young lovers. And old lovers too. The heroes and heroines of everyday life. I never imagined then that I would become a published fiction writer. This is my second volume of short stories. *The Street and Other Stories* was published in 1992.

Writing short stories suits my lifestyle. I am usually very busy. It is hard to fit fiction-writing time into an activist schedule. But when I can do it I find the writing experience very rewarding. Apart from my family, I spend a lot of my time in the company of comrades. I have always seen my activism in part as a team effort. I am a team player. I like to think I am a team builder. So I work a lot with others. I believe in the collective. And while I enjoy the company of my friends and comrades, it is refreshing to be on my own and to live in my own head and create the characters who inhabit these pages. Writing is a solitary process. I like that.

I have long admired those folks who can write music and songs or carry tunes in their heads. Musicians are magical people. Painters and photographers also have their place in the arts. Filmmakers. Sculptors. Singers. Poets. Dancers. Actors, too. But writers who can create plays or novels or poetry are special because words are special. We are lucky in Ireland that we have one of the world's oldest written languages – the Irish language. We also have a lively, living oral tradition in both Irish and English. And while the English language in Ireland is more dominant for obvious reasons, it is a form of English drawn from and influenced by the Irish language. They tried to destroy our language. We Hibernicised theirs. I hope these stories are part of that tradition. Some tell a story which may not often be told. Or heard. If readers recognise themselves or others in these pages, that will please me greatly. The essence of storytelling is to uplift, inform, distract and move the reader. To tell their story. Everyone deserves to tell or have their story told.

Storytelling can take many forms. Féile an Phobail (@FeileBelfast) in West Belfast is a wonderful example of this. Born at the height of the conflict, after some dreadful incidents, Féile was a communal response to the awful and untruthful propaganda being peddled by the establishment about the people who live in the west of Belfast city. Some of the stories in this collection are set there. Féile was, and is, a celebration of creativity, resilience, good humour, civic ambition, inclusivity, fun and hope. It is now the largest community arts festival in these islands. That tells its own story.

Writing in Ireland is more democratic now than it used to be. Censorship once was rife. Most of our celebrated writers were banned, from Edna O'Brien to Joyce and many others. And if books weren't suppressed 'legally' by the new Irish state after partition, the Church, before and after partition, pressured the faithful not to read certain books. Books were burned by zealots, their authors denounced from the pulpit. Nowadays no one would countenance such behaviour; although my publisher, the late Steve MacDonogh, was prevented from advertising *The Street and Other Stories* and other books of mine on RTÉ, the state public service broadcaster. That decision was upheld by the High Court in July 1993.

Irish women writers have carved out their own space in

Irish book publishing in the recent past. So too have tales of the urban working class, not least because of the writings of Roddy Doyle. Authentic stories from the North about the conflict are not so prevalent, especially from former political prisoners or activists, although my friends Bobby Sands, Danny Morrison, Síle Darragh and Gerry Kelly, Jim McVeigh, Daniel Jack, Mairtín Ó Muilleoir, Tony Doherty, Jake Jackson, Barry McElduff, Laurence McKeown, Pat Magee, Jaz McCann, Ella O'Dwyer, Brian Campbell and others have established themselves as authentic storytellers in Irish and English, and Tom Hartley has distinguished himself as a credible historian, particularly of Belfast's chequered past.

The act of writing intrigues me. These stories are works of the imagination. Some may be drawn from my own life experience or are influenced by it. But where they actually come from, how they take shape, who the characters are, how the ending emerges is a mystery to me because sometimes that happens by itself. The stories and the people in them seem to take on a life of their own. Do I write for myself? To a certain extent. But not entirely. I would probably write even if my work was never published. But truth to tell, and on reflection, I write mostly for the reader. That's part of the magic of it, if it's done properly. The words which are born in the mind of the writer are transferred to the page and come alive in the mind of the reader. Hopefully. From one imagination to another. That's the whole point of it.

And if you can make them laugh or cry? Make them believe? That's special. Make the reader happy and take them out of themselves. Empower them. Give them hope. Get them to imagine. To remember. And maybe to go on and write or tell their own stories.

Perhaps this is all too pretentious an aim for this modest little selection of stories. If so ignore it. The stories will stand or fall on their own. They are yours. If you don't like them, give them to someone who might.

Gerry Adams
August 2021

BLACK MOUNTAIN

Belfast has hills. Apart from its people – well, most of its people – the hills are what make this city a special place. They are not high hills. They are modest in their inclines. Hardly mountains, although we claim them as such. The Black Mountain or Sliabh Dubh. The Divis and Colin Mountains or An Colann and An Dubhais. Wolf Hill and Cave Hill or Beann Mhadagáin. There are other hills across the metropolis. The Craigauntlet and Castlereagh hills. These slopes hug Belfast in one long, soft, green embrace. They are the backdrop to the city and the main natural feature, particularly of the west of Belfast.

Tom and Harry are two of Belfast's people. I have known them since our schooldays. They were always close and that closeness has endured beyond their youth, through their working lives, their marriages and beyond, into the autumn of their existences. They survived the conflict, the house raids, riots and decades of military occupation. They were both arrested a few times, but that was a rite of passage for young men growing up in those days. They came through it all. But what makes Tom and Harry unique is not just their relationship with each other but their connection with the Black Mountain, which is central to their lives. They walk there every week. Sometimes every day, if the weather permits. For as long as I have known them, it is an important part of how they spend their time. When they were younger they ran there. Back in the day. Loping up the Black Mountain's green slopes and clambering up its rocky inclines. Sometimes barefoot or in the plastic sandals which were all the rage when we were children. Unlike me, they have persisted with these perambulations. Except for the time when it was too dangerous to venture there, day in and day out these two old pals wander up on to the heights above their neighbourhood.

Nowadays their journey is more of a dander than a walk. A dander is a very leisurely, sometimes hands-in-the-pockets saunter. It should not be confused with a ramble. A ramble could take forever. It may also involve stops at public houses and could include other ramblers who may join in for part or all of the ramble. I have done that myself. Sometimes it was planned. Other times it was an accident. Always it was very enjoyable. A dander is usually fairly short. Tom and Harry rambled the odd time, when they were young, but now they prefer a wee dander. And they rest frequently. And always, if they get that far, they sit in the Hatchet Field and ruminate on matters of importance to themselves. The Hatchet Field, so-called because of its hatchet shape, is a fine vantage point up towards the horizon high on the mountainy slope. Nowadays, by the time they reach it they need a good rest. Sprawled on a heathy bank amid the bracken, they are masters of all they survey. Here amid the uncertainties of life is certainty. Like their friendship, it has endured. And they are comfortable about that. Sometimes.

'The good weather puts everybody in good form,' Harry remarked. 'Isn't it grand?'

He and Tom were sitting in their usual spot. Black Mountain was their eyrie. Belfast sprawled below them. Its narrow-terraced, peace-wall-bisected streets, new apartment blocks, church spires and old mills stretched out until, yellow cranes dominating, their city dipped its feet into the untroubled grey waters of Belfast Lough. In the distance the coast of Scotland shimmered in the clear warmth of a fine day. To the south they could see the Mountains of Mourne and the hills of South Armagh. North-east of that the glimmer of Strangford Lough winked at them.

'Thon's our house,' Tom said as he has said many, many times, pointing down at the Murph.

Harry ignored him. The mountain slope was loud with birdsong. All around them a carpet of bluebells almost on their last legs gave way to verdant green young bracken.

'Remember when we were wee lads we used to pick primroses up here and bring them home,' Tom continued.

'I do surely. My ma used to put them in a milk bottle on the scullery window,' Harry replied.

'You mean the kitchen,' Tom corrected him.

'No, I mean the scullery,' Harry said. 'And there's a place up behind us where we used to get wild strawberries.'

'Why do you say scullery instead of kitchen?' Tom enquired with mock earnestness.

'I don't say scullery instead of kitchen,' Harry responded with great patience. 'In our house these days we have a kitchen. In those days we had a scullery. I don't call our kitchen the scullery, do I?'

Tom didn't answer.

'Well, do I?' Harry repeated.

'Nawh, you don't,' Tom eventually conceded.

'Well, if I don't call our kitchen the scullery, I'm not going to call our scullery the kitchen. I call it a scullery because it was a scullery!'

'You don't need to take the needle,' Tom retorted. 'Youse Falls Road ones always cry poverty. I was only reminiscing about the primroses. You knew my ma kept the ones I got her in a vase in the kitchen but you just wanted to get in your wee dig about the milk bottle and the scullery. You'll be telling me next about the cold water tap and the toilet in the yard.'

'Well, why shouldn't I?' Harry asked in an offended tone. 'Thems the way things were.'

'Well, they're not like that any more.'

'They are for some people.'

'But not for us! These are good times for us.' Tom raised himself up on his elbows. 'Look,' he continued, 'when you were here as a wee lad collecting wild flowers for your mammy did you think you would do all the things and see all the things you've seen?'

'No,' Harry conceded.

'We've been walking these hills for over fifty years now, on and off?'

'Yup,' Harry agreed reluctantly. 'In good times and bad.'

'Well, you know you're not going to get another fifty years.'

'I don't know about that,' Harry said with a wry smile. 'I have a death wish. I wish to die in my hundred and fortieth year.'

'Your bum's a plum,' Tom scoffed. 'You sound like a buck eejit and you know it. The point is you're lucky to be able to sit here on this fine day and look down on all this.' He waved expansively at the vista which surrounded them. 'The point is to appreciate it all. There's no use whinging and whining all the time.'

'Look,' Harry turned to him, 'I'm the one that always appreciates it all. You think I came up the Lagan in a bubble? You're the caster upper, the contrary one, the gurner, the whinger, the dark cloud. And now you're starting to get on my wick. You get on your soap-box just because I used the word scullery' – Tom raised his hands in frustration and glared at Harry – 'and because my ma put bluebells in a milk bottle,' Harry continued. 'I was gonna go on and say that it's because of my memories of things like that that I appreciate how things have improved.'

'Okay.' Tom smirked. 'Were you or were you not gonna go on to recall the hard times you had? Were you gonna go on and tell me about getting up early to go for pillowcases of bread down in Kennedy's Bakery in Beechmount? Were you or were you not gonna go on to recall the big snow of 1963 and how you cut out bits of oilcloth to use as insoles in your shoes because they had holes in them? Were you or were you not gonna retell how youse had coats on your beds instead of quilts in your house? And,' he concluded, 'were you or were you not gonna tell how big boys from Westrock stole your snake belt? Or after internment morning, about the way the Paras put you in the back of one of their jeeps and used you as cover when they drove around the district?'

'I was not,' Harry protested. 'That's something you and the Brits had in common. They don't understand ordinary people. They think everybody thinks the way they think. As if we have no minds of our own. Just like you. With you it's your way or no way.'

Despite his resentment at being compared to the Brits, Tom kept his cool. 'That's how you know you've lost the argument,' he replied evenly. 'You and I both know that the Brits could never win because you just can't come into someone's home place, with all that means, and order them about and expect them to comply.'

'I'm not asking you to comply,' Harry countered. 'Just stop being so contrary. I'm allowed to remember times past without you accusing me of being miserable about it. I'm not miserable about it.'

'Well, chance would be a fine thing,' said Tom with a sigh. 'The point is that was then. This is now. So live in the nowness. Listen to the birds. Breathe the pure mountainy air. Stop gurning. Live in the moment. And appreciate it. You were all set to launch into the five sorrowful mysteries. All set to ruin this lovely day.'

Harry turned away in frustration. 'Would you ever give my head peace?' he raged, raising his voice in frustration. 'How could anyone enjoy the day with you givin' off about everything. You're a real gabshite today. You're like an oul doll.'

'That's sexist,' Tom shot back.

'Let's go home,' Harry said.

'Aye,' Tom replied. 'You're a pain in the arse today. Can't even have a discussion without you taking the needle. You're like a big long drink of misery. It's well seen you're kitchen-house reared.'

'No, I'm not! And you know it.'

They tramped off together, descending the Black Mountain

slowly and arguing furiously, just as they did when they were only ten years old. Meanwhile, the birdsong continued unabated. The flora and the fauna ignored them. The mountain was a silent witness to their bickering.

And Belfast, basking below, paid no heed.

Eventually, at the top of the Mountain Loney, the steep road down to Ballymurphy, they stopped to draw breath.

Tom broke first. He was feeling a wee bit contrite. 'I didn't mean to annoy you so much up there. Let's not fall out. Isn't it wonderful weather?' he volunteered hesitantly.

'Go hiontach,' Harry conceded reluctantly. 'Wonderful.'

Tom has a habit of stating the obvious. But he was right. The weather was gorgeous. A big blue sky stretched over them. The sun beaming down. The Black Mountain was verdant, its greenness highlighted by the sunshine.

They made their way slowly homewards, crossing the Springfield Road at the Top of the Rock.

'I would love a beer,' Harry proclaimed. 'An ice-cold lager. From Belgium or Germany or the Nordic countries. A natural ice-cold lager. Without chemicals.'

Tom looked closely at him. Harry was usually a Guinness man.

'In a big glass. With the condensation on the outside and a good white head on top. Ahhh,' Harry sighed, gulping with the effort as he imagined the drink coursing down his throat.

They were nearly home.

'I have some lager in the shed since Christmas,' Tom confessed.

'Ah,' Harry said, 'I thought I saw it when I borrowed your spade.'

'When did you borrow my spade?' asked Tom.

'Last week,' Harry replied.

'What for?'

'To dig holes for the fence poles for my chicken run.'

'Ah … When are you getting chickens?'

'I'm working on it. I have to pick my moment very carefully. Otherwise I'm snookered. I can't ask until I know I'll get a yes.'

'So did you touch the beer?'

'I did not. I touched nothing but the spade. I wouldn't mind getting ducks as well,' he reflected as they cut down to Divismore. 'Only, ducks like water, and I don't think I would get away with digging a pool out the back. Getting the chicken run done will be a big enough challenge to my relationship with her who must be obeyed. I'm waiting for the minute when she says she would love a free-range egg. Then I'll pounce. It's a matter of patience,' he concluded thoughtfully, 'and timing.'

'My granny used to keep chickens in the coalhole,' Tom recalled. 'But not ducks. I like duck eggs.'

'How many beers have you?' Harry asked. 'And how did they survive so long?'

Tom ignored his question. 'I ate an ostrich egg once,' he continued. 'I've a cousin working at the azoo. He gave it me. Very strong. Like a big duck egg. I used a pint glass as an egg cup. And a soup spoon to eat it.'

'I'd have fresh chicken eggs every day if I got chickens,' said Harry. 'I might even give you some.'

'Fear maith thú. That deserves a beer. Here we are now.'

Tom pulled up two chairs at the back of the house. His intention was to drag it out and make Harry squirm before offering him a drink, but by now he had a drought on him, so he went into his shed and came back out with the golden, bubbling lagers. From where they sat, Black Mountain was in plain view. They rested contentedly looking up at its green slopes.

'You know,' said Harry, 'the way an oul' dog gets up after lying down for a while? You know how it gets up and stretches and gives itself a wee shake. Then it might give itself another wee shake. And another wee stretch. Its coat seems to give a wee shiver. It might yawn as well. Then it slowly danders off?'

'Aye,' said Tom, slowly wiping the condensation off his glass while listening intently to Harry.

'Well,' Harry continued, 'I think the Black Mountain is like an oul' dog sprawled out deep in slumber. I often wonder what we would do if it got up and stretched itself and then dandered off.'

Tom said nothing for a long minute as he looked up at the mountain. And then at Harry. The Black Mountain was omnipresent in the lives of the people who lived below it. Some hardy souls still live at the top of the Loney, and it wasn't so long ago that a family farmed in the Hatchet Field. Beyond its dark ridge there are old medieval remains, ring forts, ancient quarries where flint arrow and spear heads are still to be unearthed. There are archaeological ruins, old lazy beds. Remnants of human existence since time began. Fairy rings, too, for those who believe in fairies. There are hares and rabbits and pine martens, all types of birds. Bogland and moorland. Mountain meadows and steep rock faces. Mountain streams. Heather and every variety of wild flowers. Tom and Harry were exceptional. They knew every inch of the dark mountainy slopes, its ridges and gullies, its sheep tracks and high passes. Most days, except for the years of military occupation, they looked down from the mountain, never tiring of the vista below them.

In the poorly appointed housing estates at the foot of the mountain, people lived their lives looking up at it. Some, like the working poor in places like this over the centuries, lived tough lives, weighted down by poverty and disadvantage. Perhaps some of them did not look up too often. But the community in the face of adversity became close, mindful of those who lived lives of grinding misery. Local leaders organised and agitated, hopeful that change would come. Then conflict erupted and the Black Mountain's slopes echoed to the sound of gun-shots and explosions, and the stench of CR and CS gas and smoke contaminated the mountain air. British troops dug in and built fortifications overlooking the neighbourhood. They surveyed everything. Every house. Every man and woman. Children even. Every day and most nights they sallied forth to suppress the local populace, including Tom and Harry and their neighbours.

The conflict, now thankfully over, left some of their friends scarred. Others did not survive. Divisions remain. The Black Mountain was impervious to it all. From Neolithic to modern times, from when the first boulder was laid in the wall of a ring fort until the last brick was laid in the new Springhill estate, the Black Mountain witnessed everything. Throughout all those centuries, Tom reflected, it was unlikely that anyone had ever compared the Black Mountain to a sleeping dog. Only Harry could think of that, he concluded.

'I used to think our walks on the mountain kept us sane. Now, listening to you, I'm not so sure. You know there's wiser locked up.' Finally, he sighed patiently, raised his drink and saluted his friend. 'Sláinte, Harry. I'm sure if the Black Mountain could talk it would have some mighty tales to tell, but let me tell you something – that mountain is not going anywhere.'

'I know that,' said Harry. 'But that doesn't mean I can't

imagine things. It's like my chickens. Between the two of us, I know I might never get to have chickens. But that's not the point. I can imagine having them. And the colours their feathers might be, and if I had a rooster would he annoy us all crowing at dawn, and would someone complain, and would the peelers come out to mess me and the chickens about? Would I let some of the eggs hatch out so that we would have wee chicks, wee younkers? That's what keeps me going. Imagining things. Wee things like a chicken run or big things like the mountain leaving us. That's what keeps us alive. Imagining. You mark my words. If we lose our imagination we lose everything. Existing is not living. Sure, our Black Mountain walks kept us sane. But our imaginations kept us alive. Through all the troubles. In all the hard times. That's why we could never be beaten. They couldn't stop us imagining life without them. You know that. You knew a better life was possible. Or you imagined it. And they couldn't stop you. If they had done that, we'd be beaten dockets. But we're not.' He also raised his drink. 'Sláinte,' he said, a little abashed now after his little speech. 'Up the Murph.' He downed half his glass in one long gulp. 'Go raibh maith agat.' He smiled, lifting the glass again towards Tom.

'Fáilte,' Tom replied with a wicked grin. 'Big Mick gave them to me for you just before Christmas.'

Harry looked at Tom in disbelief. 'Did Big Mick give you anything else for me?' he snarled.

'Nawh,' Tom said. 'Just the pils. It's lucky I forgot about them or we wouldn't be able to have them today.'

'Aye,' Harry relented after a minute's quiet reflection. 'That's true. Let's crack open another couple.'

'A bird never flew on one wing,' said Tom.

They sat quietly for an hour or so looking up at the mountain, minding it, as Harry put it, and enjoying the sun. And the beer. Two old pals. No one to interrupt them. Their squabble was forgotten as they listened to the children playing in the street and a neighbour cutting his hedge. The cheerful jingling tune from an ice-cream van meandering its way along Springhill Avenue added to the lazy sunny mood. Soon dinner-time drew near and Harry made ready to go.

'Good luck with the chickens,' Tom said to him.

'I'll need luck with herself first,' said Harry.

'There's that right enough,' said Tom. 'Do you think you'll be able to go up the mountain for another dander tomorrow?'

'Aye,' Harry said. 'No problem. Give me a shout when you need me. By the way, does that cousin of yours who gave you the ostrich egg still work in the azoo?'

'Nawh,' Tom said. 'But Big Mick knows a man who knows a man who has alligator eggs.'

Harry shook his head. 'Nawh,' he said. 'I'll stick to Rhode Island Reds, if you don't mind. Thanks again for the beer. Even if it was me own. It rounded off a fine day.'

'Aye,' Tom agreed. 'Now we've finished yours I'm going to get stuck into mine.'

Harry stopped in his tracks. 'You cannot be serious.'

'I'm only jokin'.' Tom laughed.

Harry looked doubtful. 'I don't know whether to believe you or not!' he exclaimed.

Tom eased him through the door. 'I'm only keeping you going. See ya,' he said. 'Tomorrow about twelve,' he shouted at Harry's departing figure.

'Slán,' called Harry.

A fine day indeed, Harry thought to himself as he meandered homewards, where he had planked a few other bottles of beer that Big Mick's mate Wee Mick had left for Tom and himself. Big Mick and Wee Mick ran the local off-licence for a local businessman, Peter O'Property. Peter's real name was O'Toole but everybody called him O'Property behind his back on account of the real estate he had gathered up since the ceasefires. Big Mick and Wee Mick were discreetly generous with his wares to selected off-licence customers.

So after his short walk home, Harry poured himself a scoop. He too seated himself outside, the Black Mountain still the vista that towered above him. Meanwhile, Tom made his way back to the shed where he gathered up another bottle of the secreted lager. One of the ones Harry didn't get. He returned to his seat facing the mountain and poured himself another glass. Then, with a satisfied little sigh, he raised it in salute to his absent pal. 'Sláinte, Harry, old friend.'

And there, dear reader, we will leave them. In the shadow of Black Mountain, where they have lived all their days. Each drinking the other's beer and enjoying it all the more because of that.

Tomorrow on Black Mountain is another day to look forward to. Especially if you're lucky and have the ability to imagine things.

FIRST CONFESSION

One night a week we used to go for our religious instruction to confraternity down in Clonard Monastery, and if we left early we could spend the bus fare on sweets. We cut down the Springfield Road and joined hundreds of other boys in the chapel. To me Clonard was a wondrous place with high, high ceilings and a huge high altar. The altar boys wore long red soutanes and white gowns. The priest's incense spiralled upwards through the shafts of sunlight which came slanting down from stained-glass windows at the very top.

It wasn't a long service. Father McLaughlin, who was in charge of the confraternity, got up and made a joke or preached a sermon and then we sang a few hymns. I didn't mind it at all; in fact, I found parts of it good fun. As Father McLaughlin conducted the whole chapel full of young fellows, we would sing 'Tanto Mergo, make my hair grow'. Every section of boys had a prefect, and we had to be careful in case we'd be caught.

It was evening by the time we came out of 'confo', and the evening had a different feel, with shadows coming, the day having cooled off; we could sense the change, and things became quieter as we embarked on a rambling return home through territory we regarded as our own long-extended playground

We walked up the road, often stopping at the Flush River. Here beside the cotton mill there was a deep ravine, and often we slid down its high slopes right down to the river. Although we weren't allowed in the river, we were forever going into it. However, one of us was found out once when, having dried himself off, he went up home.

'You were in the river,' his mother said as soon as she saw him.

'No,' he lied, 'I wasn't.'

'You were,' his mother said, pointing to his head and the back of his clothes, which were decorated with white patches. There had been bleach in the river that day and he was rightly caught.

Once some wee lads stoned us at the Flush and we ran like anything; somebody said they were Protestants, but I didn't know what they were stoning us for. Up above the Flush a school stood off the road behind a tall wall, and opposite it were two terraces of houses, a small street and a shop; the people there were all Protestants except for one fella we used to call to sometimes if his father wasn't in.

Carrying on towards home, it was all green fields, and as we passed the Springfield dam we stopped to watch the swans, the water herons and, at different times of year, the ducks.

Opposite the Monarch Laundry on the right-hand side lay the Highfield estate and the West Circular Road where mostly Protestants lived; above stood an Orange hall. Away on up lay more fields: Huskey's on the left-hand side of the road, Farmer Brown's and Beechie's on the right. On yellow houses here a date indicated that they had been built a hundred years or so before.

Then we arrived on home ground: the Murph. Down the slope, the steps, Divismore Park and our house. And if we were slow coming up, having played at the Flush too long, when we reached as far as Divismore Park we might hear the long shouts of our Margaret: 'Geeeerrrryyy, you're a-wanted!' and 'Paaaaddddyyy, you're a-wanted!' The sounds might be heard too of others out shouting for Joe or Harry or Frank. Then the lamps were lit as Divis Mountain began to fade and the stars appeared.

Sometimes we would stand, put our heads straight back and look up at all the thousands and millions of stars. One night Joe Magee's dad brought us just about half a mile above the Murph to listen to the corncrakes. That was beautiful, and from a height we had a view down over the city of Belfast; then we put our heads back and looked up at the sky, all the time hearing the corncrakes.

The priest told our class that we had to tell all our sins

in confession. I wondered about that. How could you tell all your sins? Every single one? I started to try to take notes when I was committing a sin, which was fair enough because I had a week to go till my first confession, but all the sins, of my whole life? Sean Murphy, who sat in the desk beside me, said it was only mortal sins; venial sins didn't really matter. Sean said that Protestants got it easier: they didn't have to go to confession; they didn't have to tell their sins. But then, Protestants weren't going to get to heaven, he said.

The whole class went down to St Peter's; we marched down in twos, filed into the pews, with their cold, shiny seats. As one by one we genuflected in the side aisle, we moved to sit on the bench either side of the confession box, and as the line dwindled we were carried forward into the confession box.

The boy coming out smirked at me as he held the door open. I knelt down in the semi-gloom as the door slammed behind me; above me there was a small ledge and from beyond the ledge I could hear the mumble of a man's voice. A moment later I heard the slam of something being drawn closed, and then above my head an aperture opened and a friendly adult voice boomed manfully down on me. 'Good morning, my son.'

'Bless me, Father, for I have sinned. This is my first confession.' I hesitated.

'Go on, my son,' the voice encouraged me.

'I gave backcheek to my mother five times, Father. I gave cheek to my granny twice, Father. I wanted to kill my sister Margaret four times, Father.'

'You wanted to kill your sister Margaret?' the voice asked.

'Yes, Father.'

'And when was that?'

'Well, once last year, Father, in the summer, and then on Christmas Day when she opened up my stocking, and then on Easter when she broke my egg, and then yesterday, Father.'

'And does your sister Margaret annoy you?'

'Yes, Father.'

'Well, you know you're going to have to be more patient.'

'Yes, Father. Oh, and I said a bad word, Father, fifteen times.'

'What did you say?'

'I said "frig", Father. Father, I robbed an orchard, once. And me and my friends tied thread to oul' Ma Doran's door and we played "kick the door" all night ...'

'Is that all, son?'

'No, Father. I hit Terence McManus. He was hitting our Paddy, Father. Our Paddy always gets me into trouble. He said that Terence McManus kicked him and my da sent me out to hit Terence and Terence is bigger than me but I bled his nose. I didn't mean to, Father ...'

'That's all right, my son,' the voice intoned patiently. 'Go on.'

'And I beat Billy Dunne in a fair dig. He took our Paddy's kitten and my da sent me out to get it back.'

'What happened then?'

'Billy hit me with a brick in the back of the head and I smashed my teeth on the ground when I fell. I got him later with a hurley stick.'

'Is that all?'

'Our Paddy's kitten got its head caught in a tin of stewing steak and it died. I cursed at our Paddy that day. I got my teeth broke over him, Father. For nothing.'

'Is there more?'

'Well, Father … I've cheated at marleys sixty-seven times.'

'How did you do that?'

'Everybody does it, Father. I move my man when I'm taking a shot and –'

'Sixty-seven times?'

'At least sixty-seven times, Father.'

'Could it be more?'

'It could, Father.'

'Go on, my son.'

'That's all, Father.'

'Well now, I want you to say a good act of contrition and for your penance I want you to be more patient with your sister and say one Our Father and three Hail Marys.'

'Thank you, Father.'

His voice mumbled the comforting words in the dark

above me as I said a good act of contrition. There was an instant of silence when I finished. Then,

'God bless you, my son.'

'God bless you, Father.'

The shutter slid closed above me with a little thud. I heard the slam of another being drawn open in the other confession box at the other side of the priest. I levered myself slowly up off my knees and fumbled for the door behind me. I came immediately face to face with the image of the crucified Christ which hung on a cross to one side of the shutter which separated me from the priest. For a second I felt truly sorry for all my sins. Every one of them. I pressed my lips against the crucifix and then, pushing open the confessional's door, I stepped piously out into the aisle.

BLUEBELLS

When Nora opened the door to her hotel room near Amiens Street station, the little patterns of bluebells on the wallpaper caught her eye. They looked familiar, but she couldn't figure out why. She'd taken an early train from Belfast to arrive in time for the first day of a training course at Liberty Hall organised by her union. She was looking forward to it. New faces, new ideas. The capital city. Nora liked Dublin.

She unpacked her clothes, but was drawn back to the wallpaper. She looked closely at it, ran her hand over the circular bouquets of bluebells on the pale-pink background. It was like seeing a face in a crowd she couldn't quite place. But then it came to her. The street in West Belfast from her childhood. The room she shared with her little sister, Sarah. Not much money in the house. Bare wooden floorboards before that became fashionable. No oilcloth or carpet in their room, but that same lovely pink wallpaper covered with bluebells just beside their bed.

'What are bluebells for?' Sarah had once asked her. They

were lying in bed on a bright Saturday morning. No school. No work. A lie-in.

'What do you mean, what are they for?' Nora asked her. Sarah was studying the bluebell patterns curiously. Nora turned in the bed so that they were almost nose to nose. Taking her sister's little face between her palms she kissed her gently on the forehead.

'I mean, what are bluebells for, WaaWaa?' Sarah giggled, kicking the bedclothes off them both and trying to escape from Nora's hug.

'Bluebells are for love,' Nora said. 'Miss Thompson taught us that in Saint Louise's. Patrick Kavanagh wrote it. It's in one of my favourite poems. So there you go. You didn't know your big sister knew poetry, did you?'

All the while she tried to hug Sarah, and Sarah resisted, kicking, squealing and twisting in the bed and trying to tickle her in retaliation.

'Don't you dare call me a WaaWaa,' Nora repeated again and again, laughing and squealing almost as much as her younger sister.

The two of them giggled and wrestled together like this until their mother shouted up to them to come downstairs for breakfast. On Saturdays that meant a special treat. A fry. Bacon, sausage, fried egg with fried soda and potato bread. Black and white pudding. Served with lashings of HP brown sauce. The two sisters eventually came down into the kitchen, still giggling and giddy after their exuberant bout of horseplay.

Their mother greeted them with a smile. 'I don't know which of you is the biggest child!' She laughed.

That was more than thirty years ago. The bluebells brought it back to her. Sarah had two wee girls of her own now. Nora was godmother to one of them.

That night in her hotel room she had a dream which woke her with a start. She sat bolt upright in the strange bed. The dream was terrifyingly real, but Nora couldn't remember what it was about. It seemed to disappear as she tried to find it – only the fear remained. She stretched her hand out from beneath the sheets and once again touched the bluebell pattern on the wallpaper. It stood out slightly from the pink background. The bluebells, she recalled vaguely, had been there, too, in the dream.

It was still deep in the night. She would need some sleep to get through the long day of meetings and classes at Liberty Hall the next day. The noise of the city street floated up to her room; the sound of a train chugged and rattled its way into her consciousness and comforted her somehow. She lay back down and drew the sheets over her and eventually fell back into a troubled sleep.

She woke a little late in the morning and had to rush through a shower and breakfast to get to the first session at Liberty Hall. The dream came to her sometimes, just a gentle nagging at the edge of her consciousness as she went through the day, but the schedule was too tight for her to have time to dwell on it.

That night she slept soundly. No dreams, or at least none that troubled her. The following morning she awoke early, well rested and in good form. She stretched and did the breathing exercises she liked to do if she had time before she got out of bed, but the sound of a creaking floorboard outside her door jarred against her good mood. She felt a tightening in her chest and a sudden darkening in her head. She stared at the bluebell wallpaper while the creaking floorboard again intruded on her consciousness. A mild panic gripped her for a split second. She swallowed hard, her gaze focused on the blueness of the blue-bells imprinted on the pinkness of the wallpaper. The floor-board creaked again, though she knew this time it was her imagination – all was quiet outside her door. She gripped the bedclothes, took a deep breath and sat up in the bed. Then she went into the bathroom and looked at herself in the mirror. She was so tense and serious it almost made her laugh. 'Get a grip,' she said to her reflection. She forced herself to smile.

On the last night she and all her colleagues from the course went out to a music session at The Ferryman's. She felt much more at ease now in Dublin compared to her first visits, when the war was on and her Belfast accent seemed to raise suspicions. Now there was a peace process, there was much more coming and going between north and south, and even the president was a woman from Ardoyne. It was a good night in The Ferryman's, a grand send-off before they all dispersed to their homes, but even when the craic and the music were mighty, her dream niggled at the back of her mind.

The next morning she took the train back home to Belfast. There was to be a gathering that night at An Culturlann on the Falls Road with her brother Joe and all four sisters to celebrate her mother's birthday. Her mother had been unwell in recent years. Heart problems, some unexplained dizziness. They'd all been worried about her as they watched her failing slightly, fading a wee bit, seeming to move unwillingly away from them step by step. As she travelled north on the train Nora remembered the old house, the cardinal-red tiles in the kitchen, the white bread and margarine, the condensation on the walls, her father in the living room eating his dinner from a plate on his knees, her sisters plaiting each other's hair, and Joe trying to read as their mother moved around the small space in nervy, anxious movements. From sink to table to cooker. From child to child. Holding them all together. Reminding them even through the troubled years with British army raids and Joe sometimes in prison how much they had to be grateful for with a nice four-bedroomed house while so many others had so little.

As the seascape of North Dublin slipped past and merged into Meath and then Louth, the gentle motion of the train heading northwards lulled her into a half-doze, half-daydream in which she was once again a wee girl playing with her friends.

Out in the road with them she felt free. She loved the backdrop of the Black Mountain, the lightness of the evening sky as dusk invaded its space, the shrieks and squeals of the children playing. She revelled in the intensity of the small group of girls as they skipped or hopped or jumped in competition or the excitement of running free on the green, the wind in her face and her long hair bouncing behind her as she chased or was chased by the boys. She loved the wildness, the exuberance, the thrill of the running and dodging, the twisting this way and that to avoid outstretched clutching hands or feet and legs. She loved the stumbling and falling after being tripped and the delight at winning. She was lightly made up, starting to stretch, all long legs and arms, but she was fast on her feet so she won quite a lot that summer of 1964 when she was twelve years old.

Then the bus would arrive and she would watch anxiously for her father, mindful not to let the others see. If he wasn't drunk, she would greet him as he passed. 'Da, have you any odds?'

'You have me robbed, wee girl,' he would reply, fumbling in his pockets and carefully extracting pennies from among the loose change. 'Here youse are. One d for each of youse.'

'Thanks, Mr Devlin,' her friends would chorus.

'Thanks, Da,' she would giggle, her eyes brightening and

her mouth widening in a grateful smile. Then they would dash to McKee's house shop for handfuls of penny mix-ups or gobstoppers, sweetie lollies or Black Jacks.

But if her da was drunk, her girlfriends would chant as he made his unsteady trek from the bus stop on the main road to their house down the drive. 'Omo Daz drunk. Omo Daz drunk. Omo Daz drunk.' Deirdre Flynn and Máire O'Toole usually started the mantra in a low whisper. Too low for her father to hear but loud enough for Nora. It was embarrassing, humiliating even. It made her run off to hide in a neighbour's garden. Her father would stumble past the girls, barely pausing as he asked, 'How youses doing the night, wee dolls? Where's our Nora? Anybody see our wee Nora?'

Her father had been dead for ten years by this time. It had come suddenly after an accident at a building site where he worked as a labourer. A fall from scaffolding. She watched the scenes pass through her memory until sleep finally took her just as the train crossed the border and into the last shortish stretch home.

Her friends all had their own families now, except Nora. After leaving school, she had gone to work as a cleaner in the Royal Hospital down the Falls Road, but had taken classes run by Father Des Wilson in his house in Springhill. Her sense of justice awakened, she took part in prisoners' rights campaigns during the hunger strikes in Long Kesh and Armagh women's prison. Her confidence grew. Her union work brought her the offer of a job to be a union official. She'd had a few relationships through the years, but none had lasted. She had nights out with her old girlfriends from childhood and lived on her own in a flat she liked across from Casement Park. She was independent and, she thought, content.

Her mother was at the head of the table at An Culturlann when Sarah arrived. They were all there before her, children, spouses, grandchildren. They hadn't been gathered together in the same place since Christmas. Their mother was a little frail but happy to see them. They were all aware that the chances for such gatherings were diminishing. They took turns sitting beside her. When it was Nora's, she handed over a present she'd bought in Dublin and told her mother a little of her time there before asking, 'Ma, do you remember the wallpaper in my room? The one with the bluebells on it?'

'Of course I remember. I loved that wee room. That paper was dear, mind you. Rosaleen McLarnon, God rest her, gave it to me on the never-never. Why do you ask that?'

Nora looked into her mother's face for some sign, a sign of *what* she didn't quite know, but a clue, perhaps, to what had disturbed her days and nights in Dublin, some sense that there was a reason for it and that she wasn't going crazy. But her mother betrayed nothing by her expression, so Nora just said they had the same wallpaper in her hotel and told her mother about the instructors and her colleagues, the scenes in the streets, the last night in the pub. She never mentioned her dream.

After the meal they all went to Sarah's house for a few drinks and a sing-song. Joe started it. All Norah's sisters sang. And their mother. Even some of the grandchildren, after some coaxing. In between there were calls for Nora to sing. 'Give us a song, Skinny Me Link,' called Joe. 'Come on, Melodeon Legs,' shouted Sarah. 'Big Banana Feet,' added her sister Sinead. They were all names they'd called her when she was a child. She managed to avoid singing, but then it was nearly time to go and her mother said, 'You'll have to sing now, Nora. I've to get home to me bed. Sing "You Are My Sunshine". Your da used to love hearing you singing that, especially if he had a few drinks. C'mon Nora. In memory of your daddy. And for me birthday.'

She looked at her mother. She saw all the lines time and worry had put on her face, her slight shortness of breath. She had the beginnings of that look of helplessness which comes sometimes with age but that she could never have afforded when they were small and needed her. Nora didn't want to sing at all, and she especially didn't want to sing that song. But she couldn't refuse her mother. Not on her birthday.

So Nora sang, and as she did so, a tension like that brought about by her dream rose inexplicably within her. Everyone joined in the chorus: 'You make me happy when skies are grey. You'll never know, dear, how much I love you. Please don't take my sunshine awaaaay ...'

They were all smiling and swaying but it was all Nora could do to get through it. At the end she started to cry.

'Ach, look at our wee Nora.' Her mother smiled. 'Oul' softie! Getting all sentimental on us.'

Nora wiped her eyes and tried to smile back at her.

The party broke up then. A taxi was called for Joe and their mother. Later, as Sarah and Nora hugged their good-byes, Sarah looked at her quizzically. 'What was that about?' she asked.

'I'm grand,' Nora assured her. 'The wine was too much for me.'

'Well, why don't we go out for a few more next week-end? Just the two of us. Would you be up for that?'

'Aye.' Nora smiled, pleased at her sister's concern for her. She loved them all, but felt closest to Sarah.

'But no singing!' Sarah joked. 'You are my sunshine ...' she lilted.

'Especially not that!' Nora hugged her tightly again. 'I hate that song.'

'So do I,' Sarah blurted out.

Nora looked at her sister searchingly, as she had looked at her mother when she'd asked about the wallpaper, as if there might be something there that would explain her own feel-ings to her. 'What do you mean?' she asked.

'Oh, nothing, nothing. I'm only having you on. You're

easy wound up,' said Sarah. 'Now you've got to go. Mammy's in the taxi waiting for you. Joe said they'd drop you home on the way up the road. Away on with you. I'll phone tomorrow and we'll hook up. Okay?'

'Okay,' Nora said. 'Love you. Thanks for a lovely party.'

That night Nora awoke again with tears running down her cheeks. In a quiet little echo of her memory she heard Deirdre Flynn and Máire O'Toole reciting their little mantra: 'Omo Daz drunk. Omo Daz drunk.'

She lay sobbing, clutching her pillow. Her core dissolved in a torrent of tears. She begged for some way out of this thing that she couldn't understand. She never got back to sleep.

When she got to her office the next morning she looked exhausted and her eyes were rimmed in red. She made herself coffee. She sat. She tried to calm herself but her hands were shaking.

Her friend Alice, at the next desk, watched her. Finally she reached across and laid her hand on Nora's arm. 'Are you all right?'

'I'm not great,' Nora said. She bit her lip. Even this kindness filled her eyes again with tears. 'Maybe I'm having the menopause. On the verge of HRT. Or heading for a nervous breakdown. I feel myself going down for no good reason.'

'Since when?'

'Just since I went to Dublin.'

'Did something happen there?'

'I saw some wallpaper with bluebells!' They both laughed in spite of themselves. 'It was like the wallpaper at home when I was a child. Then I had a dream, the wallpaper, I couldn't make it out, but it scared me.'

'Could be a flashback,' Alice suggested. 'Something in your childhood. Some childish hurt got buried there. But it doesn't need to be a bad thing.'

Nora looked at her. She knew as soon as Alice said it that it was a bad thing. 'I think it's something to do with my da. He was okay, except ...' Nora hesitated.

Alice looked directly into Nora's eyes.

She started to cry again. 'Except when he was drunk,' she said. 'Then he was mean.'

'How? What did he do?'

'I don't know,' she blurted out. 'That's the problem.'

'Well, you shouldn't let it get you down now. Drink makes some people like that. But that was then. This is now. Think on his good points. Think on good times youse had together. C'mon, it isn't like you to be carrying on like this ... Did youse have a good time at your mammy's birthday party? Did she enjoy it?'

'Oh, she had a ball,' Nora replied, her mood lightening a little.

'Was there a sing-song?'

'There was, yeah. We always have that.'

'And you?' said Alice. 'Did you sing?'

'I did.' Nora laughed, but the tears came again as she remembered the song her father always asked her to sing. Her fingers tightened on the handle of her cup until her knuckles turned white.

Alice reached across and took her free hand. 'C'mon, love,' she murmured, 'you're never like this.'

Nora sniffed. She clasped Alice's hand. Took a deep tear-filled breath. 'I know. I know, Alice. I hate being like this. It's all the fault of those bloody stupid bluebells!' She was laughing and crying at the one time, clutching Alice's hand and gripping her coffee cup as if her life depended on it. 'Me and Sarah are going out this week. For a wee drink or two. Maybe I'll get to the bottom of it then,' she said.

But they never got their drink. Before the weekend came their mother collapsed. A neighbour who used to look in on her found her and called an ambulance. She was still alive when she arrived at the hospital, but after a massive stroke she died in the middle of the night. Nora was the first there and her brother and sisters followed. They'd watched her health failing but none of them imagined that the end would come so quickly. Nora entered a whirlwind of funeral arrangements and hadn't time to think of her own problems.

The wake was in Sarah's house. Two of their uncles and an aunt and their families arrived back into Belfast from England and all the old neighbours gathered. Black bow on the door, the mirror covered with a white cloth, clock stopped at 3.45, the time of the passing. Sorry for your troubles. Decades of the rosary to please the priest. Wreaths. Countless cups of tea and sandwiches. Tears and laughs. Stories told and retold. Family fables passed on. Mother the centre of all their attention. Mother dead. Stretched out in her fine coffin. Grandchildren – the older ones inconsolable and the younger ones fascinated by their granny's still form – off school and in everyone's way. It all passed in a blur.

The storytelling went on into the early hours, but finally everyone went home and Sarah and her family went to bed. Nora was alone. With the first signs of dawn coming in through the windows, she sat beside her mother's coffin. She looked into her face, held her cold hand. The finality of it came to her fast and heavily. With both parents dead she was alone in a way she had never been before. Scenes from the past came to her, but not those she'd grown accustomed to. They came up from somewhere within her, but she felt as if she was seeing them for the first time. They were not the scenes of family fun and teasing and sibling rivalries and boisterous gatherings they'd all recounted when they got together, but were instead unhappy, disturbing.

And in among them her dream came back to her. She was back in her old bedroom with the bluebells on the wall. The door was open. She was in bed with Sarah, who was asleep. She could hear her gentle rhythmic breathing. She saw the dark shape of her father coming closer. His breath was heavy with drink. She heard her father's insistent, coaxing, whispering tones. It was both frightening and familiar. Then beyond him she saw her mother in the door.

'Leave that child alone,' she hissed. 'Don't you dare go near my child. You're never to touch any child of mine. Now get out.'

Her father obeyed. For a second she caught the look on his face. He was crying.

And so was she. She was back in her sister Sarah's front room. Beside her mother's coffin. The room was bare of furniture except for a row of chairs for mourners and a wee table draped in white linen adorned with blessed candles. The blinds were drawn but already the light was filtering into the room. She stood up. Stood beside her mother's coffin. She was sobbing violently. Her body convulsed, flooded with grief for all that had been done to her and could never be undone. She gripped the side of the coffin and looked down at her mother.

'Mammy, you knew! You knew, didn't you? Why didn't you say? Why didn't you stop it? You stopped him once. But then you went on as if nothing happened. Why didn't you talk to me? He was sick. But you? What did you do? How could you not say something? Ask me if I was all right? Ask me if anything was wrong? If my da was doing anything on me? I'd have stopped it myself but I was protecting wee

Sarah. Keeping him away from her. How stupid. I only see it now when it's too late to do anything about it. But you were the grown-up. You were the only one could have protected me. All those years! Not a word from you!' She swayed over the coffin, the tears streaming, choking her. 'Do you see your daughter? Cracks up over a song. Crying in the night because of dreams of her da. I'm falling apart, Mammy. What am I to do? You can't help me now. What was your silence for? For him? The neighbours? Us?'

She felt a movement beside her. It was Sarah. She'd heard everything. They grabbed on to each other. Nora held her fiercely. Something inside both of them gave way and they lost themselves in a storm of weeping. An uncontrollable hearts-broken tsunami of tears. They cried together in each other's arms beside their mother's coffin until they had nothing left. Then, arms entwined, the two of them stood exhausted in a long silence.

'I thought I was the only one,' Sarah eventually said. Quietly. In a whisper.

Nora pulled back. She held her sister by the arms and looked into her eyes. 'What do you mean?' she asked, fearing the answer.

'Me. I thought it was only me,' Sarah repeated.

'No!' cried Nora. She pulled her sister close again. 'Not you too! I thought I was keeping him away from you. And all the time he −'

'I know,' Sarah said. 'But don't blame yourself. You always minded me, from when I was a wee one.'

'I wanted to, I tried, and then look what happened, he –'

'But I'm all right now. Truly.'

'And look at me. A hopeless mess.' Nora tried to smile.

Sarah wiped the tears from her sister's eyes and smoothed her hair. Then she took her face between her hands and kissed Nora gently on the forehead just as Nora had kissed her when she was small. 'I love you, Nora,' she said.

'I love you too, sister.'

'At least we have each other.'

'Yes, yes,' said Nora, 'we do,' the tears still spilling from her eyes.

They pulled apart, drying their eyes, trying to raise a laugh at the state they were in.

'And today?' said Sarah. 'Mammy's funeral. All those people. Can you manage?'

'Yes. I promise. You go on now. Get a bit more sleep before the long day. Just leave me here a wee while.'

'Are you sure?'

'Yes. Much better now. You'll see.'

But she wasn't better, not entirely. She didn't know when or if it would be possible for her to be better entirely. For now she was seething. Angry beyond words. At what had happened to her, but above all at what her father had done to Sarah. She slipped out the front door. It was liberating to get into her car. She didn't know where she was going. The Falls Road was quiet. As she drove, the presence of the Black Mountain, a constant in her life, was visible as she accelerated past street openings. Then before her was Milltown Cemetery. The gates were open. She drove through and parked below the republican plot. Then she walked to her father's grave. The gravediggers had not arrived yet to open it for her mother's coffin. She stood transfixed at the foot of his memorial.

'Jimmy Devlin. Loving husband. Devoted father.'

That's what it said. Soon her mother would be buried with him.

'Dirty rotten stinking oul' bastard,' said Nora.

Then she stepped over the low surround and stood on his grave. 'Bastard!' she shouted. 'It wasn't Mammy's fault at all. It was you! You controlled her. You. You're good for nothing. You stinking bastard.'

She turned her face up to the sky and screamed it again. 'Dirty stinking oul' bastard!'

Then she started to stamp on the grave. First one foot at a time. Then two feet. Jumping. Stomping. Kicking. Screaming.

Behind her on the M1 early morning traffic began to crowd the motorway. Birds startled by her shouting rose from the Bog Meadows and flew excitedly in sudden bewilderment. The Black Mountain was the backcloth to it all, as it had been to many human events since time began. Nora was oblivious. Her pounding of the grave slowed to an almost rhythmic dance.

'Omo Daz drunk. Omo Daz drunk. Omo Daz drunk,' she repeated. Again and again. Until she was exhausted. Until her voice quietened to a breathless whisper.

She stood motionless for an instant on the grave. Her chest was heaving. She slowly stepped back on to the pathway. Stood for a minute. Then she left and went back to Sarah's.

To bury their mother.

THE LESSON

Mickey Grogan, seventy-six years of age, handed over a copy of the *Andersonstown News* to his grandson Tommy. It was opened at an article that had clearly upset him. They were in the snug by the main bar in Muldoon's.

'Did ya see this?'

Tommy read it while his grandfather watched closely for his reaction. It told of how a fifteen-year-old local boy named Declan Byrne had been found hanged in his own room after prolonged bullying at school. He was a promising student. Quiet, but well liked. There was a picture of him above the text, smiling, sitting between his parents at Christmas.

Tommy handed the paper back to his grandfather. He shook his head, sighed. 'That's painful,' he said.

'Aye.'

'What might he have grown up to be? He looks a lovely, innocent lad.'

'Exactly so.'

Tommy was a twenty-one-year-old student teacher. His and his grandfather's regular routine was to pass their Saturday afternoons together. Ever since he'd got his driver's

licence a few years back Tommy would borrow his father's
car and pick the old man up for their afternoon out. Tommy
didn't drink and his granda was content with a few bottles
of stout. Sometimes, if the weather was good, Tommy took
him to watch the football training session or a club game if it
was on at Corrigan Park. They usually adjourned afterwards
to the bar in Naomh Eoin's for a wee while. Then the talk
was all about hurling and football with all the Johnnies –
the Naomh Eoin men – joining in, sometimes along with
supporters of the visiting team. Tommy's granda enjoyed the
banter and good-natured backstabbing of those occasions.
But when he wanted a quiet chat with Tommy he preferred
Muldoon's and the wee snug. It was obvious to Tommy that
this was such a day.

'That's what I wanted to talk to you about. It got me
thinking, remembering … There's no tolerance of bullying
now, sure there's not, Tommy?'

'We're trained to watch out for it. We encourage kids to
talk about how they feel. But as you can see from this poor
lad, it's still a problem. A big problem. We're always telling
them that it's okay not to be okay.'

'See, that's it. When I was young there was very little talk of
it. You'd never hear about the mental health of the young – or
anyone else for that matter. But especially the young ones.
That's what was wrong with us. There was plenty of bullying
and stress but nobody talked about it. We used to get slapped

regularly in school. All the teachers had a leather strap. Barbaric when you think about it. And no one said a word. You wouldn't get away with that nowadays with your pupils, would you, Tommy?'

'Nope, Granda,' he agreed, 'but we regret it sometimes. It would make teaching easier. It's a pity they did away with corporal punishment.' He smiled.

'Not a bit of it,' the old man upbraided him. 'It was a disgrace. Grown men walloping wee boys. And wee girls too. Girls got caned regularly. Not that there were any girls at our school but your granny, God rest her, could vouch for the way she and her classmates were treated. A bloody disgrace.'

'Granda, I'm only winding you up.' Tommy laughed again. 'Take it easy.'

His granda ignored him. 'So I was remembering, thinking, like I said. That boy in the paper put me in mind of something that happened long, long ago, when I was a schoolboy myself. I wanted to tell you because it's about teaching. And that's not all it's about.'

'What else is it about, Granda?'

'You'll soon see,' he said. He poured the stout carefully into his glass. 'I had a classmate by the name of Joe McKee. A quiet wee lad. Didn't stand out in the crowd. He just melted into it. No harm in him. For some reason the teacher, a man by the name of Mulligan, took umbrage at Joe. Picked on him all the time.'

'What was Mulligan like?'

'A bad-tempered bully. Getting on in years. A carnapatious oul' shitehawk with a drink problem. One day he called Joe up from his desk.

'"Come up here, McKee," he bellowed. "Come up to the front and let the rest of the boys see the state of your shoes."

'So Joe shuffled up from his desk and Mulligan caught him by the ear and pulled painfully upwards so that he was forced to stand on his tiptoes.' The old man paused reflectively and took a little sip of his Guinness before continuing. '"Have you no polish in your house, McKee?" Mulligan shouted, all the time jerking Joe's ear. "Don't you know Saint Martha's boys are supposed to be turned out clean and tidy in a way that shows respect for our school and encourages others to do the same? Well, answer me, McKee? Don't you know that? Isn't that in your Saint Martha's Boys' Charter? To be clean and tidy!"

'Joe said nothing. The pain in his ear was excruciating. The embarrassment was worse.

'"Mr McKee has lost his tongue, boys, hasn't he? Not only does he let Saint Martha's down, not only does he let me down, but he lets you, his classmates, down also coming in here like a tramp. Look at my shoes, McKee."

'Mulligan forced Joe to swivel around, still on his toes, and then pushed his head downwards. He was a big man, heavy set and volatile. Joe could smell sweat and chalk and tobacco

and a whisper of whiskey off him. He could feel Mulligan's
fingernails cutting into his ear. He thought he was going to
faint. He was making a huge effort not to cry. Some of the
lads had laughed at first, but now they were dead quiet.'

Tommy had rarely heard his granda talk like this. It was
almost as if he was back in the classroom again.

'"Look at my shoes, boy!" roared Mulligan again. Joe was
bent double. He'd have fallen if Mulligan hadn't such a fierce
grip on his ear. All he could see were Mulligan's brown
brogues, buffed to a high shine.

'"Sir, you're hurting me, sir," he eventually hissed between
clenched teeth. "Please, sir," he repeated while trying to
straighten up.

'"What did you say, McKee?" Mulligan taunted him. "I
can't hear you down there, boy! I told you to look at my
shoes. So look at them!" he demanded, spitting the words
out. "Look … at … them. Now … look … at … yours.
What do you see? You see good manners, respect and pride
in appearance versus dirt, no manners and ill-rearing. You
would think you were trailed up. You mark my words, boy.
No good will ever come of you. Now get out of my sight."

'And with that he jerked his hand away and propelled Joe
back towards his desk.'

The old man paused again, as much, Tommy could see, to
catch his breath as anything else.

'But that wasn't enough for him, Tommy,' he continued.

'That excuse for a master stood in front of us and laid on more abuse.

'"Now," he said, brushing his fingers along his sleeves and down his hands as if he was washing them, "I don't want any boy in my class coming in here like McKee. He might be a tramp but Saint Martha's boys are not tramps. We have respect for ourselves. If we don't respect ourselves nobody else will! Is that clear, McKee?"

'Joe raised his eyes from his desktop and mumbled, "Yes, sir."

'"Speak clearly, boy. What did you say?"

'"Yes, sir," Joe repeated, loudly this time.

'"Well, stop your snivelling. Let this be a lesson to you. Let this be a lesson to you all." The oul' bastard glowered slowly and silently at the class. Not one boy had the temerity to look at him. Not one. We were cowed, subdued, eyes down and faces averted. Joe's face was red. He could feel a pounding in his head. His ear felt as if it was hanging off. He was barely able to avoid sobbing.'

Tommy listened intently. His grandfather was silent again. Lost in thought.

'What happened then, Granda? Did he report him?'

'He did not. That's what I'm trying to tell ya. He tried to bury it in himself. He went home. His ma was over a stovetop filled with steaming pots, making dinner for them all, when he reached under the sink for the biscuit box containing the tins of polish and brushes. She did everything, that woman, since Joe's da died when he was just a baby.

'"Joe," she said, "I hope you didn't go out this morning with your shoes like that. Will you go on outside to clean them? I need to get the dinner finished before the rest of them come in. Lily and Martie'll be starving and I'm way behind."

'"Okay, Ma," he said.

'"Thanks, son." She smiled. "You're a good lad."

'Joe sat out in the backyard and wiped the dirt off his shoes before plastering them with polish. He was trying to buff a shine onto them when his older brother, Martie, passed by him. "Hiya, Joe. How's she cutting? You got a date tonight?"

'"Ma," Martie said when he returned to the scullery, "our Joe needs a new pair of shoes. I'll take him downtown on Saturday and buy him a pair. I took a few quid off the book-ie's."

'Martie'd become the breadwinner since he left school and started work at the building trade, to the great relief and gratitude of their ma, with Joe and their sister Lily still at school.

'They ate their dinner in the living room, plates balanced on their knees. Afterwards Joe made the tea and Lily joined him at the sink to wash the dishes. It was then she noticed his sore ear. She leaned in to inspect it.

'"What's happened your ear, Joe?" she asked. "It's very red."

'Joe blushed and pushed her away. "I hurt it playing football," he said.

"'Ma!" Lily shouted. "There's something wrong with our Joe's ear."

"'I'm all right," Joe protested. He shied away as Martie joined them.

"'What's wrong, Joseph? You talking when you should have been listening? Let's see your war wounds."

"'I got whacked in the school yard," Joe said. "Jimmy Blair's big head."

'Joe suffered in silence as the three of them peered at his ear.

"'Put Germolene on it," his mother ordered. "It'll clean out that wee cut."

'Martie was about to apply it when he stopped to take a closer look. "You say young Blair hit you with his head? This is more of a tear than a bump, Joe. That's a nasty bruise as well. You telling me the truth?"

"'It was Jimmy Blair," Joe stammered. "I swear, Martie."

"'When you say *I swear* I know you aren't telling the truth. Tell me what happened, please.'"

Tommy's granda paused here for a moment, shook the bottle before him and found it empty. He fished a couple of notes from his pocket. 'Here, Tommy, run up and get me another bottle of stout, would ya? And something for yourself.'

'How did your friend handle that, Granda?' Tommy asked when he was back with the drinks.

'He was mortified. Nothing worse in them days than to be found out. Even if you'd done nothing wrong there was some shame in it. But he had no choice. They dragged it out of him. So he told them the story of his dirty shoes, of Mulligan pulling him to the front of the class and of how he had treated him. Martie was livid. So was Lily. "He can't be allowed to get away with that," she exclaimed.

'"I'll get an hour off tomorrow and have a word with him," said Martie.

'Poor Jimmy,' the granda said. 'He saw the hard look in his brother's eyes. He saw the whole disastrous scene play out in his mind. Martie wasn't as big as Mulligan but he was tall and lean and fit from his work on the building sites and his twice-weekly training session at the local boxing club. His mother so far had said nothing to dissuade Martie. The situation had gone beyond Joe's control, but he dreaded the consequences.

'Next morning he went to school early. His shoes were shiny. He was subdued. His ear still hurt, but he wasn't thinking about that. He could think only of Martie, and also Mulligan. He sat quietly while Mr Mulligan commenced the day's lessons. He tried not to attract attention to himself, but he knew it wouldn't be long until Mulligan would be picking on him. And he was right.

'"McKee," roared Mulligan.

'Joe lowered his eyes.

'"McKee, speak when you are spoken to. Come here, boy."

'"Yes, sir." Joe got hesitantly to his feet.

'"Ah, McKee. You polished your shoes. Good boy!"

'Joe stood at the front of the class. His classmates had fallen silent.

'"You've learned your lesson, McKee. Shiny shoes. Respect. See, boys?" Mulligan gestured to the class. He put his arm around Joe's shoulder and leaned slightly against him. "See! Even a tramp can be taught manners. He might not be capable of a lot but young McKee has learned how to polish his shoes."

'He turned Joe around and examined the back of his neck. "What's this on your ear, boy? Eh? What's this?"

'Joe felt his lower lip tremble. He felt like he was going to pee his pants. It seemed to him that every one of his classmates was staring at him. He felt Mulligan's breath against his cheek. The stale smell of drink and tobacco threatened to make him vomit. "It's Germolene, sir," he stammered in a whisper.

'"Speak up, boy!" Mulligan guldered. "Speak up!"'

At this point Tommy's granda turned to him and asked, 'Can you guess what happened next?'

'Martie arrived in and sorted out Mulligan?'

'Nearly right, Tommy. But it wasn't Martie. It was his

74

mother. It seems she'd thought about it overnight. She wanted to protect both her sons: Joe from further humiliation and Martie from trouble with the peelers. She was determined to get there first. We saw her before the master or Joe. Joe told me afterwards that he felt his mother's presence before he saw or heard her. Mulligan was surprised as well. He was so preoccupied with goading Joe that she was in the classroom and halfway across the floor before he saw her. By then it was too late.

'"Let go of my son," she snapped at him. "Let him go, you big good-for-nothing hallion. You ignorant galoot. Let him go now."

'Mulligan released Joe, who took a step back so that his mother was face to face with his tormentor. Well, she would have been face to face if she was a foot taller. But Mrs McKee was undaunted. She glared up at him and reached up to tap him in the chest with a clenched fist. He stepped back. Joe could see his classmates craning forward as his mother berated Mulligan.

'"Don't you ever ill-treat a child of mine, or any other child for that matter, again. Call yourself a teacher. There's better men in the Children's Hospital."

'She advanced on him again but this time Mulligan caught her by the wrist. "Madam," he hissed. "I'll have the police on you. You cannot come into my class like this —"

'Mrs McKee pulled free. "And you cannot demean or

bully children," she retorted. "Get the police. Go on. Send for them and explain my Joe's ear to them. Go on. Get them."

'Mulligan took a step towards her but pulled up when the door burst open and Martie came in dressed in his working clothes. "What are you doing here, Ma?" he exclaimed. "I said I'd sort this out."

'His mother didn't budge. She continued to glower at Mulligan. He towered above her. "I think you have drink taken, my good man," she accused him.

'Mulligan turned from the mother to Martie and saw the hard, cold look in his eyes. He retreated, bumping against Joe in the process. He tripped and fell awkwardly on to his knees. A boy at the back of the class let out a loud whoop. Somebody else laughed. Mulligan tried to scramble to his feet and fell over again, red faced and breathing heavily.

'"Help him up, Martie," Mrs McKee instructed her son. "He's like a big girl's blouse. Only good for bating wee boys and threatening women."

'Martie reached down and pulled Mulligan to his feet. By now the class was in uproar. We hadn't a day as good as that in years. Or ever.

'"We're going to the headmaster now, Mulligan. You can explain to him how you teach children."

'Then, turning on her heel, she pushed Martie and Joe out the classroom door in front of her. Mr Mulligan followed them silently. But he never went to the headmaster's office.

Rumour had it he ended up in Walsh's pub downtown. Our class got the rest of the day off. Joe was a hero. A month later the talk was that Mr Mulligan took early retirement.'

'Not a day too soon,' Tommy remarked.

His grandfather said nothing as he sipped at his Guinness. But he looked satisfied.

'You know that story well, Granda,' said Tommy.

'Hard to forget.'

'Even how Mulligan smelled when he caught Joe by the ear.'

'Sure we all knew that.'

'How did you know what happened in the house that night?'

'He told me. I know him to this day. He opened a shop in Andytown. His son runs it now.'

'Is it a shoe shop?' Tommy asked with a smile. 'You called him Joe and then in the middle of the story you called him Jimmy.'

'Did I? I must be getting old. There was another lad went by that name.'

'Didn't your da die when you were a baby, Granda? Didn't you have an older brother who boxed? Is the story about you?'

The old man looked at Tommy for a long while, then he clinked glasses with his grandson. 'You have me read. You see, that's the problem right there, Tommy. I covered up the important bit. Kept it to myself. Told you a fib. Even after all these years I held back. I wanted to tell you about Mulligan when I read about that poor young lad, Declan Byrne. But even then I didn't tell you it was me. That's a big lesson for me today. That and the fact that I was blessed with a mother with a brave heart.'

He finished the last of his Guinness. 'Who knows how I'd have wound up had my ma not come to the school that day. Maybe I'd have had the same fate as young Byrne, or some other kind of mess in my head. Things here in the North were different in those days. The whole lot of us here pressed to the ground, just the way Mulligan pressed me down. You keep taking it and saying nothing and it's like drinking poison. But my ma stood up for me. That saved me. Saved a lot of us. Our whole class saw how a wee woman who believes in her own strength can bring down a bully.'

He stepped back to regard his grandson. 'Your generation is a bit different. You don't have that fearful, hopeless look a lot of us had back in the day when we were your age. But still young Declan Byrne slipped through the net. If only he had spoken to someone. I'm sure someone would have stood up for him if they had known he needed help. But I'm one to talk. I didn't tell my ma what happened the first time and even now, sixty years later, I didn't tell you the full story the first time. Try never to make that mistake, Tommy. Don't keep things like that to yourself. You never know when you might need someone to stand up for you. Or when you might need to stand up for them.'

'You've always done that, Granda. You were always there for me, just like you're here now telling this story.'

They made their way out of the pub. Outside on the pavement, Tommy stopped as his granda pointed down at his feet. 'Every time I polished my shoes over the years I thought of oul' Mulligan. And sometimes I felt just a wee bit sorry for him. He came out of this the worst. All because my ma stood up for me. Nothing bates that.'

Tommy reached out to his grandfather and hugged him. The old man was embarrassed. Standing outside Muldoon's where all the world could see them. But he was pleased as well.

'Instead of going straight home I'll run you over to the club now, Granda. Just for an hour. Rossa are playing Lámh Dearg. We'll catch the second half.'

'Aye,' his granda said with a smile. 'That should be a good game. And we'll have another yarn next Saturday.'

THE PRISONER

Seamus remained seated despite the perfunctory effort by the prison officers to get him to stand as the judge sentenced him to ten years for possession of a revolver and six rounds of ammunition. His seat was in the dock of Belfast Court House on the Crumlin Road. The efforts to get him to stand were only for show because republican defendants in this court without a jury rarely stood for the judge. Over the years battering and batoning them to do so had failed and then petered out almost completely. For that Seamus was glad.

The judge didn't look at him. Even though he himself was being disrespectful, Seamus thought that was out of order. An ignorant wee bastard. Seamus's family was in the public gallery. They applauded as he was escorted below the dock. He could hear Síle, his wife of two months, shouting, 'Well done, Seamus.'

He couldn't see them but as he ducked down the narrow stairs out of sight he raised a clenched fist defiantly. 'Up the 'RA!' he shouted.

'You got off light,' one of the screws said to him as he locked him in a holding cell. 'Your solicitor will be here shortly. Yours is the ninth case he lost this week,' he chuckled.

Seamus said nothing.

His solicitor, Timothy Dooley, was very cheerful for a man who had lost nine cases. 'You got off light,' he said also. 'If you'd been charged with possession with intent you would have been snookered. Ten years is a good result. I think we should appeal the severity of the sentence. The bullets didn't fit the gun so that has to count for something. Here.' He passed a packet of Fruit Pastilles to Seamus.

Seamus was glad to get them. His mouth was dry. He thanked Mr Dooley. He was a decent man, reduced in his legal endeavours to going through the motions on the judicial conveyor belt that served no justice with its special laws that deposited mainly young men in Long Kesh and other prisons. Still, he did his best, Seamus thought resignedly. It wasn't his fault. It was the system.

'They'll bring you back to the prison reception to get properly processed and then you'll be transferred to Long Kesh. I spoke to Síle and your parents. Síle says she'll be up for a visit tomorrow.'

He stood up. Seamus did likewise. They shook hands and Seamus watched as Mr Dooley was escorted back up to the courthouse again. He hadn't long to wait before he himself was escorted in the opposite direction, in handcuffs, back through the tunnel which burrowed below the Crumlin

Road, joining the court to the prison.

He felt deflated. Worried about Síle. They were only just married. Ten years was a long time for her to wait for him. And for children, if they were lucky enough to have some when he got out. He knew Síle really wanted a baby. So did he, but he reasoned that his longing for a child wasn't the same as Síle's. A man's wants or needs aren't the same as a woman's, and men didn't generally have a biological clock to worry them. Or so Seamus told himself in the long hours of doing nothing in his cell except thinking about what the future might bring for the two of them.

But Síle was strong. He knew that. That's why she was in the IRA. He had known she was a volunteer long before they were married. It was she who had asked him to keep the weapon in their house. Just for a few days. It was his name on the rent book, so he was the one who was charged. He thanked his lucky stars for that. He was glad the two of them weren't in the dock. He knew she felt sore about him taking the rap for the gear, but what could she do? No point in both of them going down. Better him in prison than her, he thought.

Their house was raided as part of a saturation search of their neighbourhood. About a hundred homes were done and a dozen or so arms found, most of them like the one in their house – not much use. Not that Seamus would have known, but Síle had told him it was just a training weapon.

She had also promised him, when he was only a few weeks on remand, that she would do nothing which might put her at risk. She said she wasn't leaving the army and he hadn't asked her to. Seamus wasn't a volunteer himself but he was as good as any volunteer, quietly doing what he could to help his local unit.

He was glad to be out of the Crum. Glad to get the trial over him. Remand was stressful. The Crum was a decrepit old jail, overcrowded and claustrophobic. The republican remand prisoners were on forty-seven-hour lock-up, which meant they only had one or, if lucky, two exercise sessions every two days. There were two young lads – about nineteen years old – in the cell with Seamus. They were nice lads. From the country, culchies. But they talked non-stop about their cases and played a local music station from morning to lights out, while Seamus spent most of his time reading any books he could get his hands on and doing his best not to let them get on his nerves too much.

At least that was all behind him now, he thought, as the prison van – which used to be called the paddy wagon – transported him and other newly sentenced felons up the M1 to the Kesh.

Síle, meanwhile, had made her way home. She, her parents and Seamus's parents, along with his younger brother and sister, had walked down the Crumlin Road after a few minutes with Mr Dooley. He was doing his best to be positive as he explained the appeals process, if Seamus decided to follow that course.

'He got off light. A different judge might have given him fifteen years,' he said.

'That's easy for you to say,' Síle retorted, before regretting her sharpness as Mr Dooley's smile crumpled.

A decade or so of similar scenes had done little to stiffen him against the annoyance of his clients' families on the odd occasion some of them gave off to him. Most suffered in silence.

Síle moved quickly to soften her words. 'He won't have to do it all anyway, Mr Dooley. He'll be out before we know it. You did your best. Thank you very much.'

They shook hands. Outside the sun was shining. People were strolling, laughing, living their everyday lives. She felt like she was on a different planet from them. All the pent-up strain since the arrest landed on her. She felt exhausted. Seamus's parents offered her dinner, but she put them off to the following day, after the visit. She just wanted to go home. When she got there she kicked off her shoes and slumped back on the settee. The house was quiet. Not a sound. She started to cry. Not just for herself. For Seamus. Bloody Brits. Being locked up and having to sacrifice your youth was just part of the way of life nowadays for people in communities like theirs.

She had no regrets about taking a stand with her friends and neighbours. A life of resistance. Living under occupation wasn't easy but acquiescing to or ignoring what was happening wasn't an option for her.

She didn't cry for long. It was more nerves and the realisation that Seamus and she would be separated for some time. He would be locked up by now, anyway, in his new accommodation, probably in his bed, she thought. So she locked up the wee house they had shared for only a wee while and got ready for bed herself.

At least she wouldn't have to go to the Crum. She hated going there, making her way across town usually on her own. She brightened up at the thought of the visit to the Kesh the following day. Many other local women were in the same boat, she reflected, although that was little comfort. But there would be a bit of craic anyway on the way up on the bus. A minibus full of women, some with children, messing and slagging. Guldering and laughing at each other. Keeping their spirits up. That was now a way of life for many of them.

'So, missus, time to get used to being a grass widow,' she told herself as she settled into bed. 'Good night, Seamus,' she whispered. 'Oíche mhaith, love.'

'Time to get up, Seamus.'

'Maith go leor, John. What's the time?'

'Eight o'clock and all is well.'

'Thanks. Be there now.'

Seamus stretched out on his narrow cot. John slept in the bunk above him. He always got up when the screws opened the hut doors at seven thirty. That way, he said, he and some of the older hands got into the showers first. 'Before all the rowdies,' as John put it.

There were thirty prisoners in the hut. There were three huts just like the one John and Seamus lived in and a half-hut. They housed almost a hundred men. The huts sat along one side of a tarmacked yard surrounded by high wire fences. These cages in turn were themselves surrounded by more wire fences, watchtowers and searchlights. This was Long Kesh prison camp. Prisoners were detained there. Some were internees, held indefinitely without charge or trial. The others, in the part of the camp where Seamus was held, had been subjected to a non-jury special courts process.

The majority of these prisoners were long-termers, most of them republicans, although at the top end of the camp there were two or three cages of loyalists. They were segregated from the republicans. Many of the men in Seamus's cage had been there for years. He and a handful of younger prisoners were new arrivals. Seamus found the relative autonomy of life in the cages of Long Kesh a welcome improvement on the locked-up and locked-down regime in Belfast Prison, the Crum.

The Crum was through-other and dirty. At least in Long

Kesh the prisoners could see the sky. Although, sharing a corrugated Nissen hut with so many other men was a bit disconcerting for Seamus. Like living in a dormitory. John had told him when he arrived that he could be prosecuted for cruelty to animals if he kept pigs in these conditions.

'Well, I've plenty of time to get used to it,' Seamus reminded himself. 'Ten years. And I've only been here one night.'

With that he pulled himself to the edge of his iron bed frame and sat for a few minutes. There was only a space of two feet or so between Seamus's bunk and his neighbour's, who was fast asleep. Or so it seemed. As Seamus reached for his jeans he heard incoherent muttering from beneath the blankets. That's how it had been since Seamus had settled down for slumber the night before. His neighbour talked in his sleep. Not loudly. Or in a comprehensible way. More a mumbled monologue.

Seamus struggled into his clothes, anxious not to disturb his comrades, and pulled on his boots. He lifted his wash bag and towel, tiptoed across the hut and slipped quietly through the heavily fortified door and out into the yard. Across from him two prisoners were jogging around the cage. Another older man was scattering bread in a corner and above him on the barbed wire a queue of sparrows and starlings waited for breakfast. Seamus strolled cheerfully towards the shower hut. He was glad to be in the fresh air. That, at least, was a blessing.

So was the shower hut being empty. Apart from John, who

stooped, naked to the waist, over a large sink slowly shaving, Seamus had the place to himself. Not that he ever thought he would see anything positive in a structure like the one he stood in now. Cold concrete floors and walls. Rough latrines. A row of shower cubicles and a stand of big Belfast sinks. Jawboxes. According to John, at times the hut would be filled with naked or half-naked men shaving or shower-ing, washing their clothes, singing and shouting, bantering and slagging. Not unlike the changing rooms at a hurling club after a training session or a game. Especially on visiting days, when there was a sense of excitement and anticipation among those prisoners who were due visits that day.

And today was such a day for Seamus. He wanted to savour it. His visit was a morning one. That's why he was up and in the shower hut so early. He wanted to avoid the rush. He wanted to be ready for Síle so he could get the most of his allotted time with her. She wouldn't have got the letter yet but he had written to her as soon as he got to the Kesh. He told her of the warm welcome from the other prisoners for him and three Belfast lads who arrived at the same time. Their slagging and good-natured banter took the edge off the brusque attitude of the prison officers who'd met them at the prison reception.

'You, 451!' one of them had barked at him. 'I'm the prin-cipal officer. I am Sir. You are a fucking number. You are 451. Leave your bag here. The governor is waiting to see you. Fall in there between those two officers.' He gestured towards two other screws who stood slightly apart on each side of a doorway into a small office.

From where Seamus stood, he could see a small man in civilian clothes seated behind a desk which was also flanked by two uniformed prison officers. He strolled over to the doorway.

'Smarten yourself up, 451,' the principal officer ordered him. 'Left, right. Left, right.'

Seamus dandered with as much bravado as he could muster while the two screws stood smartly on each side of him as soon as he entered the small office. There was only limited room, less than two steps, before he was in front of the desk.

'Aaa-teen-shun!' the principal officer barked.

The small besuited man who sat behind the desk seemed slightly embarrassed by the whole business. He looked up at Seamus from behind horn-rimmed spectacles. 'Mr McKenna?' he said quietly. He was English, with a mild plummy accent. Shuffling the papers on his desk with one hand while running his other hand across his bald head, he waited for Seamus to reply.

'Address the governor as sir,' the principal officer interjected, glowering at Seamus.

'Mr McKenna,' the governor repeated. 'You will be housed in Compound 10. Your prison number is 451. The PO will escort you to your compound. Thank you, Mr Giles.' He nodded to the principal officer. 'Goodbye, Mr McKenna.' He shuffled his papers again and looked up at Seamus. 'I hope your stay with us will be uneventful.'

Seamus hadn't been sure what to do, but it was of little matter. The PO snapped to attention. 'About turn, 451!' he roared, and the two screws who flanked Seamus about-turned and escorted him left, right, left, right back out into the reception.

As Seamus bent over to pick up his bag, the PO caught him roughly from behind and pushed him up against the wall. 'Don't you think you can come in here and fuck us about, 451, you Fenian fucker. When a prison officer speaks to you, you answer him. You understand?' He pinned Seamus's arms behind his back and shoved him towards the other screws. 'Take him to his cronies,' he snarled. And that was that.

Seamus had had no contact with the prison system since. He knew a screw would escort him from the cage to the Visits – a long series of prefab huts divided into small visiting rooms under the close scrutiny of both his escort and other screws – and as he dried himself off after his shower, he thought of the strain the coming years would put on his marriage. He knew of some relationships which had broken down. It was straightforward for a prisoner. He or she had no option but to get on with it. There were very little alternatives or temptations in Long Kesh. But outside it was different. And Síle was an attractive young woman. He knew she loved him, but what if she met someone else?

Back in the hut, John had the tea ready. He seemed to catch on to Seamus's mood. 'The first visit can be the worst one,' he said with a smile. 'Until the next bad one. If you're not careful you could put your wife on a downer. Remember, she's doing time as well. So go out there and be cheerful.'

'I'm okay,' Seamus said gruffly.

'Well, then you're a better man than me,' said John. 'I've been here five years and I've never been okay. But I make the most of it and that's all any of us can do.'

'Five years?' Seamus murmured, sipping slowly on the tea. 'Five years? How long have you to do?'

'I got life,' John said evenly. 'So I don't have a release date. And I don't have a wife either. So go out and have a good visit and don't be feeling sorry for yourself. Not on your first visit. You'll have plenty of time for that. Déan do whack – do your whack. And finish your tea. I'm away for a boowl.'

Seamus thanked John and walked with him to the door. As John went off, Seamus sat in the morning sunshine and sipped his tea. Boowl was prisoner parlance for a walk. John was one of the few prisoners who walked on his own. Most men, particularly the younger ones, walked in groups, mostly in twos, and if one of them went off on their own it was usually a cause for banter and slagging from other walkers.

This morning six prisoners were walking. Two of them, including John, were on their own. The others were in pairs.

All of them were walking anticlockwise. Seamus pondered on that as he finished his cuppa. Against the clock. Funny how everyone here walked in that direction. He was interrupted in his musing by a prison officer calling his name.

'McKenna. Visit!'

Seamus waved to him and sighed. That was all he needed. His escort was Principal Officer Giles. From his time in the Crum he knew it was unusual for a PO to act as an escort on visits. Better not to show any concern, he decided. Better not to let him ruin his first visit. So when Giles opened the gate and gestured to Seamus to take up the search position, Seamus smiled at him. 'Good morning, Mr Giles!' he said.

Giles frisked him quickly, running his hands over Seamus's chest and shoulders and then bending to run his hands up and down Seamus's outstretched legs. 'One off,' Giles called to the other prison officer who controlled the outside gate. 'One off,' he repeated as they made their way through the airlock and he and Seamus started the short journey from Cage 10 to the visiting area.

'Thank you, Mr Giles,' the other prison officer said, smiling. 'Have a good visit, young McKennna,' he called cheerfully after Seamus as he locked the gate again.

'Thanks,' Seamus stammered in surprise.

And so he did. Síle looked well. He had to wait a few minutes for her in the visiting cubicle. Then before he knew it she was standing in front of him. He reached for her and they held each other tightly without a word between them. For that short time he was oblivious to everything except her smell, the feel of her body against him and the way her hands pressed into his back. His lips brushed gently across her hair and he cupped her face in his hands. 'Come here,' he whispered and they kissed passionately.

The visit was over far too quickly. Giles didn't intrude on them. He stood slightly back from the door of their cubicle, talking to another screw at the adjoining one. Seamus and Síle stood for the entire visit, speaking in whispers and holding each other close. Síle told him of how she'd made her way home after the court. When she recalled how she felt that night, thinking of him being away for ten years, Seamus squeezed her to him and fought back the tears which threatened to unnerve him.

Then, looking into his eyes, Síle said quietly, 'I swear to stand by you. I love you and,' she smiled at him, 'I know you couldn't do your whack without me.'

So Seamus returned from the visit on a high. Back in the hut, he stretched himself out on his bunk and carefully unwrapped the tiny package that Síle had slipped from her mouth to his as they kissed at the end of the visit. These comms or teachts – from communications or *teachtaireacht* – were letters written on cigarette papers then folded tightly before being wrapped securely in cling film. There were three separate missives in Seamus's teacht. He unfolded them carefully, saving the cling film for future use. One of the notes was from Síle to him. He put it to one side. The second was for another prisoner. His wife was a friend of Síle's and, as was the custom, visitors regularly brought letters in and out for each other.

But the last one had no name on it. Seamus pondered on that. Then he slipped it under his pillow and opened Síle's note.

Seamus, when you get to read this our visit will be over so these few words are just to tell you again that I love you. I can't wait to see you and to hold you and to feel your arms around me. That's all I think of. Me and you together again. I know it seems very long before you get out, but the time will come when all this will be a memory. So you mind yourself, love. Don't worry about me. I am yours forever.

xoxo Síle

Seamus sighed. He smoothed the note gently with his finger and read it again. He savoured every word. Over and over. Until he could almost recite it, especially the last sentence. *I am yours forever.*

'You doing heavy whack?' John's voice roused Seamus from his reflections. 'Big D time. Post-visit depression.' He laughed. 'C'mon, chara. Time for walkies.'

The two of them strolled around the cage talking easily about that weekend's football fixtures. John was from North

Antrim. His passion was hurling. But he tolerated football. Seamus could see that John was making an effort to ease him into the routines of life in Long Kesh. He was grateful for that. Seamus told John that he'd had a good visit, that Síle was looking well and that she had left him some money in his tuck-shop account. 'I'm going to get some tea-bags and biscuits. Do you want anything?'

'Nope,' John replied. 'I'm well stocked up. I have my own wee routine. Every month I get Jaffa Cakes, tea-bags and Wrigley's chewing gum. Every so often I break out and get an Aero bar, a mint one. I'm easy satisfied.' He smiled and then, nodding towards a large group of screws who were congregating at the cage gates, he scowled. 'Looks like a raid. It's not often we get a raid during daytime.'

As they watched, the screws were approached by the cage OC, who was elected to represent the prisoners. Mickey Doherty was his name. He was a middle-aged Belfast man. Seamus and John watched as he and the principal officer conversed for a few minutes. Then Mickey went into the first hut ahead of the raiding party.

'Mickey will accompany them during the raid. That way there's less chance of anything being stolen,' John said to Seamus. 'They shouldn't be long. They're looking for poitín.'

The raid lasted about an hour. Fifteen minutes or so in each hut. The screws checked lockers and under beds. They sounded the floors randomly using heavy metal bars and searched the wash hut as well for good measure. Then they left. Seamus and John continued their walk until a few minutes before lunchtime. It had been an anxious week running up to his trial. Now he knew where he was. And the visit with Síle had lifted something from him. He felt peaceful for once, more relaxed, ready for a short siesta.

'I think I'll have a wee doze,' he told John.

'Me too,' said John, and the two of them flopped on their bunks.

Seamus fell instantly into a deep sleep. After what seemed like minutes he was awakened by a sharp jab in his ribs. It was Joe from the bunk opposite him. 'The OC wants you,' he said.

'Me?' Seamus asked.

'Yup! You, mo chara. Anois!'

Seamus knew the OC. He had been in the Crum for the first two months of Seamus's incarceration there, and the two of them had spent some long, slow hours together in the holding cell below the court waiting for their remand hearings. Seamus had found Mickey Doherty to be a thoughtful individual, intense and deeply committed to the republican struggle. He also recalled that the screws rarely messed Mickey about. This was his second period in prison – he had served a sentence during the early seventies. He had been elected OC, or officer in charge, of Cage 10 when he'd moved there after being sentenced to twenty years. Seamus remembered Mickey telling the judge that he was honoured to be part of the IRA and sorry only that he was caught. The judge added another five years for that. Mickey was unfazed. 'When I get to judge you I'll be much fairer than that,' he declared. 'Tiochfaidh ar lá.'

So Seamus was pleased that Mickey was looking to see him, and when they met in Mickey's hut it was clear the feeling was mutual.

As they shook hands, Mickey grinned at him. 'Well, our kid? How's it going? Sorry I didn't get to see you when you arrived. I was in the prison hospital. I hope you're settling in okay. Is John looking after you?'

Seamus told him he was doing well. 'But,' he asked, 'what has you in hospital?'

'Nothing to worry about. I'm grand,' Mickey replied. 'I'll tell you what I'm after. Did you get a comm from taobh amuigh – outside – on your visit?'

'Yup,' said Seamus. 'There was no name on it and Síle didn't tell me who it was for. I'll go get it now.'

'Okey-dokey,' said Mickey. 'See you back here.'

Seamus hurried to his hut. There was nobody about. Most of the men were in the canteen watching a film. Seamus had wanted to watch it, but it was too late now. Not to worry, he told himself. John had told him they got a film every few weeks. He lifted his pillow and felt his heart skip when he realised that the comm wasn't there.

'Fuck's sake,' he muttered to himself. Then as he pulled back the sheet he cursed again. Loudly this time, recalling the screw raid earlier that day. 'I'm in shit now,' he said to the empty hut as he stripped back his bedclothes and checked the floor space around his bunk. No comm.

Mickey was visibly annoyed, though he contained it well, when Seamus returned and explained that he couldn't find the teacht. 'What do you mean you can't find it?' was all he said before asking Seamus to go back and recheck his bed.

Seamus did so. John helped him. But to no avail. The comm was nowhere to be seen. Mickey joined them and searched the place again. By now he looked unsettled. Eventually he gave up. 'Let me talk to you a minute, Seamus,' he said. 'Outside, le do thoil.'

Once outside, Mickey told Seamus he wanted him to report to the camp adj when he arrived into the cage that afternoon on a visit. All the cages had their own command structure, which was subordinate to an overall camp council. The council took decisions on behalf of the republican prisoners, liaised with the prison administration and communicated with outside. The camp council was headed by an OC who had a small staff including an adj. He was responsible for discipline among the prisoners.

'This is a serious matter, Seamus,' Mickey continued. 'The comm was important. It should have been handed over right away. Now it looks like the screws have it and the OC will want to know how that happened. Okay? Be at the study hut at three. Just make sure you tell exactly what happened. And don't be talking to anyone else.'

The study hut was a wooden shed adjacent to the shower hut. Set aside for study purposes and Irish classes, it was also used for meetings. Seamus knocked on the door promptly at three o'clock. He had seen the adj arrive into the cage an hour or so earlier. He was a Tyrone man, Martin McNulty. Seamus didn't know him but he had heard that he was a fitness fanatic, running up to ten miles every day around the cage. Rumour had it that he wanted to introduce a fitness regime for the republican prisoners but the council felt this should be on a voluntary basis. Since he'd become adj he had introduced a range of other measures, which included weekly clean-outs of the huts and daily brushing of the yard in the republican cages.

When Seamus entered the study hut, Martin told him to take a seat. 'I'm sorry,' he said, 'to put you through all this, but we're just trying to get some sense of what happened with the comm. Tell me, le do thoil?'

So Seamus told him. It didn't take long.

'Do you know who the comm was from?' Martin asked him.

'No,' Seamus replied. 'Síle didn't say.'

'Do you think she knew?'

'Is this a wind-up?' Seamus laughed in genuine amusement.

'It's a serious question,' Martin replied. 'And it's no laughing matter. You were given a teacht from outside to deliver to us. Who has it? The screws have it, that's who! So tell me the joke? Eh? Tell me the joke and the two of us can laugh together, funny boy!'

Seamus sat back in his chair and took a deep breath. Martin was glowering at him.

'Look,' Seamus began again. 'I don't know what all the fuss is about, but it has nothing to do with me. I didn't know who the comm was for. There was no name on it. It was our first visit. We had things to talk about. So maybe Síle should have told me something and maybe she forgot, but she did nothing wrong. She didn't need to smuggle the bloody thing in anyway, so leave her out of it. It's my fault for leaving it on my leaba. But that doesn't make me Gypo Nolan. I only went for a walk – I didn't actually hand it over to the screws.' Now *he* was glowering.

'You might as well have,' Martin retorted. 'This isn't the end of this matter. Report to your OC tomorrow at noon. We'll have some sense of things by then. And change your attitude. Don't be an amadán. You're a republican prisoner. Don't behave like a squaddie.'

'And don't you behave like a sergeant major!' Seamus thought angrily to himself. But, as he told John later, he said nothing aloud.

'I didn't mind the first few questions,' Seamus said as they walked around the yard. 'But when he began the interrogation and brought Síle into it, I thought that was out of order.'

'Sometimes,' John replied, 'people end up saying more than they mean to. There is a wee cut-off between the brain and the tongue and it doesn't work all the time the way it is supposed to.'

Seamus started to chuckle. 'When did you become a Buddhist?'

'When I entered into this place I took Holy Orders. Along with a vow of celibacy. It keeps me from going mad.'

'So what should I do? What can I do?' Seamus asked him.

'When you talk to Mickey tomorrow just take it easy. Mickey is a good guy. Martin's not a bad fella either. But command is a lonely post and he has his job to do. One thing's for certain: whatever was in your comm was something important.'

'Aye. It wouldn't be like me to lose a comm that wasn't a matter of national importance. Someone up there loves me. Let's go in and I'll make your tea.'

The following morning all the talk was about the raid on the prison hospital. The trusty bringing in the containers of porridge told John, who was on breakfast duty that week, that a big raiding party had arrived at the hospital directly after lock-up the night before. The hospital was really only another cage, with two huts set up like hospital wards and another hut for medical screws and a store for pharmaceutical supplies. The raiding party took the place apart and got a stash of white coats and other gear, including an imitation revolver, hidden in a hidey hole in one of the wards.

John relayed this scéal to Seamus.

'You think there's a connection between the comm and the raid?' Seamus asked.

'Who knows?' John replied. 'But they were obviously acting on some sort of information. You'll find out soon enough. Here comes Mickey and Martin.'

'Mickey was in the prison hospital when I arrived here from the Crum,' Seamus recalled.

'I'll leave you to it,' John said. 'Don't forget what I told you. Maith go leor? Morning, Mickey. Hiya, Martin.'

Mickey nodded towards him.

Martin raised a hand in greeting. 'Maidin maith, John. Fancy a quick boowl, Seamus?'

The three of them strolled around the cage. It was a nice morning. The prison camp was slowly coming to life. A radio blared from one of the huts. Two prisoners were brushing the yard. Overhead, Seamus noticed a hawk slowly circling above one of the watchtowers. Mickey was talking in low, intense short sentences. From what Seamus could gather, the raid on the hospital had put paid to an escape plan.

'The problem is, Seamus, it was very tight. We were just waiting on the go-ahead from taobh amuigh. I was in the hospital myself putting the final touches to the plan. The comm you lost is the only way the screws could have rumbled us.'

Seamus's heart sank. He took a deep breath. He didn't know what to say. So he said the first thing that came into his mind. 'Nothing to do with me, Mickey. How could I know anything about anything? I only arrived here. Unless they knew I was bringing the comm in, and if they thought that they would have strip-searched me and Síle. So as far as I can see, they just got lucky finding the comm and all …' His words trailed off sullenly. He could see Mickey wasn't listening. Or Martin. They walked on in an awkward silence.

Eventually Martin exclaimed, 'How could you be so stupid? What kind of eejit are you? Leaving a comm on your bed like that. The height of stupidity.'

Seamus said nothing.

'It isn't that I think you had any inside knowledge of the escape or that you gave it away. Nope, that's not why I'm annoyed. It's because it's the wee things that you can't plan for or predict, those are the things that trip you up. So all the months of planning and plotting come to nought. All because somebody doesn't do what they were supposed to. And, mo chara, in this case that somebody is you. Or, at least, one of the somebodies is you. So we're going to have an enquiry. You will be put under arrest.'

'Put under arrest?' Seamus interjected. 'Put under arrest?

I can't believe you said that. I'm in fucking Long Kesh. I *am* under arrest. Would you ever catch yourself on!'

Mickey said nothing. Martin was unperturbed. He gestured to two other prisoners who were sitting outside the study hut. 'Jimmy here and Declan,' Martin continued, 'will keep guard on you. You are to be detained in the study hut until 1.30, when the enquiry starts. You will remain under detention, probably in your own hut, until the enquiry agrees its conclusions – hopefully later this evening. You are not to talk to or have contact with anyone until then. Is that understood?'

Seamus stared at him open-mouthed.

Martin concluded, 'You'll be able to get someone to represent you if the enquiry finds you are at fault. And you'll have the right to appeal. If you want to. Mickey is your OC. He will see that you get all your rights. Sin é.'

One of the two lads, the one named Declan, came alongside Seamus. 'Let's go, mucker. Lean ar aghaidh.' He opened the study hut door.

Seamus hesitated. The other lad, Jimmy, who Seamus knew from the Crum, came in behind him. 'The lunatics have taken over the asylum,' Seamus muttered.

'Ach, don't be like that,' said Jimmy. 'It'll soon be sorted out. I'll go and get you tea. One off,' he mimicked with a smile at Declan and Seamus.

When he returned with the tea, Seamus and Declan were

sitting where he had left them. In silence. Neither of them responded positively to his efforts to lift the mood.

'Give it a rest,' Declan eventually advised him.

So the three of them sat in silence until a paranoid tenseness and an awkward brittle mood enveloped them. Seamus's mind, fuelled by anger at Martin's attitude to him and the implied criticism of Síle, was racing. He knew that he had to contain himself. But that rational part of his consciousness was consumed by a jagged, blinding rage which bubbled within him. So he sat with his two comrades guarding him. Guarding him from what? he fumed to himself. And if he insisted on leaving the study hut, could they really stop him? Where could he go? Other prisoners boowled around the yard. He sat looking out at them. Looking out from his prison. His own little prison. At them walking round and round in their bigger prison.

Eventually a number of members of the camp staff arrived. They quizzed Seamus about the comm and he answered their questions with great patience. It didn't take long. About twenty minutes or so. Then they conferred in low tones while he sat stony faced just out of earshot. When their deliberations were complete, the most senior of the prisoners asked Seamus to bring his chair over to the table where the three of them were sitting.

'I'm sorry you had to go through all this,' he said. 'We have no reason to think you were implicated in any way in the escape being rumbled. We do think you should have made a bigger effort to pass the comm on to one of the cage staff, but it seems to us that it was a fluke that it was caught so you are free to go.' He smiled, stood up and stretched his hand towards Seamus. They shook hands, though Seamus said nothing.

Free to go, he thought to himself as he nodded to the other two members of the enquiry panel. Free to go? Was the irony lost on them?

Outside the study hut Declan and Jimmy stood guard. 'All right, our kid?' Declan ribbed him gently. 'You get the all clear?'

Seamus ignored him. Later he would regret being so cranky. It wasn't Declan's fault. Martin was the one who had created the problem. Officious wee bollix. That's how Seamus described him to John when they walked around the yard for the last few laps before lock-up.

'Ach, take it easy, chara. Which isn't to say that he isn't a wee bollix, but just remember, you wouldn't let Giles break you, or any of the other screws for that matter. You wouldn't let any of them break you, would you?'

'No,' Seamus replied.

'Martin might be a wee bollix but he is our wee bollix. Which doesn't mean you have to like him. But he's not trying to break you. That's not his intention. He's only doing his job. What would you do if you were him?'

Seamus said nothing.

'So let's go in,' John continued. 'Remember, it's your turn to make the tea. You'll be okay tomorrow.'

Oh no I won't, Seamus thought to himself, but he said nothing to John. He knew John was doing his best to help him. But that didn't make it any easier. No, Seamus mused. I've only nine years, eleven months and just over three weeks to do. He wondered if Síle had got safely home. It seemed like a lifetime since he'd seen her. He decided he would lie up on his bunk and recreate every minute of their visit. The way she reached for him and how they held each other tightly without a word between them. The feel of her body against him and the way her hands pressed into his back. Her scent. He also had her wee comm to read again.

'No big Ds allowed here,' John reminded him as they entered the hut. 'Except when I have one.' He grinned.

'I'm okay,' Seamus said. 'A man's gotta do what a man's gotta do,' he drawled in his best John Wayne voice.

John laughed. 'Aye, our kid. You'll do it in your sleep. The thing to remember is that we're all prisoners. You and me. Our comrades. Our families. The screws. Their families.'

'Talking of screws,' said Seamus. 'You know what Giles said to me after they found the comm when I passed him walking round the yard? I didn't twig what he meant until now.'

'What?' asked John.

'Tiochfaidh, he said. Tiochfaidh ar fucking lá.'

'Well, at least he has a sense of humour.' John laughed.

'He's a glyp,' Seamus retorted.

'He did stop an escape.' John laughed again. 'He's entitled to enjoy that.'

'Aye, I suppose that's true. I'm having an early night,' Seamus said to him, 'if you don't mind, mucker.'

'I know what you're at,' John teased him. 'You're going to lie there and think sweet thoughts about your Síle.'

'And why not? What more does a man need? After my first day here sure the rest of my time in Long Kesh is bound to be wee buns.'

'Don't count on it,' said John as they both settled down in their bunks and withdrew into that part of their imagination in which happy memories reside and which prisoners draw on to keep them sane.

In Seamus's case, his memories and his imagination were filled with one person. That was Síle.

'Good night, love,' he whispered. 'Oíche mhaith.'

DEAR JOHN

'What!' I exclaimed.

Your Man sighed sadly. He leaned back in his chair until it was tilted on two legs with its back resting against the wall of the study hut. He eased his legs out from under the table and balanced himself with his feet on the table top. He stared at the ceiling, then, swallowing hard and averting his gaze from mine, he replied, 'Sinead has left me. She's taking the kids to live in England.'

'When did you find this out?'

'Today. On the visit. Well, I found out for definite today. She talked about it before; we both did. Remember last year? When I told you she wasn't coming up because she was sick? Well, she wasn't sick. She was just browned off with the searches and the British army outside the camp, the screws on the visit, and all the messing about getting ready and the annoyance with the kids. And then before we'd know it the half hour would be up and it was time to start waiting for the next half hour – the following week.'

Your Man's tone was despondently even. He continued to stare at the ceiling.

'To make matters worse, we don't …' he corrected himself, 'we didn't live in a republican area. So she used to come up on her own in her brother's car. You know the way all our people come up on the bus, well most of them do, and they get a bit of craic and, you know, it all helps. Sinead always felt a bit of an outsider.'

'You should have said. Sure there's plenty of our people to give a wee bit of support,' I protested. 'She could have – she could still go out with Colette and Anne Marie and all that crowd. Why don't you arrange for –?'

'Nawh, mucker, it's too late,' he interrupted me. 'And don't be annoying yourself. I suggested all that. I even got my sisters to take her out. Nawh, it isn't that. Sinead just never got married for this. She got married to be married. It's not her fault. It's a wonder she stuck it so long – it's three years now. Our Sean's five and wee Mairead's nearly four. Not much of a life for any of them, is it?'

He swung his legs down off the table and hunched forward in his chair. He stared blankly at the study-hut door. I could see the tears welling up in his eyes.

'I'm going to miss the kids,' he declared eventually, sucking in his cheeks and blowing out a long, deep breath. 'That's why Sinead didn't go before this. She knew I loved the kids up on a visit.'

'Maybe it's a phase she's going through. Once it's out of her system she'll be all right,' I offered.

'Nawh,' Your Man smiled wryly at me, 'this is no phase. This is for keeps. Sinead's a realist. I've another nine years to do, you know. That's not much of a future. So we decided that we'd separate.'

'You agreed!' I exclaimed.

'Aye,' he replied. 'What did you expect me to do? I was a beaten docket. I'd no choice. Like, I'll still see the kids during the summer. They're going to come back to stay with her ma, and our ones will bring them up to see me. They'll probably have wee English accents by then. Who'd have thought it would turn out like this? Poor Sinead; poor kids. Poor me.' He gave a false little smile and then stood up.

'It's a hard oul' station.' He smiled again, a wee, sorry smile. 'C'mon and let's go for a walk. It's no use the two of us going into a big D. I'll be all right; I'm glad I got talking to somebody about it. You're the first one I've talked to except for Sinead. Just shows you the type of relationships we have in here. By the way, don't say anything to Egbert or Cedric. I'll tell them the morra.'

We pulled the door of the study hut shut behind us. It was a bright, starlit night. We paused, hesitating, unsure of ourselves.

'Are you sure she's going to go away?' I asked, more for something to say than anything else.

'Her plane left Aldergrove ten minutes ago,' Your Man answered, with a touch of impatience creeping into his voice.

'I'm sorry,' I said. 'I didn't mean to annoy you asking stupid questions.'

'It's okay. It's not your fault. It's nobody's fault. It's just the way the cookie crumbles, as my da used to say. The only problem is …'

He started to walk. I fell in alongside him.

'The only problem is, old comrade, that I love Sinead and Sinead still loves me.' He stopped in mid-stride, and for the first time he looked me in the eyes. 'You don't understand that, do you?'

I said nothing.

'Well, maybe you're right,' he continued. 'I don't understand it either. But that's what I believe, and I'm going to keep believing it,' he asserted determinedly, 'until I'm able to come to terms with this mess. Then I'll probably be ready to believe something else. Okay? But not before that. Okay?'

'Okay,' I replied.

We walked in silence.

'You know why I need to believe that?' he asked after a short while. 'You know why?' He continued without waiting for an answer. 'Because in this place,' he waved his hand expansively at the maze of wire and lights and watchtowers which surrounded us, 'in this place you need to believe in something, and right at this minute I don't have a lot to believe in. But I believe Sinead loves me.'

He glared fiercely at me. Tears of anger and frustration and sorrow welled up again in his eyes. 'She just couldn't take it. And that's not her fault. Okay?'

'Okay, old friend,' I said quietly.

'You know something else?' he asked.

'What?'

'I'm fucked.' His voice finally broke. 'Okay?'

'Okay,' I replied.

I didn't look at him. I didn't need to. I knew he was crying. Not the body-wracking, sobbing convulsions of uncontrolled and disbelieving grief; no, Your Man's tears were the silent, proud and dignified longing for a lost love. He was almost regal in his sorrow.

He didn't look at me. He didn't need to. He knew I cried with him, sad little tears of solidarity and love. No one in Long Kesh saw us weeping that night as we journeyed slowly around the yard. Or if they did we didn't notice them. We were impervious to our surroundings.

We thought only, each in our different way, of Sinead and the two kids, flying high over the Irish Sea. Your Man never mentioned her to me again, not for about two years. And she never came back.

MONICA

He could feel the cold, pale sunlight filtering into the room. He didn't need to open his eyes. He knew how the light slowly invaded the space. He knew that there was a small triangle of sky brightening the day beyond his window. He knew there would soon be a little narrow strip of light, the lightness of the dawning day, slipping beneath the blind. He thought of how welcoming and reassuring that first wakening moment had always been, even when he was a child sandwiched between his brothers on a bed piled high with his father's heavy coats in the back room of their farm in Moycullen. He always loved the luxury of waking in a warm bed and watching the day lightening around him.

But this morning he could not bear it. The familiarity no longer reassured him. On the contrary, it mocked him. He felt a heaviness on his chest and he kept his eyes shut tight. The bed was warm where he lay but he stretched his legs outside the quilt to feel the coldness of the room. He knew he had to get up but first he turned slowly towards where she used to lie. Her pillow was cold to his touch as he clasped it to his chest. He could smell her but he knew that too would fade. So as he opened his eyes to another dawn he wept silently. There was nothing else for him to do. Clutching her pillow, smelling her scent and whispering her name. That is how he awakened these mornings.

'Monica, Monica.' He said her name aloud just to hear it. 'Mon ... i ... ca.' When they used to lie together she would turn to him on mornings like this, stretch her legs across his and snuggle in against him beneath the sheets. In those days he left the blinds open so they would wake with the early morning light. The warmth of her body against his and the familiarity of her presence in the bed excited him and he would turn and clasp her as he watched the slow sun illuminate their room.

'Maidin maith, Jimmy,' she would whisper. 'Good morning.'

'Good morning yourself,' he would reply.

Sometimes he would slip his hand inside her vest to cup her breast. She would press against him as *Morning Ireland* brought them news of slaughter in Gaza and, nearer to home, stories of scandals of church and state.

'Time to get up,' he would mumble before trying to free himself from her embrace.

'Ah, you're no fun any more,' she would complain mockingly. 'What sort of a man are you?'

Then depending on his mood and the time they had, they would make love as the sunlight filled the room. Sometimes.

Other times he would swing his feet onto the cold floor and head for the toilet.

'I'm dying for a pee,' he would explain, half-apologetically.

'Ah, you're a dead loss,' she would tease him in that funny half-brogue she had developed.

He wished she was there now. He wished that more than anything. Even though he knew that could not be. But he wished it anyway. Just for a minute. That would do, he told himself and whoever it was who decided these things. Even though he had no faith in anything any more, he wished her back so that he could explain how much he needed her. How much she meant to him. How she brought balance to his existence. Just so that she would hold him again. To reassure him that all would be well, despite the radio news, the drudgery of his day and the dreariness of wet Irish winters or soft Irish summers. All would be well. Because she was. Because he wakened beside her. Because she loved him. Because she lay with him. Because she minded him. Because she gave his life purpose.

And she did.

When he returned from the bathroom she would already be at the stove.

'Put something on your feet,' he would nag her. 'You're going to catch your death of cold.'

He would finish the breakfast after he had washed and dressed while she got herself ready. That was their routine.

No longer. Now he was on his own. Now he pulled himself reluctantly into a sitting position on the side of the bed. He listened for a minute or two, resignedly, to the quietness of the house before padding to the bathroom.

'So what are you going to do now, Jimmy?' he asked himself.

'Eh, Jimmy?' he muttered aloud as he squinted at his image in the bathroom mirror.

'What are you going to do now?' he repeated as he shaved for the first time in a week.

He felt a wee bit better after that. Monica always liked the feel of his face after he had shaved. Sometimes she would reach across the table to him while they ate breakfast together. She would run her fingers across his chin and cheeks. When he protested mildly, as he invariably did, though he savoured the gentle touch of her fingertips, she would smile and tease him. 'Ah, you grumpy oul' lad. You're definitely not a morning person.'

He sighed at himself. 'Pull yourself together, Jimmy. That's what Monica would tell you. "Pull yourself together, my bold Irish man."'

He made his way to the stove. The sink was filled with dirty dishes. He started to clear up the mess. At least the water was hot. The milk in the fridge was sour. He poured it slowly down the drain and watched the clotted liquid bubble and gurgle as it ebbed around the bottom of the sink.

When did Monica go? A week ago. He realised that he hadn't listened to the news in a week. He switched on the radio and sat at their table with a cup of black coffee. The news presenter's voice was as dead-pan as ever. As if nothing had happened. He was explaining that the FTSE had fallen. Jimmy grimaced, sucking in his breath, as tears welled in his eyes. He fought against them. He hadn't stopped crying since she left. He thought he couldn't cry any more. But it now seemed part of his routine. He knew it was good for him. That it was part of the process. But he was sick of it. He was sick of tears. Sick of being unable to control his emotions. Mortified that anything would start him off. Even the FTSE Index. Monica would enjoy that. She had always told him he had to learn to let go. He told her it was a cultural thing. He was used to keeping things to himself. She was from a different culture. She didn't understand, he said. She told him he was talking balls. He was just a man. But thinking back now, he realised, for all her assertiveness, that there was vulnerability just below the surface of her remarks. But where did it come from? He didn't see it until it was too late, when she was no longer there to ask.

They'd met in the first moment of the new millennium in Eyre Square. At the stroke of midnight. He was half-drunk. In Galway city for the craic and the New Year celebrations. Checking out the talent or pretending to. He and his mates were shawaddywaddying across the square among the other revellers when the countdown to the New Year began.

'Five … four … three … two … one!'

Someone pushed him into a group of young women. And there was Monica. A little tipsy. Very beautiful. And black. He did something he had never tried to do before with a stranger. He tried to kiss her.

'Hold on, Irishman,' she said, laughing at him. 'In my country you need my father's permission before you can kiss me.'

'Ah,' he said, 'but this isn't your country, is it?'

She laughed again. 'No. But it will be.' She smiled and reached out to him. 'You can have a hug.'

And he did. Holding her in Eyre Square as the fireworks lit up the sky and everyone around them hugged everyone else and the Saw Doctors sang out 'Auld Lang Syne' and they all tried to join in. That was the start of it. When the crowd began to disperse he asked could he walk her home.

'All right,' she said. 'As far as the door.' She smiled.

There seemed some distant promise in that smile. At least he liked to see that. She had a room out beyond Salthill. They moved down Shop Street towards the river, a few calls and shouts and songs breaking out around them, the odd pop of a firework bursting in the sky. He tried to walk slowly, to drag it out, to try to make enough of a connection with her so he could see her again. A shyness natural to them both restrained them. But they were intrigued enough to leave each other an opening, to let it play out, to keep the conversation moving, to learn something of one another. Her long slender fingers and stately walk and soft voice lifted him. She liked the flash of life in his eyes. Shy and awkward though he was, she sensed an intensity behind the restraint. She liked his height, the way he moved, his blue eyes. She even liked his shyness. Maybe it was the drink. Maybe it was the night that was in it. Neither could tell.

She had arrived in Ireland a month before. She was from Somalia. She liked Ireland, she told him.

'Happy New Year,' he said to her as they parted.

'Happy New Year to you too, Jimmy.'

'Would you … I mean, can I see you again?'

'I'd like that,' she said.

'Um, how will I …?'

'You're not used to this, are you?' she said. 'Well, neither am I. But this would help.' She wrote down her number and handed it to him.

'Thanks!' he said, with an innocence that almost made her laugh.

She saw a line of very faint light to the east. 'How do you say good morning in Irish?'

'Maidin maith,' he told her.

'Maidin maith, Jimmy,' she said.

He didn't try to kiss her but there was a lightness in his step as he began the long trek home.

He was delighted with himself. Monica was happy

also. He called her the following night. He feared she might forget who he was. They arranged to meet in Dolan's. He was harder for her to reach than the night they'd walked through the city, but with questions – about him, his family, Ireland – and with the help of a few drinks, he got through it without discouraging her.

They began to meet each weekend, then more frequently. Before he met Monica, Jimmy spent his free time with his brothers Micéal and Liam at Éire Óg Gaelic Athletic Club. He didn't play any more, but he helped out with training and mentoring some of the underage teams. In his day he was a good hurler, steady and reliable. A hamstring injury laid him off a few years before he met Monica. Micéal was a class hurler, as fast as a whippet and competing for a place on the county team. Jimmy was his biggest fan. Their lives revolved around work, the GAA and the pub. Jimmy's life was particularly uneventful. Liam and Micéal had steady girlfriends. Jimmy'd had the odd one-night stand, but apart from that he had not been in a steady relationship in over ten years or so. He was tall and fit and handsome and women took an interest in him, but when they tried to talk to him and draw him out, his natural shyness took over and the words seemed to get tied up in knots whenever he tried to speak to them. Instead, he put everything into hurling.

He told Monica all this on their first date. She quizzed him about his family. He told her he was living at home with his widowed mother and two sisters. She said he should get a place of his own. It wasn't good for a man of his age not to have his own space, his independence. In her country the men were spoiled by their mothers. Even when they married they lived with their mothers. She was younger than him. He thought she was very opinionated but he didn't say so. He thought she would probably soon get fed up with him. On their third or fourth date he told her this. She looked at him without saying anything for a long while, then she told him she didn't think she would ever get fed up with him. She said he was a good man. A kind man. She said he was very good looking. He was flattered. And embarrassed. She teased him. He wasn't used to being talked to like that. She found his modesty attractive. It more than compensated for his occasional contrariness. That too, she thought, came from his shyness. She told him he had to learn to love himself. She told him to look at himself in the mirror before he went to bed that night.

'Give yourself a big smile and say "Hi, good looking."'

So he did. And he felt better for it.

She phoned him and asked if he'd done as she had told him to do. When he said he had, she made him go back into the bathroom, his mobile phone in hand, and got him to do it all over again.

He thought she was gorgeous. She thought she was lucky to have met someone so soon after her arrival in Ireland. She had never gone out with a white man before, and even though neither of them knew what way their relationship might work out, Monica was glad to enjoy a new experience and to be with someone who could keep her company in her newly adopted country. Jimmy, needless to say, born, bred and buttered in rural Galway, had never gone out with anyone like Monica before.

Later she confessed that she'd thought she would have to learn Irish to live in Ireland. 'But when I arrived here I discovered everyone talks English.'

'Not everyone,' he protested. 'In Conamara they speak Irish. And in Donegal.'

'We should live there,' she said, 'and learn Irish. You will lose more than you know if you lose your own language. I never learned mine. And now it is gone. Except for some of the elders, everyone in my family speaks English.'

That's the way she was. Passionate about things. There was also a troubled depth to her he couldn't quite fathom. At first he didn't know that she had these sensitivities, until they started to emerge in the little ways she had of responding to unkindness or, for that matter, news stories of conflict or people being treated badly. This was particularly the case when he tried to get her to talk about her life in Somalia. It was as if she felt a need to be guarded about what she revealed about her attitude to these matters. As they got to be more comfortable together she became more relaxed, but she was still reluctant to discuss her homeland – especially if they were in company or in a public place. If they were alone she would laugh off his queries, skilfully change the subject or give him opaque answers. When he realised something in her past was troubling her, he stopped pursuing what were quite innocent questions, driven only by his desire to get to know her better.

And of course there were issues which troubled her about her life before she came to Ireland. Monica was a patriotic woman who loved her native country, but she resented the way women were treated in Somalia. She was proud of the way her mother resisted this. But she was very aware that the family paid a price of social ostracisation which led to her father leaving their home. All these memories troubled her. At times, although she loved her new life in Galway and her relationship with Jimmy, she felt ashamed about leaving. She had been part of a mostly underground movement for women's rights. Her friends, as far as she knew, were still active, but sometimes she felt as if she had abandoned them. She felt like a deserter. No one who observed her confident way of going would have guessed she was carrying this guilt. Even Jimmy didn't know. But he did know that there was part of her past that she wouldn't talk about. A part unknown to him. Because that's the way Monica was.

For her part, Monica was sometimes concerned about Jimmy's shyness in company and annoyed at his occasional gruffness with her. Hurt, maybe, more than annoyed. He could be so loving at times but then, especially if he was tired or preoccupied, he would be grumpy for no good reason. It was as if he was taking his bad form out on her. When she challenged him at these times, he withdrew into a moody quietness. As if he couldn't bear to be confronted. Monica didn't like that in him but she knew she could be challenging at times. Used to saying what she thought. She knew that could be irritating. She was much more outgoing than Jimmy. More curious and outspoken. These bouts of stress between them were usually short-lived, though. Most of the time they were happy together.

Jimmy was happier than he ever had been in his adult life. Monica was quite a catch. He knew some of his friends envied him. He went out less often with them. Most of his free time was spent with Monica. They walked. She taught him to cook. He started to read again. She told him she'd like to get out of the city one day, to see the world he came from. He collected her in the morning and then drove back out to the hurling ground for a practice session with the minor team. This was the day that started to change things for her. She saw him come into his own there, with the hurl in his hand, joking with the coaches and parents, speaking gently but with authority to the players, cajoling and mentoring the young Gaels. Afternoon turned to evening and finally to a night in the pub. She met his cousins, his brothers.

His mother joined them for an hour or so. She and Monica bonded instantly.

When Éire Óg got into the county championship he took her to the game. Micéal was marked by Mickey McBrodrick, one of the most experienced backs in the county. He tried to needle Micéal throughout the match but Micéal was wise to his game plan. Except when Mickey brought Monica into it. Micéal confessed to Jimmy that he nearly lost it when Mickey taunted him. 'I see your Jimmy is riding a darkie.'

Micéal said nothing but at the end of the game, with Éire Óg the victors by three points, as they made their way off the field, he came up beside McBrodrick and jabbed him in the ribs with his hurl. McBrodrick collapsed at Micéal's feet. All pandemonium broke loose. Hurling sticks and helmets went flying through the air as McBrodrick's teammates bore down on Micéal and the rival teams tore into one another.

'Handbags at dawn,' Jimmy said to Monica as they watched the melee. 'Them Gort ones are bad losers.'

Afterwards at the victory do in McMahon's lounge bar Micéal told Jimmy what had happened.

'You did right,' Jimmy assured him. 'It would have been a mistake to hit him during the game. That's what the pup wanted. We won, thanks to you. We're the county champions – McBrodrick's heart and his ribs are broken.'

There was a great music session that night. Generations of Éire Óg supporters, players and former players and their families celebrated their victory long into the night. Someone had a flute, another a guitar, still another an accordion. The tunes began. Monica had been at such sessions before in Galway, but it was different here. There was a different look in the eyes, an excitement, a knowledge that this was where the music came from and of what it was trying to say. They went around the room, tunes alternating with songs. A teenage boy coaxed his grandmother to sing and she obligingly went into 'Óró Sé Do Bheatha 'Bhaile'. Everyone sang the chorus, even Monica. Or at least she tried.

Finally it was Jimmy's turn to sing. She was nervous for him. She'd never heard him sing before. She didn't know if he could. He began low, quietly. The song, she learned later, was 'Mo Ghile Mear'. His voice rose to its intense moments, then dropped back. His eyes were closed. There was such longing and melancholy and pride and ancientness in it. Tears came into her eyes. She couldn't believe that the shy, awkward man she'd been sitting with in pubs could make such a wondrous thing. This was when she fell in love with him. After they cleared the floor for the set dancers, Jimmy's sister coached her through the steps. It was an exuberant, joyous experience. Monica felt happy in a way she didn't remember feeling since childhood. She was the outsider, by nation, by race, but none of them made her feel that way. The music pulled them all together. They were uplifted, united and excited by its power.

Before that he'd been wondering how long it would take her to get fed up with him. He thought it was inevitable. All his experience led him to believe that this was so. But she didn't. Each became the major focus for the other. When they couldn't meet they could pass two hours or more on the phone talking late into the night. The word 'love', approached tentatively at first, began to appear in their conversations. The first night they slept together she told him she had learned the word 'anamchara'. She thought it was a beautiful word.

'Do you know what it means?' he asked.

'*Anam* is soul and *chara* means friend.'

'Well done,' he said.

'Anamchara,' she whispered into his ear. 'Forever.'

'Forever,' he said and he meant it.

Not long after that they moved in together into a rented house on the edge of the city. It was well back from the road. Up a long lane. Quiet and very beautiful. Jimmy never told Monica the cause of the brawl at the county final. Occasionally she would relate some racist incident to him. Nothing too overt. An overheard remark or the sense of a change of tone or conversation when she tried to engage with some people. Once a group of young boys shouted at her in the street and another time some teenagers taunted her. But most people were welcoming and friendly.

That suited Monica's temperament. She was open with

people once she got to know them. Sometimes that made Jimmy jealous. He was always a little reserved with people he didn't know. Although he and Monica didn't socialise much with others, when they did he would marvel at how comfortable and confident she was engaging with people. And if she left him for too long with someone he didn't know, sometimes he felt awkward and ill at ease if the discussion moved on to issues he was not familiar with. Occasionally she lost patience with him.

'Why do you behave like a stupid man? A man who goes back into his cave when he's hurt or confused. Like all stupid men. Instead of talking things out. Instead of letting go. Ah, Jimmy ...'

That was the first time she had flared up at him. In Galway. When she told him she didn't want to go out. She was too tired. At times like that Monica felt Jimmy was too set in his ways. Too used to doing his own thing, even though he was also kind and genuine. Maybe he was on his own too long and used to not having to take account of what she wanted. In her country men expected women to fit in with their plans. That was the dominant culture. The patriarchy was not as prevalent in Ireland as far as she could see, but it was there nonetheless. Jimmy was a creation of it. Even though in her country women had little rights in comparison to modern Ireland, she had a sense from listening to older women and from her studies that thirty or forty years before it would have been a different set-up.

'Let's stay in, Jimmy. I couldn't be bothered going out.'

He had stormed out and quickly regretted it. She joined him later where he sat on his own, stony faced, on the high stool, staring into his pint. She came up beside him just as he had resolved to go back to her. For some reason it annoyed him that she was the first to give in. And that she was tired looking. For her part, while Monica had a real sense of herself, she also loved him more than she could believe. She wouldn't let him take her for granted but she also wanted to prevent their relationship being soured by any friction or a thoughtless remark or action.

'You shouldn't have come out,' he said gruffly. 'I was going back.'

'Not before you get me a drink?' She smiled.

'I thought you were too tired,' he snapped, even though he knew it was the wrong thing to say. But it was said. And that was that. He was too quick with the hard word when he was annoyed. He knew that. Even before she told him about it. And she did put that to him on the walk back home as she had done before, patiently but firmly, when he reared up at her without cause. Slowly, as they got to know each other better, she started to get him to learn to relax. Nearly from when they first met, she would reflect to herself at times, his shyness and occasional lack of confidence sometimes made him a wee bit abrupt, especially if he was tired. Or as she put it once or twice, it was the Irishman in him. Spoilt by his mammy.

Monica got to know his little insecurities. They endeared him to her. She herself wasn't always as confident as she appeared and she could relate to how he felt out of his depth at times. But when she felt like that her positivity helped her through. He just felt and looked awkward. She would mock him gently when he raised this with her. But she was also sensitive to his moods and his needs. He knew that. She brought out the best in him. Essentially, she was a kind person. Although they seldom talked about Somalia, over time she seemed to lose the insecurities which were just below the surface when they first met. She appeared to be better able to cope with whatever led her to leave Somalia. And when she was stressed or when she was hurt her soft side showed. When he was hurt he wanted to fight back.

'You have to love yourself,' she said one evening. 'I mean, you have to like yourself before you can love anyone else. You have to be kind to yourself. To look after yourself. That's why I left home. I didn't want to be anyone's property. I wanted to be me. But I had to find out who *me* is.'

They were sitting together on the settee after an evening out. Monica had kicked off her shoes and had her legs tucked under herself.

'And have you found yourself yet ?' he asked.

'Not yet,' she whispered, taking his hand, 'but I found you. And your beautiful country and I'm happy that I am free here to find myself at my own pace. With you.'

They fell asleep like that, Jimmy recalled. Life was good. They grew more and more comfortable together and learned a lot about how to be a couple. A partnership. There were things unsaid, at least on Monica's part, but she was able to tell him, and more importantly herself, that she was happy. Before they knew it two years had passed. By then she had two jobs and was almost finished her studies in the university. Her student visa was due to run out. She seemed blissfully unperturbed and undaunted by her potentially illegal status. Jimmy said he would marry her, but she refused.

'I'll marry you when I'm ready to, if you'll take me, but I won't marry you because I have to. I'm happy the way we are.'

He finished his coffee. It was cold. He was surprised, when he glanced at the clock, that he had been sitting lost in his thoughts for over half an hour. He went over to the settee where she used to sit. Her absence was palpable. Her absence was everywhere. He sat back and looked around him. At her books, her CDs, her paintings. The wall hangings. But there was more to her than her possessions. They remained. But she was gone. Her presence had brought life, colour, noise into his surroundings. She had brought touch, smell, mood into his life. It was the absence of her presence that wounded him. The permanency of it. His expectation that she was only in another room, that she would re-enter his life again. Sometimes he would go upstairs to look for her. Sometimes he would open her wardrobe and bury his face in her clothes. Once he stepped into the wardrobe and wrapped himself in her things. He didn't cry that time. Instead he got quiet comfort from the scent and feel and texture of her clothing. It calmed him.

He went back into the bedroom and lay on top of the unmade bed. He knew he would have go out. Today would be difficult. He needed to compose himself. He had people to thank. Some of them were brilliant. Especially the people in Dublin. His mind slipped back to the first time they went to Dublin. It was for the All-Ireland. It was Monica's idea that they would stay afterwards until the following weekend. The match was mighty. Kilkenny won. Again. The following day they went to Kilmainham Prison to where the 1916 leaders were shot. And to the GPO. And Monica insisted on them taking the tour of Glasnevin Cemetery. To visit the graves of all your great leaders, she told him.

Her curiosity about and her admiration for their exploits and achievements touched him and rekindled his sense of national pride. Still, he was surprised when she suggested they should go to Belfast. He had never seriously thought of going to the North. For as long as he could recall, until recently, the North was about bombs and shootings and riots.

He didn't know how people survived it all and he admired them. He was glad peace had now been brokered. Everybody was. At least everybody he knew. But going up North was a different matter entirely.

Monica's mind was set. She reminded him about how he had lauded the Northern footballers, especially Tyrone and Armagh.

'Well, they did sort out Kerry,' he joked, catching on to how determined she was.

'A one-day visit,' she said. 'The early bus leaves at eight in the morning and we're back again at eight that night.'

So he gave in. And later, as they headed back southwards on the M1, he was glad he did. They had a great day. A black-taxi tour of all the places he was so familiar with from television. Monica insisted on going to Bobby Sands's grave in the cemetery off the Falls Road. She was clearly moved by that experience. She held him tightly as they stood together in the shadow of the Belfast hills and to his surprise she said a little prayer out loud. He had never heard her pray like that before. There were tears in her eyes. He had a real sense of what was passing through her in that moment. Sacrifice, struggle, war, death. They had inspired and wounded her. They had been in the balance there in that Belfast graveyard but one finally would prevail.

'Back in Somalia my mother prayed for Bobby Sands and his friends. Back in my country we needed someone to look up to. My mother was an educated woman. Sophisticated. But she had no chance to make a living that suited her education or to have the quality of life she deserved. All because she was a woman. I don't think I could ever go back there. It scares me to think about it. Girls are still subjected to genital mutilation. Barbaric. I was part of the fight against that and I made many enemies, especially among the police.'

She winced and clutched Jimmy's arm as she spoke and he was moved to see her eyes filled with tears. He held her close.

'I escaped that thanks to my mother. But many women, girls – little babies even – have that horrible, dangerous brutality forced upon them. No, I'm never going back there,' she concluded fiercely, looking at him as if seeing him for the first time. 'Thanks for bringing me here. We admired Bobby Sands. It's funny that our little group of women in Somalia fighting for women's rights would be inspired by a man. But we were. We identified with him. He made a stand. My mother was taught by Irish nuns and she knew all about Ireland. It was she who encouraged me to leave, first to France and then to Ireland. She always said women had no chance to be independent human beings in our country. She told me I would get that chance here in your country. A country with people like Bobby Sands was bound to be a good place, she said.'

'Our history of dealing with women is hardly a good one.

Your mother was obviously never here,' Jimmy retorted, only half-joking.

'No, she never was but she was right,' Monica replied, oblivious to his scepticism.'And anyway, if she was not ambitious for me I would not have met you.And where would you be then, Irishman?You'd still be a wee Irish mammy's boy!'

Jimmy loved it when she slipped into a half-brogue. For his part, he was very conscious of his own brogue as they took a walk around the Belfast city-centre shops before catching the bus for Dublin again. But nobody passed any remarks. Everyone was friendly. On the way out of the city he commended her for insisting they take the trip. 'It's bizarre that it took a mad woman from Somalia to bring me to Belfast and to Dublin to be close to some of the people who helped make Irish history. I'm glad you did.And I'm glad your mam had such a high opinion of us poor paddies.'

'So am I,' she sighed, snuggling close to him.

He had never felt happier.

They dozed most of the way along the motorway. Monica was quietly content. In the haziness of half-sleep she thought if her mother was still alive she would be delighted to know of their pilgrimage to Belfast and Bobby Sands's grave. Her mother had died in an accident two years after Monica left. That was another reason why she would never go home. She never said it to Jimmy, but she never fully believed that her mother's death was accidental. By that time she had emerged as one of the leading public advocates for an end to female genital mutilation and for women's rights. After her death there was a short-lived campaign for a public enquiry into the circumstances but the government ignored it. Some of her friends from the underground women's movement were arrested. Monica's feeling of guilt at leaving returned. But what could she do? Without her mother, Monica felt she had no one to go home to. No. She had made her home in Ireland. This was her country now. She fell into a deep sleep cuddled close to Jimmy as the bus sped towards Dublin.

Then a few miles across the border the bus slowed down to negotiate a roadblock just north of Dundalk. It was a very low-key affair. When the bus stopped a garda officer clambered awkwardly aboard and made his way up along the seats, scrutinising the passengers as he proceeded. When he came to where Monica and Jimmy sat together he stopped and asked her for her ID.

'Have you any form of identity, miss?' he asked almost apologetically.

Jimmy was flummoxed. 'She's with me,' he said hastily.

'I can see that, sir. No need to get annoyed. Once I see her ID you can be off about your business and I'll be off about mine. Have you any ID, miss?'

Monica gave him her student visa as Jimmy remembered, with a sinking feeling, that it had expired months ago when her course finished.

'This is out of date, miss,' the garda announced. 'Have you an up to date one? If you haven't you'll have to come with me. Please.'

Jimmy protested. In vain. Other people on the bus were looking at them. Monica felt a desperate sense of dread. Hardly woken from her sleep, she was perplexed and couldn't quite understand what was happening. She became untypically flustered when Jimmy challenged the police officer.

'Is it because she's black that you picked on her? The only black woman on the bus and you pick on her!'

'I'm only doing my job –'

'My arse!'

'The young lady will have to accompany me, sir.'

'I'm coming,' Monica said, anxious that Jimmy wouldn't get into trouble.

'And I'm coming with you,' Jimmy asserted. He could see she was alarmed and embarrassed at being the centre of attention.

'As you wish,' the garda said. 'Is this your bag, miss?' He stepped aside to let them pass and then reached up to retrieve Monica's bag from the overhead rack before escorting them off the bus and into a waiting garda car.

They spent the night in the station in Dundalk. Monica in a cell, Jimmy in the waiting room. He got a local solicitor who explained little could be done once it was clear that Monica had no visa. He was surprised that they had crossed the border.

'I know,' Jimmy agreed. 'It was a spur of the moment decision. We were in Dublin for a break after the big game and we took a day trip. Monica has been in Galway with me for over two years now, and not a bit of bother from anyone.'

'She's likely to be deported,' the solicitor told him. 'The Minister for Justice has really tightened up on illegal aliens.'

'Christ, man – she's not from Mars. She's not an alien.'

'She is in the eyes of the law. Ten people were deported last month. She'll probably get bail in the morning and a set timeframe to sort out her affairs and leave or get a visa from the Department of Justice to stay.'

And so it was that Jimmy and Monica caught the train that afternoon back to Dublin. They had a month to sort things out. The solicitor gave them the contact details of a migrants' advocacy group in the capital. 'They'll get you all the help you need,' he assured them.

The next few weeks were a blur. Thinking back, Jimmy didn't know how they survived it. The advocacy group launched a publicity campaign in support of Monica's application for a visa. Her photograph appeared in many newspapers and on TV. Two TDs gave their support and some anti-racist groups picketed the Department of Justice. Her application was turned down because her studies were finished, but the advocacy group had a solicitor who specialised in immigration cases and she made an application to the High Court. Monica was given an extended period of bail.

Jimmy noticed how the weight had dropped off her. They were staying in Dublin with a young woman who worked for the advocacy group. He took time off work to lobby. He wasn't confident about it, although when he was talking about Monica's case he was lucid and passionate. But he wasn't suited to all the waiting about, to the red tape and bureaucracy. He hadn't the patience for it.

And he didn't know Dublin. Galway was a walking city and he was familiar with it, but Dublin was a place apart. It was big and gridlocked and confusing and, in late October, wet and miserable. Dirty Dublin, as the country people would say, and Jimmy could see why as he tramped around the city centre in the rain. Monica was miserable also. Jimmy saw the change in her. Sometimes she would show her old positive side but a lot of the time she was withdrawn and quiet. He knew she was nervous about going back to Somalia.

'I'm going with you,' he said.

'Don't talk nonsense,' she said gently. 'What would my bold Irish man do in Somalia? You'd be homesick for the hurling and the soft days. I know. It's different coming to a place you want to be in and –'

'I want to be with you.'

'No, Jimmy.'

Jimmy tried to make her smile. 'Éire Óg wouldn't be the county champions with that approach. We can still win the court case.'

But even as he said it, he found it hard to believe.

As the date for the High Court hearing drew closer Monica drew more into herself. Jimmy could see it. He challenged her.

'It's your imagination, Jimmy. I love you.'

'Well then marry me, Monica, marry me.'

'No, Jimmy. Not under duress. Not like this.'

He was right when he said she was withdrawing from him. Monica knew that. But she couldn't help herself. Her happiness was shattered. She did think of marrying him as he asked. But that's not the way she was. She had seen too many forced marriages, loveless marriages, arranged marriages which became toxic and arid. Or abusive. That's not what she wanted. Even if it started as they were now, obviously in love and happy together, she still questioned and doubted the future if it was based on a marriage of convenience. What if Jimmy's love faded in time? What if he treated her the way some men treated their wives. She hated how her mother was abandoned.

No, Monica didn't want to be locked into an arrangement like that, in which she started at a disadvantage. Getting married to get residency was not for her. It would be far from the partnership she envisaged and which, until now, she had enjoyed with Jimmy. For her such a marriage was out of the question just as much as Jimmy's other proposal that they go to Somalia together. She was certain she was going back into real danger. She would definitely be questioned by the police about her activities before she left. Her concerns about her mother's death returned. Is that what would happen to her? She said nothing of this to Jimmy. Long, moody silences punctuated their normally talkative relationship. No matter how hard Jimmy tried, their connectedness became a little ragged. A little stilted. Moody. Stressed. She knew he was trying. But that made her feel worse. Brittle. Despondent. Edgy. She told herself that she was protecting them both. She was preparing for the worst. It was for the better. Her distance from him lengthened and the gap between them deepened.

They tried to make contingencies for different scenarios but their discussions never got very far. Once Monica broke down completely. She sobbed incessantly. Jimmy had never seen her like that before. She was always the strong one, the confident, cheerful one. He was the awkward culchie. Now she was inconsolable and he wasn't much better.

That was the night before they had to go to court for Monica's hearing. Liam and Micéal and Jimmy's sisters, Áine and Máire, came up to be with them, along with a few friends from Moycullen. All of them found the Four Courts intimidating. Monica's case took an hour. She lost. Jimmy saw her afterwards. They clung together until the prison warder told him the visit was over. She was to be detained until her deportation could be arranged.

'I love you, Jimmy,' she told him.

'We have a visit tomorrow,' he said. 'See you then.'

He never saw her again. Alive. He was summoned to the detention centre early the following day to identify her remains. She had hanged herself in the showers.

So he made himself get up off the bed again. He pulled on a heavy coat and a woolly hat and went out to meet the day. That's what she would expect him to do. Monica was the best thing that ever happened to him. He consoled himself with that. And as usual she got her own way. Jimmy smiled to himself wryly as he pulled the front door behind him.

She got her own bloody way, he told himself. She got to stay in Ireland. If it wasn't so fucking serious it would make you laugh. He looked up at the grey washed sky and then, hunching his shoulders against the wind, he set off down the road.

'Monica, Monica.' He whispered the words into the wind. 'Mon … i … ca … What am I going to do without you?'

HEAVEN

'That is a wren. Yes, that wee one.'

Billy and Niamh were sitting quietly in his garden. Whispering. Billy was eighty-three. Niamh was five. They were watching his bird table. That is why they were whispering. They didn't want to disturb the birds.

It was a lovely day. Billy's garden was at the back of his house. He had two little rows of vegetables and a patch of green grass. But a very old apple tree, which still gave fine cooking apples, and a cluster of beautiful roses were in pride of place. The birds loved the apples. And Billy loved the birds. So did Niamh.

When the apples were ready Billy and Niamh would collect them all up. Well, nearly all of them. Billy always left some for the birds. The rest they gave to the neighbours. And every house at their end of the street had apple cake and apple crumble. Some of the older people even made potato apple cake. Billy loved potato apple. Niamh loved apple cake with warm custard.

'Why do you call it a wren?' Niamh asked.

'Because that's its name.'

'But why?'

'Because that big one is a starling. And the other two beside it. And you know the sparrow. But the wee one is a wren.'

'But why? Who gives the birds their names?'

'Probably comes from the Latin,' Billy said thoughtfully.

Niamh wasn't impressed. 'What's the Latin?' she queried.

That is how Billy and Niamh spent their time together. Niamh was all about questions. And Billy took time to answer them. Billy was a kind man. A widower. Living on his own. He was a good handyman. Any time Niamh's mother had something that needed fixed it was Billy who did it. He rewired sockets. Hung doors. One time he soldered the handle back onto Niamh's mother's favourite pot and she was delighted.

She would send dinner in to Billy a few times every week. 'A wee bit of dinner for you, Billy.'

'Ach, you shouldn't have,' he would say.

And if Niamh was with her mammy he would say, 'Ach, Niamh. And how is my wee girl doing today? Sit down there beside me.'

Niamh would sit on the tiny little chair that Billy had made decades before for his own children. It also served his grandchildren. But Niamh was the one who used it most often, out in the garden if the weather was good or in Billy's back room while he had his wee bit of dinner.

The little wren that Billy had identified was one of a pair who had a nest in the garden wall. Billy showed it to Niamh one day. He told her she should never touch a bird's nest until the birds had stopped using it. And she should never ever touch birds' eggs unless the birds had abandoned them. He also showed her the house martins' nests up in the eves at the gable of his house.

These were special times for Billy. They were also special times for Niamh.

Then Billy died. He passed away quietly while asleep. No fuss. No bother. Just the way he would have wanted it. Niamh's mammy broke the news to Niamh. She sat her down and explained to her that Billy had gone away.

'Away where?' asked Niamh.

'He's gone to heaven,' her mother explained.

'Where is heaven, Mammy?'

'It's a nice place people go when they die.'

'Right,' said Niamh.

Then she went back to playing with her dolls.

Billy was waked for a few days. His family and the neighbours gathered and old friends called to pay their respects. Niamh's mother was in and out making sandwiches and tea and washing up the cups and plates. Niamh would go with her. But only as far as the door. She refused to go into the house. If there were other children there, some of them were sent out to keep her company. They tried to coax Niamh indoors but she was resolute. She was too young to fully understand what had happened to Billy but she knew it was something profound.

'Do you not want to say goodbye to Billy?' Niamh's mother asked her on the morning of Billy's funeral.

'Mammy, when will Billy be coming back?' Niamh replied.

'Niamh, love, he's not coming back,' her mother told her gently. 'I told you. He's in heaven.'

'Mammy, what is a Protestant?'

Niamh's mother was perplexed. And amused. As she told Niamh's daddy later, she could hardly keep her face straight. 'A Protestant? Did you say a Protestant, Niamh?'

'Yes, Mammy,' Niamh said patiently. 'Ceara Elliot says that Billy is a Protestant and that Protestants don't go to heaven. Only Catholics get to heaven.'

'Billy wasn't a real Protestant,' Niamh's mother stammered. 'He gave up religion a long time ago. He believed in human beings. He had no time for Protestant or Catholic stuff or any of that sort of carry-on. Billy was nothing. If he was anything he was a Christian,' she added thoughtfully.

'Well, Mammy, if Billy was nothing, how will he get to heaven?'

'He was a good man. That's how. Good people get to heaven. So are you going to go in now to see him and to say your goodbyes?'

'No, Mammy,' said Niamh.

The next year Niamh started school. She was nervous at first but braved it out and she had the comfort of being picked up every day by her mammy's Auntie Leah, who took her home to her little bungalow near the school and gave her orange juice and custard creams and told her stories until Niamh's mammy or daddy collected her after finishing work.

Auntie Leah was very old and walked with great deliberation.

'Like a tortoise,' Niamh teased her one day.

Auntie Leah thought that was very funny. She started to refer to herself as Niamh's oul' tortoise when the two of them walked together. Sometimes Niamh skipped ahead, but as time went on and Leah got a little slower, Niamh understood it was because she was old, and she held back and grasped Leah's hand and walked beside her, asking her questions about whatever came into her head. She noticed that Leah loved to talk about when she was a young woman and especially loved talking about going to dances.

'We'd meet at Aldo's fish and chip shop,' said Leah. 'All dolled up to the eyebrows.'

Niamh's eyes lit up as she pictured Leah and her friends. 'Can I go to a dance, Auntie Leah?' she asked.

'You'll have to wait a wee while yet, love.'

'Well, can I go to Aldo's?'

'You surely can,' said Auntie Leah, and the next day they went there together. It's there yet at the top of the Donegal

Road. The Continental. Or the Conto to local people. Niamh had ice cream. Real Italian ice cream. They sat together at a little table.

'The best thing for us then was the showbands, Niamh,' Auntie Leah told her. 'Better than the boys!'

'What's a showband, Auntie Leah?'

'They played rock, country, even ceilidh music. They had flashy suits. We just lived for them. I especially loved Joe Dolan and Roly Daniels.' She leaned in across the table and began to sing softly to Niamh, 'It's you. It's you. It's you …'

All the staff and customers in Aldo's stopped and watched and listened to the old lady sing to the small child. Niamh wasn't a bit put out or embarrassed by Auntie Leah's singing in a public place. She loved it. Especially when Leah stood up, burled around and raised one hand with her finger stabbing the air while the other hand held an imaginary microphone.

Auntie Leah went through the whole song and when she finished everyone at Aldo's applauded. Some even stood. Later that night when Niamh told her mammy what had happened, it was as if Leah had been singing in the Grand Opera House.

Then one day, not long after this, on their way back from school Auntie Leah stopped suddenly and clutched hold of Niamh's arm. 'I haven't a breath, love,' she gasped.

Niamh helped her home and, although Leah rallied when she got to sit for a while in her favourite armchair, by the time Niamh's mammy arrived to collect her, Auntie Leah was breathless once again. Niamh's mammy phoned for an ambulance and for Niamh's daddy to take her home while her mammy went to the hospital with Auntie Leah.

'Why did she have to go to the hospital?' Niamh asked her father. 'Can I visit her? When will she get out?'

One question followed the other the whole way home.

That night when he put her to bed she reached up to him and he hugged her tightly. 'Will Auntie Leah be okay?' she asked him.

'Yes, my wee love. You say a wee prayer for her.'

She snuggled down in her bed as he kissed her gently on the forehead. 'I love Auntie Leah,' she said as he quietly slipped out of the room.

It was her mammy who told her that Auntie Leah was dead. Niamh took this news quietly and in a matter-of-fact way. It was as if she'd known this might happen. She thought to herself that she would never see Leah again. That's what happened to Billy. He disappeared out of her life. She missed him. And she didn't know why this should be so. Why did grown-ups just go and never come back?

'Is Auntie Leah in heaven as well?' Niamh asked her mammy.

'Yes, Niamh, she is.'

'Will she be with Billy?'

'Yes, I'm sure she will. They would be having a wee talk

and he would be asking about you and Auntie Leah would be telling him that you're a very good girl and that you miss him and your wee talks.'

'Can I go to see Billy in heaven?' Niamh asked. 'And Auntie Leah?'

'No, Niamh,' her mother said hurriedly, sweeping Niamh up in her arms and hugging her tightly. 'No, love. You are not going to heaven. You are staying here with us. We couldn't do without you. You have to grow up to be a big girl and help me. Billy is happy in heaven. And Auntie Leah. They were old and ready for heaven. You're not. So no more questions for the night. Time for bed. Away you go up to your bath. Oíche mhaith, love.'

'Oíche mhaith, Mammy.'

Niamh's parents didn't put her under any pressure to go to Auntie Leah's wake. She said she didn't want to go and that was that. She missed Leah picking her up after school. And she missed her wee stories about the olden days. She enjoyed school, she had good friends there, but Billy and Auntie Leah stayed in her mind. She talked about them to her mammy. They had gone to this place called heaven. But where was it?

It was Niamh's Mamo Anne who took over picking Niamh up from school the way Auntie Leah used to. Kitty, the dinner lady in her school, was one of her Mamo Anne's friends. She always had a wee chat with Kitty if Kitty was about when she collected Niamh. Kitty called her Niamh's mammy's mammy. Kitty was a very kind woman. She made all the school boys and girls feel special and she always made sure they all ate their school dinners and that no one messed anyone else about. In Kitty's school canteen no one was left out, but she always made a special fuss of Niamh when she served her because Mamo Ann had been her friend since they were girls. Niamh liked her.

Mamo Anne had a habit of saying 'whatyoucallhim' or 'whatyoucallher' when she was talking about someone and couldn't remember their name, and as it happened Kitty had a great gift for mimicry, so once when Niamh had passed through the dinner line Kitty said in a voice exactly like Mamo Ann's, 'Niamh, do you know Jimmy Whatyoucallhim in your class? He sits beside wee Bridie Whatyoucallher?'

Kitty laughed uproariously at the expression on Niamh's face as she looked around for Mamo Anne. Then when she realised it was Kitty she chuckled and giggled, especially when Kitty warned her in mock seriousness not to tell her mamo. Of course that was the first thing Niamh told her when Mamo turned up.

It seemed to Niamh that these old people weren't really old at all. That's what she told her mammy. Maybe their bodies were old and slowed down but that was all. They weren't really *old* old. Not the way they joked about and carried on and made up stories to make her and themselves laugh. Kitty was really good at that.

'She loves a good slegg,' was the way Niamh put it.

'Better laughing than crying,' her mammy replied with a smile.

Then one morning Niamh's teacher told the children about Kitty when they arrived into class. Kitty had been in a car accident. Niamh knew what she was going to say once she heard the words 'and Kitty died in hospital last night'. Niamh knew that their teacher was going to tell them that Kitty was in heaven. And she did. That afternoon when Niamh's mother collected her at school, Niamh told her Kitty was away to heaven as well.

'I know, love,' her mother said. 'It's terrible. Kitty was a great wee woman. She was one of your granny's best chums. She told your granny she gave you extra custard with your trifle in the school dinners.'

'And, Mammy, she gave me and my friend Grainne biscuits. The same ones that Billy used to have. Digestives. And she imitated my mamo. Did Kitty know Billy?'

'I don't know, love. We're going to call to Kitty's house to pay our respects on the way home. It's the only chance I'll get so I need you to be very, very good. We won't stay long, and I'll make you a special dinner when we get home.'

'I don't want to go, Mammy,' Niamh said.

'Why not?' her mother asked her gently. 'You didn't go to Billy's house after he died or to your Auntie Leah's either.'

'I don't know, Mammy.' Niamh hesitated. 'The two of

them went to heaven. Nobody seems to come back from there. Since Billy went I've never seen him again. Or Auntie Leah. So now Kitty is away to heaven also. So I won't see her either. Ever again. One minute they're my friends and they're here. The next minute they're away.'

Her big blue eyes filled with tears as her mother reached for her and held her close. 'That's why you wouldn't go to Billy or Auntie Leah's, love? But they're still your friends. You can always say a wee prayer to them,' her mammy said.

Niamh knuckled her hands into her eyes and sniffed away her tears. 'Heaven must be very far away if no one who goes there is able to get home again,' she said.

Her mammy just hugged her tighter and smiled, and as always that made Niamh feel better.

When they got to Kitty's house Niamh hesitated at the front door.

'Now, Niamh,' her mother coaxed her gently and bent down to lift her, 'don't be a baby. Come up to me now.'

They went into the house. Niamh was in her mammy's arms. The living room was empty except for a large coffin sitting on trestles along the wall opposite to them. The blinds were drawn but the strong sunshine filtered its light through the whiteness of the blind and illuminated the room. It lit up the coffin and the mass cards lined up below it in rows. Niamh could see the little pictures of Jesus and his mother Mary. She could see Kitty stretched out in the coffin. She was still and pale, her arms across her chest and her fingers entwined in blue rosary beads. Niamh clung even tighter to her mammy's neck.

The sound of adult voices and clinking dishes came from the kitchen but no one there heard Niamh and her mammy in the living room. Niamh held her breath and scrutinised it all. Two candles placed on a small table beside the coffin gave off a faint musky scent. As they approached the coffin and Kitty she whispered, 'Mammy?'

'What, love?'

'Is Billy here?'

'What would Billy be doing here?'

Niamh looked at Kitty and then at her mother. 'Or Auntie Leah? Is she here?'

She looked all around the wake room with her big blue curious eyes. 'Mammy,' she whispered. 'Mammy … is this heaven?'

A GOOD CONFESSION

The congregation shuffled its feet. An old man spluttered noisily into his handkerchief, his body racked by a spasm of coughing. He wiped his nose wearily and returned to his prayers. A small child cried bad-temperedly in its mother's arms. Embarrassed, she released him into the side aisle of the chapel where, shoes clattering on the marble floor, he ran excitedly back and forth. His mother stared intently at the altar and tried to distance herself from her irreverent infant. He never even noticed her indifference; his attention was consumed by the sheer joy of being free, and soon he was trying to cajole another restless child to join him in the aisle. Another wave of coughing wheezed through the adult worshippers. As if encouraged by such solidarity, the old man resumed his catarrhal cacophony.

The priest leaned forward in the pulpit and directed himself and his voice towards his congregation. As he spoke they relaxed, as he knew they would. Only the children, absorbed in their innocence, continued as before. Even the old man, by some superhuman effort, managed to control his phlegm.

'My dear brothers and sisters,' the priest began. 'It is a

matter of deep distress and worry to me and I'm sure to you also that there are some Catholics who have so let the eyes of their soul become darkened that they no longer recognise sin as sin.'

He paused for a second or so to let his words sink in. He was a young man, not bad looking in an ascetic sort of a way, Mrs McCarthy thought, especially when he was intense about something, as he was now. She was in her usual seat at the side of the church, and as she waited for Fr Burns to continue his sermon, she thought to herself that it was good to have a new young priest in the parish.

Fr Burns cleared his throat and continued. 'I'm talking about the evil presence we have in our midst, and I'm asking you, the God-fearing people of this parish, to join with me in this Eucharist in praying that we loosen from the neck of our society the grip which a few have tightened around it and from which we sometimes despair of ever being freed.'

He stopped again momentarily. The congregation was silent: he had their attention. Even the sounds from the children were muted.

'I ask you all to pray with me that eyes that have become blind may be given sight, consciences that have become hardened and closed may be touched by God and opened to the light of His truth and love. I am speaking of course of the men of violence.' He paused, leant forward on arched arms and continued.

'I am speaking of the IRA and its fellow-travellers. This community of ours has suffered much in the past. I know that. I do not doubt but that in the IRA organisation there are those who entered the movement for idealistic reasons. They need to ask themselves now where that idealism has led them. We Catholics need to be quite clear about this.'

Fr Burns sensed that he was losing the attention of his flock again. The old man had lost or given up the battle to control his coughing. Others shuffled uneasily in their seats. A child shrieked excitedly at the back of the church. Some, like Mrs McCarthy, still listened intently, and he resolved to concentrate on them.

'Membership, participation in or cooperation with the IRA and its military operations is most gravely sinful. Now I know that I am a new priest here and some of you may be wondering if I am being political when I say these things. I am not. I am preaching Catholic moral teaching, and I can only say that those who do not listen are cutting themselves off from the community of the Church. They cannot sincerely join with their fellow Catholics who gather at mass and pray in union with the whole Church. Let us all, as we pray together, let us all resolve that we will never cut ourselves off from God in this way and let us pray for those who do.'

Fr Burns paused for the last time before concluding. 'In the name of the Father and the Son and the Holy Ghost.'

Just after communion and before the end of the mass there was the usual trickling exit of people out of the church. When Fr Burns gave the final blessing the trickle became a flood. Mrs McCarthy stayed in her seat. It was her custom to say a few prayers at Our Lady's altar before going home. She waited for the crowd to clear.

Jinny Blake, a neighbour, stopped on her way up the aisle and leaned confidentially towards her. 'Hullo, Mrs McCarthy,' she whispered reverently, her tone in keeping with their surroundings.

'Hullo, Jinny. You're looking well, so you are.'

'I'm doing grand, thank God. You're looking well yourself. Wasn't that new wee priest just lovely? And he was like lightning, too. It makes a change to get out of twelve o'clock mass so quickly.'

'Indeed it does,' Mrs McCarthy agreed as she and Jinny whispered their goodbyes.

By now the chapel was empty except for a few older people who stayed behind, like Mrs McCarthy, to say their special prayers or to light blessed candles. Mrs McCarthy left her seat and made her way slowly towards the small side altar. She genuflected awkwardly as she passed the sanctuary. As she did so the new priest came out from the sacristy. He had removed his vestments, and dressed in his dark suit, he looked slighter than she had imagined him to be when he had been saying mass.

'Hullo,' he greeted her.

'Hullo, Father, welcome to St Jude's.'

His boyish smile made her use of the term 'Father' seem incongruous.

'Thank you,' he said.

'By the way, Father ...' The words were out of her in a rush before she knew it. 'I didn't agree with everything you said in your sermon. Surely if you think those people are sinners you should be welcoming them into the Church and not chasing them out of it.'

Fr Burns was taken aback. 'I was preaching Church teaching,' he replied a little sharply.

It was a beautiful morning. He had been very nervous about the sermon, his first in a new parish. He had put a lot of thought into it, and now when it was just over and his relief had scarcely subsided, he was being challenged by an old woman.

Mrs McCarthy could feel his disappointment and resentment. She had never spoken like this before, especially to a priest. She retreated slightly. 'I'm sorry, Father,' she said uncomfortably, 'I just thought you were a bit hard.' She sounded apologetic. Indeed, as she looked at the youth of him she regretted that she had opened her mouth at all.

Fr Burns was blushing slightly as he searched around for a response.

'Don't worry,' he said finally, 'I'm glad you spoke your

mind. But you have to remember I was preaching God's word, and there's no arguing with that.'

They walked slowly up the centre aisle towards the main door. Fr Burns was relaxed now. He had one hand on her elbow, and as he spoke he watched her with a faint little smile on his lips. Despite herself, she felt herself growing angry at his presence. Who was this young man almost steering her out of the chapel? She hadn't even been at Our Lady's altar yet.

'We have to choose between our politics and our religion,' he was saying.

'That's fair enough, Father, as far as it goes, but I think it's wrong to chase people away from the Church,' she began.

'They do that themselves,' he interrupted her.

She saw that he still had that little smile. They were almost at the end of the aisle. She stopped sharply, surprising the priest as she did, so that he stopped also and stood awkwardly with his hand still on her elbow.

'I'm sorry, Father, I'm not going out yet.'

It was his turn to be flustered, and she noticed with some satisfaction that his smile had disappeared. Before he could recover she continued, 'I still think it's wrong to exclude people. Who are any of us to judge anyone, to say who is or who isn't a good Catholic, or a good Christian for that matter? I know them that lick the altar rails and, God forgive me, they wouldn't give you a drink of water if you were dying of the thirst. No, Father, it's not all black and white. You'll learn that before you're much older.'

His face reddened at her last remark.

'The Church is quite clear in its teaching on the issue of illegal organisations. Catholics cannot support or be a part of them.'

'And Christ never condemned anyone,' Mrs McCarthy told him, as intense now as he was.

'Well, you'll have to choose between your politics and your religion. All I can say is if you don't agree with the Church's teaching, then you have no place in this chapel.'

It was his parting shot and with it he knew he had bested her. She looked at him for a long minute in silence so that he blushed again, thinking for a moment that she was going to chide him, maternally perhaps, for being cheeky to his elders. But she didn't. Instead she shook her elbow free of his hand and walked slowly away from him out of the chapel. He stood until he had recovered his composure, then he too walked outside. To his relief she was nowhere to be seen.

When Mrs McCarthy returned home her son, Harry, knew something was wrong, and when she told him what had happened he was furious. She had to beg him not to go up to the chapel there and then.

'He said what, Ma? Tell me again!'

She started to recount her story.

'No, not that bit. I'm not concerned about all that. It's the end bit I can't take in. The last thing he said to you. Tell me that again?'

'He said if I didn't agree then I had no place in the chapel,' she told him again, almost timidly.

'The ignorant good-for-nothing wee skitter,' Harry fumed, pacing the floor.

Mrs McCarthy was sorry she had told him anything. 'I'll have to learn to bite my tongue,' she told herself. 'If I'd said nothing to the priest none of this would have happened.'

Harry's voice burst in on her thoughts. 'What gets me is that you reared nine of us. That's what gets me! You did your duty as a Catholic mother and that's the thanks you get for it. They've no humility, no sense of humanity. Could he not see that you're an old woman?'

'That's nothing to do with it,' Mrs McCarthy interrupted him sharply.

'Ma, that's everything to do with it! Can you not see that? If he had been talking to me, I could see the point, but you? All your life you've done your best and he insults you like that! He must have no mother of his own. That's all they're good for: laying down their petty little rules and lifting their collections and insulting the very people —'

'Harry, that's enough.'

The weariness in her tone stopped him in mid-sentence.

'I've had enough arguing to do me for one day,' she said. 'You giving off like that is doing me no good. Just forget

163

about it for now. And I don't want you doing anything about it; I'll see Fr Burns again in my own good time. But for now, I'm not going to let it annoy me any more.'

But it did. It ate away at her all day, and when she retired to bed it was to spend a restless night with Fr Burns's words turning over again and again in her mind.

Choose between your politics and your religion. Politics and religion. If you don't accept the Church's teachings, you've no place in the chapel. No place in the chapel.

The next day she went to chapel as was her custom, but she didn't go at her usual time, and she was nervous and unsettled within herself all the time she was there. Even Our Lady couldn't settle her. She was so worried that Fr Burns would arrive and that they would have another row that she couldn't concentrate on her prayers. Eventually it became too much for her and she left by the side door and made her way home again, agitated and in bad form.

The next few days were the same. She made her way to the chapel as usual, but she did so in an almost furtive manner, and the solace that she usually got from her daily prayers and contemplation was lost to her. On the Wednesday she walked despondently to the shops; on her way homewards she bumped into Jinny Blake outside McErlean's Home Bakery.

'Ach, Mrs McCarthy, how 'ye doing? You look as if everybody belonging t'ye had just died. What ails ye?'

Mrs McCarthy told her what had happened, glad to get talking to someone who, unlike Harry or Fr Burns, would understand her dilemma. Jinny was a sympathetic listener and she waited attentively until Mrs McCarthy had furnished her with every detail of the encounter with the young priest.

'So that's my tale of woe, Jinny,' she concluded eventually, 'and I don't know what to do. I'm not as young as I used to be ...'

'You're not fit for all that annoyance. The cheek of it!' her friend reassured her. 'You shouldn't have to put up with the like of that at your age. You seldom hear them giving off about them ones.' Jinny gestured angrily at a passing convoy of British army Land Rovers. 'They bloody well get off too light, God forgive me and pardon me! Imagine saying that to you, or anyone else for that matter.'

Jinny was angry, but whereas Harry's rage had unsettled Mrs McCarthy, Jinny's indignation fortified her, so that by the time they finally parted Mrs McCarthy was resolved to confront Fr Burns and, as Jinny had put it, to 'stand up for her rights'.

The following afternoon she made her way to the chapel. It was her intention to go from there to the parochial house. She was quite settled in her mind as to what she would say and how she would say it, but first she knelt before the statue of Our Lady. For the first time that week she felt at ease in the chapel. But the sound of footsteps coming down the aisle in her direction unnerved her slightly. She couldn't look around to see who it was, which made her even more anxious that it might be Fr Burns. In her plans the confrontation with him was to be on her terms in the parochial house, not here, on his terms, in the chapel.

'Hullo, Mrs McCarthy, is that you?'

With a sigh of relief she recognised Fr Kelly's voice. 'Ah, Father,' she exclaimed. 'It is indeed. Am I glad to see you!'

Fr Kelly was the parish priest. He was a small, stocky white-haired man in his late fifties. He and Mrs McCarthy had known each other since he had taken over the parish fifteen years before. As he stood smiling at her, obviously delighted at her welcome for him, she reproached herself for not coming to see him long before this. As she would tell Jinny later, that just went to show how distracted she was by the whole affair.

'Fr Kelly, I'd love a wee word with you, so I would.' She rose slowly from her pew. 'If you have the time, that is.'

'I've always time for you, my dear.' He helped her to her feet. 'Come on and we'll sit ourselves down over here.'

They made their way to a secluded row of seats at the side of the church. Fr Kelly sat quietly as Mrs McCarthy recounted the story of her disagreement with Fr Burns. When she was finished he remained silent for some moments, gazing quizzically over at the altar.

'Give up your politics or give up your religion, Mrs

McCarthy? That's the quandary, isn't it?'

He spoke so quietly, for a minute she thought he was talking to himself. Then he straightened up in the seat, gave her a smile and asked, 'Are you going to give up your politics?'

'No,' she replied a little nervously and then, more resolutely: 'No! Not even for the Pope of Rome.'

He nodded in smiling assent and continued, 'And are you going to give up your religion?'

'No,' she responded quickly, a little surprised at his question.

'Not even for the Pope of Rome?' he bantered her.

'No.' She smiled, catching his mood.

'Well then, I don't know what you're worrying about. We live in troubled times, and it's not easy for any of us, including priests. We all have to make our own choices. That's why God gives us the power to reason and our own free will. You've heard the Church's teaching and you've made your decision. You're not going to give up your religion nor your politics, and I don't see why you should. All these other things will pass. And don't bother yourself about seeing Fr Burns. I'll have a wee word with him.' He patted her gently on the back of her hand as he got to his feet. 'Don't be worrying. And don't let anyone put you out of the chapel! It's God's house. Hold on to all your beliefs, Mrs McCarthy, if you're sure that's what you want.'

'Thank you, Father.' Mrs McCarthy smiled in relief. 'God bless you.'

'I hope He does,' Fr Kelly said. 'I hope He does.' He turned and walked slowly up the aisle. When he got to the door he turned and looked down the chapel. Mrs McCarthy was back at her favourite seat beside the statue of Our Lady. Apart from her, the silent church was empty. Fr Kelly stood reflecting pensively on that. For a moment he was absorbed by the irony of the imagery before him. Then he turned wearily, smiled to himself and left.

TELLING IT AS IT WAS

The two men looked at each other. Despite the robust tone of their discussion there was no tension between them. They knew each other well. They had been on IRA active service together. Alfie had told Michael a long time ago that he only got involved after the Brits shot one of his neighbours. He was at university at the time, enjoying his life as a student and doing well amidst the mayhem of Belfast. He was stopped on the street a few times, like most young men, by the RUC and the British army and they messed him about, calling him an Irish bastard. He got punched a few times but he was never arrested. After they checked his identity they would let him go again.

One day he attended an anti-internment rally along with his brother Paul.

'I've joined the army,' Paul told him that day.

'The army?' Alfie asked him.

'The IRA. The Irish Republican Army,' Paul replied. 'Don't say a word to anyone. Especially not me ma or da. It would kill them.'

Alfie wasn't entirely surprised by Paul's news. Not when he

reflected on it. Paul was always reading history books and he watched the news a lot. He was also friendly with the Clarkes, a well-known local republican family whose house was raided regularly. Mr Clarke was interned. A few months after Paul told Alfie he was a volunteer, he was arrested. By fluke Alfie saw the arrest. He was upstairs on the bus home when a heavily armoured British army vehicle pulled in front of the bus, forcing it to stop. The Saracen armoured vehicle crashed into a car, which was in front of the bus, pushing it off the road. There was a loud bang of metal on metal, the screeching of brakes and then shouting and screaming as British soldiers leapt out of their vehicle and swarmed around the car. It was a Ford Escort. A grey one. There were two young men in it. The Brits pulled them from the badly damaged car and started to beat them with rifle butts and batons. They were spreadeagled on the ground, crumpled together under a blizzard of blows. One of the young men was Paul. Alfie didn't know the other one. They were both bleeding from cuts on their heads and faces when the Brits eventually bundled them into their armoured pig. From his elevated vantage point on the bus Alfie could see it all. As the heavy armoured back door was pulled shut on Paul, he glanced upwards, his bloodied face contorted in a grimace. Their eyes met. Then the Brit vehicle revved up and sped away.

Alfie got off the bus. He was shaken although he made sure not to show any emotion. He felt guilty. As if he had let his brother down.

'Brit bastards,' the bus conductor said to him as he stepped down. 'I wouldn't like to be those two lads.'

Alfie said nothing. He went home and told his parents what he'd seen. As Paul had predicted, they were both upset. His mother told Alfie to go and sit in their Aunt Rita's house in the next street. His father went to call a solicitor from the phone in Henry's pub at the corner.

'They'll be raiding here before long,' his mother said. 'Bad enough one son in the barracks. You can come back when they leave.'

When Alfie got back after the Brit raid their home was wrecked. Everything was turned inside out. They had broken down the front door, and Alfie's bedroom door hung off its hinges. Paul was released, along with the other lad, forty-eight hours later.

The solicitor had told them in advance that was probably what would happen. 'They have nothing on them. Paul was out for a drive with his friend Paddy. The car belongs to Paddy's father and he was fully qualified and insured to drive it.'

Neither Alfie nor his parents had ever heard of Paddy before, but Paul stuck to his story when he got home, battered and bruised, from the barracks. Paddy was a friend from work, he said, and they were just out for a wee spin. Alfie said nothing.

Later that week he told Paul how he had witnessed his arrest from the bus. He didn't ask Paul what he and Paddy were doing. There was no point. And anyway he didn't want to know.

'Just to let you know, Paul, I won't be joining the 'RA. I agree with their aims but ...' he hesitated, 'I couldn't kill anyone. Not even a Brit soldier.'

Six months later the Brits killed Mr Gillen, their neighbour. His wee dog was barking at a passing patrol and running and snapping at the soldiers' legs. He did that every day a patrol came into the street. Mr Gillen went out to bring him in, and as he bent down to gather up the mutt, the officer in charge of the patrol shot Mr Gillen in the head. He died instantly.

There was rioting all that night in the neighbourhood. Alfie had known Mr Gillen since he was born. He was one of his da's friends, a quiet, decent man who never married. Everyone was incensed when the British army described him as a gunman who had opened fire on their patrol. They said a mob had taken his weapon away. All lies.

Alfie didn't sleep that night. Instead he made his way down to the corner and watched youngsters throwing stones and the occasional petrol bomb at Brit Land Rovers. That's no use, he thought to himself.

The next day he joined the IRA. That's how he met Michael.

Michael became a volunteer by a different route. He was

working abroad, in Australia. Barely out of his teens, he'd left Ireland and gone into the outback to work on the mines. He was a fit young man, reared on a farm in County Tyrone and well used to hard work. The pay was good for the dangerous job they did in harsh conditions. It was a surreal experience, far from the green, lush place he grew up in.

A cohort of mostly young men, including some Irish lads, they shacked up in a work camp in the wilderness. Three weeks working then they were off for a week of carousing and drinking weak Australian beer in Perth. Then back to work again. That's when Michael saw the first television coverage of the civil rights agitation in his home county. In a bar in Perth. He saw people he knew marching together across the TV screen. Heard them singing 'We Shall Overcome'. Saw them being attacked by the state police, the RUC.

When he first went to Australia, his intention was to stay until he had saved up enough money to come home and buy a bit of land. His father farmed a few acres but Michael's intention was to get his own plot, and his father had earmarked a nice wee farm in the east of the parish which could be bought quietly.

Michael liked Australia. He became friends with some of the native people who lived locally off the land and by doing the odd bit of casual work around the workcamp. He went hunting and fishing with them. That experience stayed with him. He loved the wilderness, nature, the bush. In later life if he was socialising and the stories were ignited by a few drinks, he always started his tales with 'I remember one time in Australia ...' His family, in particular, ribbed him a lot over that. He stayed friends for the rest of his life with some of his workmates but he never earned enough to buy the wee farm. Instead he bought a car and headed off, in 1969, driving into the sunrise, to make the long journey across Australia to catch a plane back to Ireland and Tyrone. He came home with his mind made up. There was a struggle for rights heating up in Ireland. He knew what side he was on.

He and Alfie met in prison. For seven years or so they did time together. That included sharing a cell in the H-Blocks for a time during the prison protests. They were close to Francie Hughes. Alfie was a good friend of Joe McDonnell, who also died on hunger strike. They rarely talked of those terrible times afterwards, but each of them was proud of surviving the blanket protest, the beatings and the brutality of that period. They were part of the dogged resistance that pitted prisoners against a cruel penal regime. Even though there were over five hundred prisoners in the H-Blocks at the height of the protests, they knew the resistance was personal. Every man was engaged in his own individual fight. So were the women in Armagh Prison. That's how the system tried to break them. One at a time. And that's how they resisted. One at a time.

When they were released they both reported back, separately, to the IRA for active service. As it turned out, they ended up in the one unit. They both were active in the bloody years leading up to the peace process. They never got arrested again. They nearly got killed a few times. And they did their share of killing. When the cessation came they were wary of it but determined to give the new mode of struggle a chance.

So Alfie and Michael had lots of time for each other. The system had failed to break them. They were older now, getting on with their lives and supportive of the development of the peace process. Michael was heavily involved in the political leadership. Alfie was on the sidelines, willing to help locally during elections or other campaigns, and an influential figure among his peer group, but content to be a supporter instead of an activist. Michael and he had been talking for an hour.

'You're asking me to go to the commission and tell them about operations I was involved in?' Alfie asked tersely. 'The bloody commission to deal with the past? The commission that the last peace talks at Stormont agreed on? Are you expecting MI5 and all the Brit intelligence crowd to come forward and tell all they know about their operations and dirty tricks, including the names of the English politicians who authorised so many killings here?'

The two men were seated in armchairs in the front room of Alfie's home. They were both of an age – mid to late forties. Alfie was dressed in jeans and a T-shirt. The man

175

opposite him was also in jeans but with an open-necked shirt and jacket.

Alfie looked into the middle distance for a long, tense minute. Then he spoke slowly and forcefully. 'I'm not going to any commission, Michael. Not now. Not ever. You go if you want. That's your choice. My war is over. I have no interest in any of that any more. You politicians have to do that stuff. You have my support but that doesn't include me talking to a commission about army operations.'

The two men looked at each other in silence for a long minute. Michael was thinking wryly and without rancour that this was typical Alfie. For his part, he was content to let Alfie give off to him. He had anticipated that Alfie would say no at the start. He wasn't surprised. He knew it was a big thing he was asking him to do.

Alfie was also thinking that this was typical Michael. No bother to him to put a proposition like that to Alfie. He must have known he would say no. Or he should have known. Then Alfie relaxed suddenly and smiled broadly at Michael. 'Don't worry,' he grinned, 'you'll get someone to go forward. But that someone won't be me. So there's no point in putting a big long face on you. Tell me how things are going with you. The only time I see you nowadays is on TV. Or when you're looking for something.'

He grinned again. Michael eventually smiled back at him. 'You always had a way of saying what you think. That's what I liked about you. Though I'm sorry you're not up for moving this process on another bit. It's disappointing, comrade.'

Alfie continued to smile. He admired Michael's patience and the slow, steady way he came at issues when he wanted to have his own way. Alfie wasn't unlike that himself. But that was when he was immersed in the twists and turns of the struggle. When it seemed that that was all that mattered. But now he had a life. He was off the merry-go-round. His focus was on the more ordinary but vital and loving relationship he had with Alice and their three children. Still, he was glad to see Michael. Even if it was only because he wanted him to do 'a wee turn', as he put it. Some wee turn, Alfie thought. But that's the way Michael was – he was in for the long haul. Alfie admired him for that, and he would help if he could. But not this time.

He smiled at his friend again. 'Michael, how long do I know you now?' he said, the irony clear in his tone. 'Don't bullshit me, mo chara. You know I've done my bit and that I'm out of it now. Things are going OK without me. Youse are doing a good job. Progress is too slow but that's the way of peace processes. It's not your fault. Between the Brits and the Unionists they obviously want to move as slowly as possible. Or not to move at all. And Dublin isn't much better … But you don't need me to tell you any of this. I support what you're doing but I've a life now and three wee ones –'

'And you want them to go through what you went through? Alfie, this is about winning the peace. About out-flanking the bigots and the dark side of the system so that your kids and everybody else's kids can have a decent future. This isn't really about the past, chara. This is about the future.'

'I know all that, Michael, but I've given you my answer. I did what I did because I believed in it. I still do. But there is only so much that a man can do. I was a good volunteer. You know how active I was. That's why you're here –'

'No, that's not why I'm here,' Michael interrupted. He paused for a second. He knew Alfie would always be straight with him. He understood why, once the armed struggle had ended, Alfie slipped back into a more passive role. He was always there during the war. In the gap of danger when called on. Even in risky ventures Alfie was the one prepared to take the big chances in order to succeed. He was one of the bravest people Michael had ever known. But after the intensity of those times had passed, it was natural that he would want to pick up the threads of life again when he got the chance. And that's what he did. Michael knew that Alfie considered himself to be one of the lucky ones. He had survived the war against all the odds. He had soldiered hard and deserved credit for that. Though Alfie never looked for credit. He never thought he was owed anything by the move-ment. Michael and he had that in common. They had lost too many friends. Too many who were not as lucky as them. So

Michael chose his words thoughtfully and carefully.

'I'm here,' he continued, 'because you were always politically tuned in. I'm here because I thought you would understand the need to keep moving things on. Our strategy needs momentum. Inertia is the death of our efforts. Our enemies know that. Including the militarists on our side.'

'Don't give me that,' Alfie countered. 'Those eejits are going nowhere. Riddled with agents. If the Dissies didn't exist they'd have to invent them. There might be some sincere people who disagree with us on the fringes of those groups, but for the most part the Brits or the Special Branch run that particular show. You don't need me to tell you that. All they can do is distract and destabilise, which is the main reason for their existence. But they're no real threat to Sinn Féin's big project.'

'Be that as it may or may not be, we are trying to deal with legacy issues, Alfie.'

'You know the Brits won't do that!'

'We can lead by example.'

'Lead who, Michael? The Brits? No chance. That's a load of horse shit and you know it. Our war is over but their wars aren't. They'll always be trying to get us in the long grass. What they used to do in Ireland they're now doing in other places using exactly the same methods. Leaving everything else aside, how could they get their forces to do that if they hung them out to dry for doing the same thing

here? The Brit system – the real government, the permanent one – won't allow that even if a benign prime minister
wanted to take an initiative.'

'*We* have to take the initiative, Alfie. You know that.
We who want the maximum change need to take the big
risks. A team rarely wins playing only in its own bit of
the field. You have to play in the other side's bit of the
field as well. Chancey. But necessary. So this isn't about
a sweet wee deal with the Brits. This is about outflanking
them. Exposing their duplicity. We've made negotiations a
mode of struggle. That means every so often making strategic
compromises. Short-term pain. But longer-term gain. We
won the war thanks to you and others. But we have to win
the peace as well. You know all this, Alfie. It's about winning
more support. Building political strength. Neutralising our
opponents ...'

Outside the room where they sat the light was draining
from the sky. The street was quiet. They could hear house-
hold sounds. Children were reluctantly being readied for
bed. Their mother's voice raised in appeal. The closing of
a door. The patter of feet on the stairs. The excited babble
of childish voices. Michael knew it was almost time for him
to go. But he didn't want to give up while there was still a
chance that Alfie might say yes.

Alfie knew Michael was on a mission. Alfie appreciated
that he hadn't come to him on a whim. It would have been

decided after a lot of consideration and Michael would have been selected as the best one to talk to him.

'I understand why you're looking to deal with the past.' Alfie smiled. 'I appreciate the reasons for doing so, and in a way I'm flattered that you came to me, but as far as I'm concerned, and as I've told you, you're talking to the wrong man. I'm happy to help with bits and pieces when you need me to but I'm not going forward to any commission and that's that. Sin é. I'm telling you it as it is.'

'OK,' Michael said, 'but do one thing for me, le do thoil?'

'What's that?'

'Promise me you'll consider what I've asked you to do. Just for the sake of old times.'

Alfie smiled. 'For the sake of old times?'

The two men sat in silence again. This time for a few minutes. The sounds from outside the room seemed to be more subdued. The children's voices came from upstairs now.

When Alfie spoke again there was a slight edge to his voice. 'Michael, the old times are done. I'm proud of what I did. I'm proud I was a volunteer. Don't get me wrong – I'm not saying we were right all the time. We weren't. I regret some of the things I did. There are things you do when you're twenty that you wouldn't do when you're fifty. But that to one side, I did the best I could and I've a clear conscience and the satisfaction of knowing I stood up against the Brits and the madness they brought to our country. But I'm also glad the war is over. It's a great achievement – mostly because of your efforts and others like you – that we can proceed without anyone else killing or being killed. Or going to jail.'

'And that's the way we want to keep it,' Michael intervened. He still had hope that Alfie could be persuaded. That was obvious from his demeanour. Alfie would be well fit to deal with the commission. Of course there would always be someone else to do that. But they needed to be willing to do so. A volunteer was always better than a conscript. Especially if the snakes in the long grass had their way.

But Alfie was not for moving. He took a deep, impatient breath. 'Michael,' he exclaimed, 'you just don't get it. You're like a dog at a bone. My war is over. Kaput! I have a life now. A family to rear.

'No, Michael.' Alfie looked earnestly at him. 'This is my last word on it.' He looked at his old comrade with a little smile. His face reddened as he continued. 'The fact is I never did anything that would be of any interest to any commission – or anyone else for that matter. I never did nothing. I was never in anything. Nobody can prove any different. And that's the way it's gonna stay. I'm telling it as it was.'

That ended the discussion. They both knew that. The two of them stood up. There was a brief awkwardness between them. Even so, they shook hands.

They had been through too much together to do anything else.

So Michael said goodnight to Alfie's wife, Alice. She was flattered that he had called and insisted on getting the kids down the stairs for a photo with their 'Uncle' Michael. Alfie took the first photo and then joined Michael, the two of them with arms full of kids in their pyjamas, easy once again in each other's company.

They left it like that, with a last comradely embrace before Michael walked back to his car.

Fact is, he and Alfie understood each other better and appreciated each other more than they ever could articulate or explain, even to each other. Even if they wanted to. That was the unspoken bond that had grown between them through their long years of activism. Something unique to them and the life they had lived. Unknown to anyone who had not been there. Unknown to anyone else.

So Michael decided it was better for him to say he'd changed his mind about Alfie being the right man for the commission. Better that than tell what Alfie had said to him. Michael understood that was Alfie's way of getting through to him. Michael knew better than anyone that Alfie had done his bit. That couldn't be taken away from him. Not by anyone and especially not by Michael. So he resolved never to repeat what had been said. It was a conversation that never happened. And maybe, Michael thought to himself with regret, as he drove away, it never should have.

THE MOUNTAINS OF MOURNE

Geordie Mayne lived in Urney Street, one of a network of narrow streets which stretched from Cupar Street, in the shadow of Clonard Monastery, to the Shankill Road. I don't know where Geordie is now or even if he's living or dead, but I think of him often. Though I knew him only for a short time many years ago, Geordie is one of those characters who might come into your life briefly but never really leave you afterwards.

Urney Street is probably gone now. I haven't been there in twenty years, and all that side of the Shankill has disappeared since then as part of the redevelopment of the area. Part of the infamous Peace Line follows the route that Cupar Street used to take. Before the Peace Line was erected, Lawnbrook Avenue joined Cupar Street to the Shankill Road. Cupar Street used to run from the Falls Road up until it met Lawnbrook Avenue, then it swung left and ran on to the Springfield Road. Only as I try to place the old streets do I realise how much the place has changed this last twenty years, and how little distance there really is between the Falls and the Shankill. For all that closeness there might as well be a thousand miles between them.

When we were kids we used to take shortcuts up Cupar Street from the Falls to the Springfield Road. Catholics lived in the bottom end of Cupar Street nearest the Falls; there were one or two in the middle of Cupar Street, too, but the rest were mainly Protestants till you got up past Lawnbrook Avenue; and from there to the Springfield Road was all Catholic again. The streets going up the Springfield Road on the right-hand side were Protestant and the ones on the left-hand side up as far as the Flush were Catholic. After that both sides were nearly all Protestant until you got to Ballymurphy.

When we were kids we paid no heed to these territorial niceties, though once or twice during the Orange marching season we'd get chased. Around about the Twelfth of July and at other appropriate dates, the Orangemen marched through many of those streets, Catholic and Protestant alike. The Catholic ones got special attention, as did individual Catholic houses, with the marching bands and their followers, sometimes the worse for drink, exciting themselves with enthusiastic renderings of Orange tunes as they passed by. The Mackie's workers also passed that way twice daily, an especially large contingent making its way from the Shankill along Cupar Street to Mackie's Foundry. The largest engineering works in the city was surrounded by Catholic streets, but it employed very few Catholics.

Often bemused by expressions such as Catholic street and Protestant area, I find myself nonetheless using the very same expressions. How could a house be Catholic or Protestant? Yet when it comes to writing about the reality it's hard to find other words. Though loath to do so, I use the terms Catholic and Protestant here to encompass the various elements who make up the Unionist and non-Unionist citizens of this state.

It wasn't my intention to tell you all this. I could write a book about the craic I had as a child making my way in and out of all those wee streets on the way back and forth to school or the Boys' Confraternity in Clonard or even down at the Springfield Road dam fishing for spricks, but that's not what I set out to tell you about. I set out to tell you about Geordie Mayne of Urney Street. Geordie was an Orangeman, nominally at least. He never talked about it to me except on the occasion when he told me that he was one. His lodge was the Pride of the Shankill Loyal Orange Lodge, I think, though it's hard to be sure after all this time.

I only knew Geordie for a couple of weeks, but even though that may seem too short a time to make a judgement, I could never imagine him as a zealot or a bigot. You get so that you can tell, and by my reckoning Geordie wasn't the worst. He was a driver for a big drinks firm: that's how I met him. I was on the run at the time. It was almost Christmas 1969, and I had been running about like a blue-arsed fly since early summer. I hadn't worked since July, we weren't getting any money except a few bob every so often for smokes, so things were pretty rough. But it was an exciting time: I was only twenty-one and I was one of a dozen young men and women who were up to their necks in trying to sort things out.

To say that I was on the run is to exaggerate a little. I wasn't wanted for anything, but I wasn't taking any chances either. I hadn't slept at home since the end of May when the RUC had invaded Hooker Street in Ardoyne and there had been a night or two of sporadic rioting. Most of us who were politically active started to take precautions at that time. We were expecting internment or worse as the civil rights agitation and the reaction against it continued to escalate. Everything came to a head in August, including internment, and in Belfast the conflict had been particularly sharp around Cupar Street. This abated a little, but we thought it was only a temporary respite: with the British army on the streets it couldn't be long till things hotted up again. In the meantime we were not making ourselves too available.

Conway Street, Cupar Street at the Falls Road end and all of Norfolk Street had been completely burned out on the first night of the August pogrom; further up, near the monastery, Bombay Street was gutted on the following night. These were all Catholic streets. Urney Street was just a stone's throw from Bombay Street; that is, if you were a stone thrower.

The drinks company Geordie worked for was taking on extra help to cope with the Christmas rush, and a few of us went up to the head office on the Glen Road on spec one morning; as luck would have it I got a start, together with big Eamonn and two others. I was told to report to the store down in Cullingtree Road the next morning and it was there that I met Geordie.

He saw me before I saw him. I was standing in the big yard among all the vans and lorries and I heard this voice shouting: 'Joe … Joe Moody.'

I paid no attention.

'Hi, boy! Is your name Joe Moody?' the voice repeated.

With a start I realised that that was indeed my name, or at least it was the bum name I'd given when I'd applied for the job.

'Sorry,' I stammered.

'I thought you were corned beef. C'mon over here.'

I did as instructed and found myself beside a well-built red-haired man in his late thirties. He was standing at the back of a large empty van.

'Let's go, our kid. My name's Geordie Mayne. We'll be working together. We're late. Have you clocked in? Do it over there and then let's get this thing loaded up.' He handed me a sheaf of dockets. 'Pack them in that order. Start from the back. I'll only be a minute.'

He disappeared into the back of the store. I had hardly started to load the van when he arrived back. Between the two of us we weren't long packing in the cartons and crates of wines and spirits and then we were off, Geordie cheerfully saluting the men on barricade duty at the end of the street as they waved us out of the Falls area and into the rest of the world.

Geordie and I spent most of our first day together delivering our load to off-licences and public houses in the city centre. I was nervous of being recognised because I had worked in a bar there, but luckily it got its deliveries from a different firm. It was the first day I had been in the city centre since August; except for the one trip to Dublin and one up to Derry, I had spent all my time behind the barricades. It was disconcerting to find that, apart from the unusual sight of British soldiers with their cheerful, arrogant voices, life in the centre of Belfast, or at least its licensed premises, appeared unaffected by the upheavals of the past few months. It was also strange as we made our deliveries to catch glimpses on television of news coverage about the very areas and issues I was so involved in and familiar with. Looked at from outside through the television screen, the familiar scenes might as well have been in another country.

Geordie and I said nothing of any of this to one another. That was a strange experience for me, too. My life had been so full of the cut-and-thrust of analysis, argument and counter-argument about everything that affected the political situation that I found it difficult to restrain myself from commenting on events to this stranger. Indeed, emerging from the close camaraderie of my closed world, as I had done only that morning, I found it unusual even to be with a stranger. Over a lunch of soup and bread rolls in the Harp Bar in High Street, I listened to the midday news on the BBC's Radio Ulster while all the time pretending indifference. The lead item was a story about an IRA convention and media speculation about a republican split. It would be nightfall before I would be able to check this out for myself, though a few times during the day I almost left Geordie in his world of cheerful pubs and publicans for the security of the ghettos.

The next few days followed a similar pattern. Each morning started with Geordie absenting himself for a few minutes to the back of the store while I started loading up the van. Then we were off from within the no-go areas and into the city centre. By the end of the first week the two of us were like old friends. Our avoidance of political topics, even of the most pressing nature, that unspoken and much-used form of political protection and survival developed through expediency, had in its own way been a political indicator, a signal, that we came from 'different sides'.

In the middle of the second week Geordie broke our mutual and instinctive silence on this issue when with a laugh he handed me that morning's dockets. 'Well, our kid, this is your lucky day. You're going to see how the other half lives. We're for the Shankill.'

My obvious alarm fuelled his amusement.

'Oh, aye,' he guffawed. 'It's all right for me to traipse up and down the Falls every day, but my wee Fenian friend doesn't want to return the favour.'

I was going to tell him that nobody from the Falls went up the Shankill burning down houses but I didn't. I didn't want to hurt his feelings, but I didn't want to go up the Shankill either. I was in a quandary and set about loading up our deliveries with a heavy heart. After I had only two of the cartons loaded I went to the back of the store to tell Geordie that I was jacking it in. He was in the wee office with oul' Harry the storeman. Each of them had a glass of spirits in his hand. Geordie saw me coming and offered his to me.

'Here, our kid, it's best Jamaicay rum. A bit of Dutch courage never did anyone any harm.'

'Nawh, thanks, Geordie, I don't drink spirits. I need to talk to you for a minute …'

'If it's about today's deliveries, you've nothing to worry about. We've only one delivery up the Shankill, and don't be thinking of not going 'cos you'll end up out on your arse. It's company policy that mixed crews deliver all over the town. Isn't that right, Harry?'

Harry nodded in agreement.

'C'mon, our kid. I'll do the delivery for you. Okay? You

can sit in the van. How's that grab you? Can't be fairer than that, can I, Harry?'

'Nope,' Harry grunted. They drained their glasses.

'I'll take a few beers for the child, Harry,' Geordie said over his shoulder as he and I walked back to the van.

'You know where they are,' said Harry.

'Let's go,' said Geordie to me. 'It's not every day a wee Fenian like you gets on to the best road in Belfast –' he grabbed me around the neck '– and off it again in one piece. Hahaha.'

That's how I ended up on the Shankill. It wasn't so bad, but before I tell you about that, in case I forget, from then on, each morning when Geordie returned from the back of the store after getting his 'wee drop of starting fuel', he always had a few bottles of beer for me.

Anyway, back to the job in hand. As Geordie said, we only had the one order on the Shankill. It was to the Long Bar. We drove up by Unity Flats and on to Peter's Hill. There were no signs of barricades like the ones on the Falls, and apart from a patrolling RUC Land Rover and two British army jeeps, the road was the same as it had always seemed to me. Busy and prosperous and coming awake in the early winter morning sunshine.

A few months earlier, in October, the place had erupted in protest at the news that the B-Specials were to be disbanded. The protesters had killed one RUC man and wounded three others; thirteen British soldiers had been injured. In a night of heavy gunfighting along the Shankill Road, the British had killed two civilians and wounded twenty others. Since then there had been frequent protests here against the existence of no-go areas in Catholic parts of Belfast and Derry.

Mindful of all this, I perched uneasily in the front of the van, ready at a second's notice to spring into Geordie's seat and drive like the blazes back whence I came. I needn't have worried. Geordie was back in moments. As he climbed into the driver's seat he threw me a packet of cigarettes.

'There's your Christmas box, our kid. I told them I had a wee Fenian out here and that you were dying for a smoke.'

Then he took me completely by surprise.

'Do y'fancy a fish supper? It's all right! We eat fish on Friday as well. Hold on!'

And before I could say anything he had left me again as he sprinted from the van into the Eagle Supper Saloon.

'I never got any breakfast,' he explained on his return. 'We'll go round to my house. There's nobody in.'

I said nothing as we turned in to Westmoreland Street and on through a myriad of backstreets till we arrived in Urney Street. Here the tension was palpable, for me at least. Geordie's house was no different from ours. A two-bedroomed house with a toilet in the backyard and a modernised scullery. Only for the picture of the British queen, I could have been in my own street. I buttered rounds of plain white bread and we wolfed down our fish suppers with lashings of Geordie's tea.

Afterwards, my confidence restored slightly, while Geordie was turning the van in the narrow street I walked down to the corner and gazed along the desolation of Cupar Street up towards what remained of Bombay Street. A British soldier in a sandbagged emplacement greeted me in a John Lennon accent.

''Lo, moite. How's about you?'

I ignored him and stood momentarily immersed in the bleak pitifulness of it all, from the charred remains of the small houses to where the world-weary slopes of Divis Mountain gazed benignly in their winter greenness down on us where we slunk, blighted, below the wise steeples of Clonard. It was Geordie's impatient honking of the horn that shook me out of my reverie. I nodded to the British soldier as I departed. This time he ignored me.

'Not a pretty sight,' Geordie said as I climbed into the van beside him.

I said nothing. We made our way back through the side streets on to the Shankill again in silence. As we turned in to Royal Avenue at the corner of North Street he turned to me.

'By the way,' he said, 'I wasn't there that night.'

There was just a hint of an edge in his voice.

'I'm sorry! I'm not blaming you,' I replied. 'It's not your fault.'

'I know,' he told me firmly.

That weekend, subsidised by my week's wages, I was immersed once more in subversion. That at least was how the Unionist government viewed the flurry of political activity in the ghettos; and indeed a similar view was taken by those representatives of the Catholic middle class who had belatedly attached themselves to the various committees in which some of us had long been active. On Monday I was back delivering drink.

We spent the week before Christmas in County Down, seemingly a million miles from the troubles and the tension of Belfast town. For the first time in years I did no political work. It was late by the time we got back each night and I was too tired, so that by Wednesday I realised that I hadn't even seen, read or heard any news all that week. I smiled to myself at the thought that both I and the struggle appeared to be surviving without each other; in those days that was a big admission for me to make, even to myself.

In its place Geordie and I spent the week up and down country roads, driving through beautiful landscapes, over and around hilltops and along rugged seashores and loughsides as we ferried our liquid wares from village to town, from town to port and back to village again; from market town to fishing village, from remote hamlet to busy crossroads. Even yet the names have a magical sound for me, and at each one Geordie and I took the time for a stroll or a quick look at some local antiquity.

One memorable day we journeyed out to Comber and from there to Killyleagh and Downpatrick, to Crossgar and back again and along the Ballyhornan road and on out to Strangford where we ate our cooked ham baps and drank bottles of stout, hunkering down from the wind below the square tower of Strangford Castle, half-frozen with the cold as we looked over towards Portaferry on the opposite side, at the edge of the Ards Peninsula. We spent a day there as well, and by this time I had a guide book with me written by Richard Hayward, and I kept up a commentary as we toured the peninsula, from Millisle the whole way around the coast-line and back to Newtownards. By the end of the week we had both seen where the Norsemen had settled and the spot where Thomas Russell, 'the man from God knows where', was hanged, where St Patrick had lived and Cromwell and Betsy Grey and Shane O'Neill. We visited monastic settlements and stone circles, round towers, dolmens and holy wells. Up and down the basket-of-eggs county we walked old battle sites like those of the faction fights at Dolly's Brae or Scarva, 'wee buns' we learned compared to Saintfield where Munroe and seven thousand United Irishmen routed the English forces, or the unsuccessful three-year siege by the Great O'Neill, the Earl of Tyrone, of Jordan's Castle at Ardglass. And in between all this we delivered our cargoes of spirits and fine wines.

This was a new world to me, and to Geordie, too. It was a

marked contrast to the smoke and smell and claustrophobic closeness of our Belfast ghettos and the conflicting moods which gripped them in that winter of 1969. Here was the excitement of greenery and wildlife, of rushing water, of a lightness and heady clearness in the atmosphere and of strange magic around ancient pagan holy places. We planned our last few days' runs as tours and loaded the van accordingly so that, whereas in the city we took the shortest route, now we steered according to Richard Hayward's guide book.

On Christmas Eve we went first to Newry where we unloaded over half our supplies in a series of drops at that town's licensed premises. By lunchtime we were ready for the run along the coast road to Newcastle, skirting the Mournes, and from there back home. At our last call on the way out to the Warrenpoint Road, the publican set us up two pints as a Christmas box. The pub was empty, and as we sat there enjoying the sup, a white-haired man in his late sixties came in. He was out of breath, weighed down with a box full of groceries.

'A bully, John,' he greeted the publican. 'Have I missed the bus?'

'Indeed and you have, Paddy, and he waited for you for as long as he could.'

Paddy put his box down on the floor. His face was flushed. 'Well, God's curse on it anyway. I met Peadar Hartley and big MacCaughley up the town and the pair of them on the tear and nothing would do them boys but we'd have a Christmas drink and then another till they put me off my whole way of going with their céilí-ing and oul' palavering. And now I've missed the bloody bus. God's curse on them two rogues. It'll be dark before there's another one.'

He sighed resignedly and pulled a stool over to the bar, saluting the two of us as he did so.

'John, I might as well have a drink when I'm this far and give these two men one as well.' He overruled our protests. 'For the season that's in it. One more'll do youse no harm. It's Christmas. Isn't that right, John? And one for yourself and I'll have a wee Black Bush meself.'

'Will you have anything in the Bush, Paddy?'

'Indeed and I'll not. Now, John, if it was Scotch now I'd have to have water or ginger ale or something, but that's only with Scotch. I take nothing in my whiskey!'

We all joined him in his delighted laughter.

'What way are youse going, boys? Did you say youse were going out towards Newcastle?' the publican asked us.

Geordie nodded.

'Could you ever drop oul' Paddy out that road? He has to go as far as Kilkeel, and by the looks of him if he doesn't go soon he'll be here till the New Year.'

'No problem.' Geordie grinned. I could see he was enjoying the old man who was now lilting merrily away to himself.

'De euw did eh euw, did eh euw did del de.'

'Paddy, these two men'll give you a wee lift home.'

Paddy was delighted. 'Surely to God, boys, but youse is great men so youse are. Here, we'll have another wee one before we go. A wee *deoch don dorais*. All right, John?'

'Indeed and it isn't,' John told him. 'Kate'll be worrying about you and these two lads can't wait. Isn't that right, boys?'

'Well, let it never be said that I kept men from their work,' Paddy compromised. 'A happy New Year to you, John.'

The three of us saluted our host and retreated into the crisp afternoon air.

'It'll snow the night,' our newfound friend and passenger announced, sniffing the air. I was carrying his box.

He did a jig, to Geordie's great amusement, when he saw that we were travelling in a drinks van.

'It'll be the talk of the place!' He laughed as we settled him into the passenger seat while I wedged myself against the door. Geordie gave him a bottle of stout as we pulled away.

'Do you want a glass?' I asked. 'There's some here.'

'A glass? Sure youse are well organised. Youse must be from Belfast! No, son, I don't need a glass, thanks all the same. This is grand by the neck. By the way, my name's Paddy O'Brien.'

We introduced ourselves.

'You'll never get a job in the shipyard with a name like that,' Geordie slagged him.

'And I wouldn't want it. 'Tis an Orange hole, begging your pardon, lads, and no offence, but them that's there neither works nor wants.'

To my relief Geordie guffawed loudly, winking at me as he did. For the rest of the journey Paddy regaled us with stories of his mishaps in black holes and other places.

'I wouldn't like to live in Belfast. I'll tell youse that for sure. I worked there often enough, in both quarters, mind you, and I always found the people as decent as people anywhere else. I was at the building and I went often enough to Casement Park, surely to God I did, for the football and some grand games I saw, but I wouldn't live there. Thon's a tough town!'

'It's not so bad,' I said loyally, while all the time looking beyond Paddy and past Geordie to where Narrow Water flashed past us and the hills of County Louth dipped their toes in Carlingford Bay.

'No, give me the Mournes,' Paddy persisted. 'Were youse ever in the Mournes?' He emphasised 'in'.

'Nawh,' we told him. Geordie began to enthuse about our week journeying around the county.

'Sure youse have a great time of it,' Paddy agreed. 'I'll come with youse the next time. Work? Youse wouldn't know what work was. But, boys, I'm telling youse this. Don't be leaving this day without going into the Mournes. There's a road youse could take, wouldn't be out of your way, so it wouldn't. After youse drop me off, go on towards Annalong on this road, and a wee bit outside the village on the Newcastle side there's a side road at Glassdrummond that'll take you up to Silent Valley. It's a straight road from here right through to Glassdrummond, boys. Youse can't miss it.'

'That sounds good to me,' Geordie agreed.

'Well, that's the best I can do for youse, boys. Come back some day and I'll take youse on better roads right into the heart of the mountains, but it'll be dark soon and snowing as well and my Kate'll kill me, so the Silent Valley'll have t'do youse. You'll be able to see where youse Belfast ones gets your good County Down water from to water your whiskey with and to wash your necks.'

'Is Slieve Donard the highest of the Mournes?' I asked, trying to find my faithful guide book below Paddy's seat.

'Donard? The highest? It'll only take you a couple of hours to climb up there; but, boys, you could see the whole world from Slieve Donard. That's where St Donard had his cell, up on the summit. You'll see the Isle of Man out to the east and up along our own coast all of Strangford Lough and up to the hills of Belfast and the smoke rising above them, and beyond that on a clear day Lough Neagh and as far as Slieve Gallion on the Derry and Tyrone border. And southwards beyond Newry you'll see Slieve Gullion, where Cúchulainn rambled, and Slieve Foy east of there, behind Carlingford town, and farther south again you'll see the Hill of Howth and beyond that again, if the day is good, the Sugar Loaf and the Wicklow Mountains'll just be on the horizon.'

'That's some view,' Geordie said in disbelief.

Paddy hardly heard as he looked pensively ahead at the open road. 'There's only one thing you can't see from Donard, and many people can't see it anyway although it's the talk of the whole place, and even if it jumped up and bit you it's not to be seen from up there among all the sights. Do youse know what I'm getting at, boys? It's the cause of all our cursed troubles, and if you were twice as high as Donard you couldn't see it. Do youse know what it is?'

We both waited expectantly, I with a little trepidation, for him to enlighten us.

'The bloody border,' he announced eventually. 'You can't see that awful bloody imaginary line that they pretend can divide the air and the mountain ranges and the rivers, and all it really divides is the people. You can see everything from Donard, but isn't it funny you can't see that bloody border?'

I could see Geordie's hands tighten slightly on the steering wheel. He continued smiling all the same.

'And there's something else,' Paddy continued. 'Listen to all the names: Slieve Donard or Bearnagh or Meelbeg or Meelmore – all in our own language. For all their efforts they've never killed that either. Even most of the wee Orange holes: what are they called? Irish names. From Ballymena to Ahoghill to the Shankill, Aughrim, Derry and the Boyne. The next time youse boys get talking to some of them Belfast Orangemen you should tell them that.'

'I'm a Belfast Orangeman,' Geordie told him before I could say a word. I nearly died, but Paddy laughed uproariously. I said nothing. I could see that Geordie was starting to take the needle. We passed through Kilkeel with only Paddy's chortling breaking the silence.

'You're the quare craic,' he laughed. 'I've really enjoyed this wee trip. Youse are two decent men. Tá mise go han buíoch daoibh, a cháirde. I'm very grateful to you indeed.'

'Tá fáilte romhat,' I said, glad in a way that we were near his journey's end.

'Oh, maith an fear,' he replied. 'Tabhair dom do lámh.'

We shook hands.

'What d'fuck's youse two on about?' Geordie interrupted angrily.

'He's only thanking us and I'm telling him he's welcome,' I explained quickly. 'Shake hands with him!'

Geordie did so grudgingly as the old man directed him to stop by the side of the road.

'Happy Christmas,' he proclaimed as he lifted his box.

'Happy Christmas,' we told him. He stretched across me and shook hands with Geordie again.

'*Go n'éirigh an bóthar libh,*' he said. 'May the road rise before you.'

'And you,' I shouted, pulling closed the van door as Geordie drove off quickly and Paddy and his box vanished into the shadows.

'Why don't youse talk bloody English?' Geordie snarled savagely at me as he slammed through the gears and catapulted the van forward.

'He just wished you a safe journey,' I said lamely. 'He had too much to drink and he was only an old man. It is Christmas after all.'

'That's right, you stick up for him. He wasn't slow about getting his wee digs in, Christmas or no Christmas. I need a real drink after all that oul' balls.'

He pulled the van roughly in to the verge again. I got out, too, as he clambered outside and climbed into the back. Angrily he selected a carton of whiskey from among its fellows and handed me a yellow bucket which was wedged in among the boxes.

'Here, hold this,' he ordered gruffly. As I did so he held the whiskey box at arm's length above his head and then, to my surprise, dropped it on the road. We heard glass smashing and splintering as the carton crumpled at one corner. Geordie pulled the bucket from me and sat the corner of the whiskey box into it.

'Breakages.' He grinned at my uneasiness. 'You can't avoid them. By the time we get to Paddy's Silent bloody Valley there'll be a nice wee drink for us to toast him and the border *and* that bloody foreign language of yours. Take that in the front with you.'

I did as he directed. Already the whiskey was beginning to

drip into the bucket.

'That's an old trick,' Geordie explained as we continued our journey. He was still in bad humour and maybe even a little embarrassed about the whiskey, which continued to dribble into the bucket between my feet on the floor. 'The cardboard acts as a filter and stops any glass from getting through. Anyway, it's Christmas and Paddy isn't the only one who can enjoy himself,' he concluded as we took the side road at Glassdrummond and commenced the climb up to the Silent Valley.

The view that awaited us was indeed breathtaking, as we came suddenly upon the deep mountain valley with its massive dam and huge expanse of water surrounded by rugged mountains and skirted by a picturesque stretch of road.

'Well, Paddy was right about this bit anyway,' Geordie conceded as he parked the van and we got out for a better view. 'It's a pity we didn't take a camera with us,' he said. 'It's gorgeous here. Give's the bucket and two of them glasses.'

He filled the two glasses and handed me one.

'Don't mind me, our kid. I'm not at myself. Here's to a good Christmas.'

That was the first time I drank whiskey. I didn't want to offend Geordie again by refusing, but I might as well have for I put my foot in it anyway the next minute. He was gazing reflectively up the valley, quaffing his drink with relish while I sipped timorously on mine.

'Do you not think you're drinking too much to be driving?' I asked.

He exploded.

'Look, son, I've stuck you for a few weeks now, and I never told you once how to conduct your affairs; not once. You've gabbled on at me all week about every bloody thing under the sun and today to make matters worse you and that oul' degenerate that I was stupid enough to give a lift to, you and him tried to coerce me and talked about me in your stupid language, and now you're complaining about my drinking. When you started as my helper I didn't think I'd have to take the pledge *and* join the fuckin' rebels as well. Give my head peace, would you, wee lad; for the love and honour of God, give's a bloody break!'

His angry voice skimmed across the water and bounced back at us off the side of the mountains. I could feel the blood rushing to my own head as the whiskey and Geordie's words registered in my brain.

'Who the hell do you think you are, eh?' I shouted at him, and my voice clashed with the echo of his as they collided across the still waters.

'Who do I think I am? Who do you think you are is more like it,' he snapped back, 'with all your bright ideas about history and language and all that crap. You and that oul' eejit Paddy are pups from the same Fenian litter, but you remember one thing, young fella-me-lad, youse may have the music

206

and songs and history and even the bloody mountains, but we've got everything else; you remember that!'

His outburst caught me by surprise.

'All that is yours as well, Geordie. We don't keep it from you. It's you that rejects it all. It doesn't reject you. It's not ours to give or take. You were born here same as me.'

'I don't need you to tell me what's mine. I know what's mine. I know where I was born. You can keep all your emotional crap. Like I said, we've got all the rest.'

'Who's we, Geordie? Eh? Who's we? The bloody English queen or Lord bloody Terence O'Neill, or Chi Chi, the dodo that's in charge now? Is that who we is? You've got all the rest! Is that right, Geordie? That's shit and you know it.'

I grabbed him by the arm and spun him round to face me. For a minute I thought he was going to hit me. I was ready for him. But he said nothing as we stood glaring at each other.

'You've got fuck all, Geordie,' I told him. 'Fuck all except a two-bedroomed house in Urney Street and an identity crisis.'

He turned away from me and hurled his glass into the darkening distance.

'This'll nivver be Silent Valley again, not after we're finished with it.' He laughed heavily. 'I'm an Orangeman, Joe. That's what I am. It's what my da was. I don't agree with everything here. My da wouldn't even talk to a Papist, nivver mind drink or work with one. When I was listening to Paddy I could see why. That's what all this civil rights rubbish is about as well. Well, I don't mind people having their civil rights. That's fair enough. But you know and I know if it wasn't that it would be something else. I'm easy come, easy go. There'd be no trouble if everybody else was the same.'

I had quietened down also by now. 'But people need their rights,' I said.

'Amn't I only after saying that!' he challenged me.

'Well, what are you going to do about it?' I retorted.

'Me?' He laughed. 'Now I know your head's cut! I'm going to do exactly nothing about it! There are a few things that make me different from you. We've a lot in common, I grant you that, but we're different also, and one of the differences is that after Christmas I'll have a job and you won't, and I intend to keep it. And more importantly, I intend to stay alive to do it.'

'Well, that's straight enough and there's no answer to that,' I mused, sipping the last of my whiskey.

Geordie laughed at me. 'Typical Fenian,' he commented. 'I notice you didn't throw away your drink.'

'What we have we hold.' I took another wee sip and gave him the last of it.

'By the way, seeing we're talking to each other instead of at each other, there's no way that our ones, and that includes me, will ever let Dublin rule us.'

The sun was setting and there were a few wee flurries of snow in the air.

'Why not?' I asked.

''Cos that's the way it is.'

'What we have we hold?' I repeated. 'Only for real.'

'If you like.'

'But you've nothing in common with the English. We don't need them here to rule us. We can do a better job ourselves. They don't care about the Unionists. You go there and they treat you like a Paddy just like me. What do you do with all your loyalty then? You're Irish. Why not claim that and we'll all govern Dublin.'

'I'm British!'

'So am I,' I exclaimed. 'Under duress 'cos I was born in this state. We're both British subjects but we're Irishmen. Who do you support in the rugby? Ireland, I bet! Or international soccer? The same! All your instincts and roots and –' I waved my arms around at the dusky mountains in frustration '– surroundings are Irish. This is fucking Ireland. It's County Down, not Sussex or Suffolk or Yorkshire. It's us and we're it!' I shouted.

'Now you're getting excited again. You shouldn't drink whiskey,' Geordie teased me. 'It's time we were going. C'mon; I surrender.'

On the way down to Newcastle I drank the whiskey that

was left in the bucket. We had only one call to make, so when I asked him to, Geordie dropped me at the beach. I stood watching as the van drove off and thought that perhaps he wouldn't return for me. It was dark by now. As I walked along the strand the snow started in earnest. Slieve Donard was but a hulking shadow behind me. I couldn't see it. Here I was in Newcastle, on the beach. On my own, in the dark. Drunk. On Christmas Eve. Waiting for a bloody Orangeman to come back for me so that I could go home.

The snow was lying momentarily on the sand, and the water rushing in to meet it looked strange in the moonlight as it and the sand and the snow merged. I was suddenly exhilarated by my involvement with all these elements, and as I crunched the sand and snow beneath my feet and the flakes swirled around me, my earlier frustrations disappeared. Then I chuckled aloud at the irony of it all.

The headlights of the van caught me in their glare. My Orangeman had returned.

'You're soaked, you bloody eejit,' he complained when I climbed into the van again.

He, too, was in better form. As we drove home it was as if we had never had a row. We had a sing-song – mostly carols with some Beatles numbers – and the both of us stayed well clear of any contentious verses. On the way through the Belfast suburbs Geordie sang what we called 'our song'.

O Mary, this London's a wonderful sight,
There's people here working by day and by night:
They don't grow potatoes or barley or wheat,
But there's gangs of them digging for gold in the street.
At least when I asked them that's what I was told,
So I took a hand at this digging for gold,
For all that I found there I might as well be
Where the Mountains of Mourne sweep down to the sea.

We went in for a last drink after we'd clocked out at the store, but by this time my head was thumping and I just wanted to go home.

As we walked back to the van Geordie shook my hand warmly.

'Thanks, kid. I've learned a lot this last week or so, and not just about County Down. You're dead on, son,' he smiled, 'for a Fenian. Good luck to you anyway, oul' hand, in all that you do, but just remember, our kid, I love this place as much as you do.'

'I know,' I said. 'I learned that much at least.'

He dropped me off at Divis Street and drove off waving, on across the Falls towards the Shankill. I walked up to the Falls. That was the last I saw of Geordie Mayne. I hope he has survived the last twenty years and that he'll survive the next twenty as well. I hope we'll meet again in better times. He wasn't such a bad fella, for an Orangeman.

THE SNIPER

Seán, uncomfortable with squatting for so long in one position, eased himself carefully up on one knee and slowly rubbed his cramped limbs.

Below him, back gardens were crisscrossed by fluttering, flapping shirt- and nappy-laden clothes-lines stretched between back-to-back houses. Seán, above the clothes-lines, hedges, coal-holes and back doors, had a clear, wide-angled view of the street.

He could see ten, no, twelve houses on one side and fourteen on the other side of the street. He could easily see the windows of number 36, where the blind was drawn on the front bedroom window. He reminded himself to check that blind every few seconds. No use getting lackadaisical.

The kids in number 40 were late going to school; they must have slept in. He watched three youngsters dashing out of sight along the street. When, he mused, they got to the lamp-post they would be 140 yards from where he was perched. His eyes searched and found the white rag tied, waist high, to the lamp-post, then swung back to check the blind on number 36. It was still drawn. Other windows stared back blankly at him.

Number 36 seemed different. The drawn blind, like a dropped eyelid in the face of the house, was almost winking at him – one of those conspiratorial winks that seem to go on for a long time.

The sound of a shovel scraping coal into a bucket swung his attention once again to the back gardens. He chided himself for not immediately tracing the source of the noise, in fact for not seeing the source before it scraped its way into his attention. Mrs O'Brien, he smiled to himself, as the smoke curled lazily from her chimney to be lost against the haze of the Black Mountain.

Mrs O'Brien paused, coal bucket in hand, and peered over her hedge into the neighbouring garden. Her voice, raised to a shout, carried easily to where Seán crouched: 'Are you there, Maggie?' Twice she shouted, before the door opened and Maggie came out. They stood, Mrs O'Brien with coal bucket in hand, on opposite sides of the dividing hedge, chatting. Seán's gaze swung away from them up towards number 36 again. It remained as before, the blind in the same position.

All these homes could do with a new coat of paint, he decided. Especially that one, the red one with the cracked window. Like the brown one below that, it definitely deserved a fresh coat. His gaze paused momentarily at a neat row of green vegetables. Jimmy Graham's lettuces seemed to be coming along well, and Da Grogan's spuds. He smiled to himself, then watched intently as a black and white cat picked its way stealthily towards an open dustbin where a few scrawny starlings quarrelled over bread wrappings and discarded tin cans.

The sound of a motor-car brought him back to the street and to number 36. The blind was up. The window with its bright curtains glared glassily back at him. Forgetting the cramp in his legs, he checked the piece of wood which held open the slate, forming the slot through which he peered. Hurrying now, he eased a round into the breech of the heavy rifle which straddled his legs. He raised it up so that the muzzle nosed through his slated peep-hole. He squinted along the sight, zeroing in on the white rag which bandaged the lamp-post, and thumbed off the safety catch. One hundred and forty yards, give or take a few feet. He had checked it himself, scrambling over hedges and wire fences to pace out the distance. Beneath him, in the innards of the house, a doorbell rang. Seconds later, a head appeared at the open trap-door.

'It's dark in here,' a voice complained. 'Where are you Seán?'

Seán didn't turn round. The transition from daylight to the gloom of the attic would have upset his vision. 'I'm here,' he muttered.

'The car's below,' said the voice, relieved at seeing Seán's dim shape wedged below the roof tiles against a heavy joist.

'Okay,' Seán replied, 'I won't be long.'

'I'll wait below,' said the voice, but Seán's attention, now that the car had arrived and his run-back was clear, was riveted to the street before him. His heart pounded heavily against his ribs. The cramp in his legs had returned, and as he strove to exorcise these distractions a quiet stillness seemed to settle on the deserted street.

It was a feeling he would never get used to. The whole area, the houses, unanimous in their silence. The gardens, even the streets themselves, seemed to be holding their breath. Every time he got the same feeling. How many times was this?

He smiled grimly to himself. Concentrate. Don't let your attention wander. That's the way to get yourself killed. Maybe that would be better than killing? He was surprised at the suddenness of the thought.

He squinted again along the length of the rifle as he considered this question and his response to it. It was a question which had come into his head off and on during the last few months. Not about getting killed. He wasn't into getting killed. No way. If it happened it wouldn't be by choice. He surveyed the scene before and below him. Nothing had changed. Was it right to kill?

No, he told himself, it wasn't right to kill. But there was no choice.

Of course there was a choice. No one forced him to do

what he was doing. He could leave now. Leave? What good will it do, staying there? No one would know and no one could complain. He'd have done his best.

He swung his attention back to the task before him. It might or might not be right to kill, but sometimes it was necessary. He considered that proposition. The people he was trying to kill were better armed, better equipped, better trained than he was. There were also more of them.

And they would have no compunction about killing him. He settled himself back, pushing the doubts and imponderables out of his consciousness. They should not be here, he reminded himself. It was his country, not theirs. They didn't belong. They were the enemy. They gave him no choice except to fight. And in fighting it was necessary to kill.

He crouched now, blocking out thoughts of everything but what he was to do. Though he knew these other thoughts would return. Maybe it was good that they did. He could smell, or thought he could almost smell, the tension. They would certainly be able to sense his own fear. There would be scores of British soldiers. He tried not to think of that. He was well covered. Better not to worry. It was too late now anyway. It would not be long.

Then into view came the first of a patrol of green-uniformed soldiers. They moved cautiously forward on both sides of the street, covering one another, snuggling into their flak jackets and arching their rifles to point at the grey jerry-built houses which mutely and sullenly surrounded them. The leading soldier was walking by number 36. Seán studied him with a vague disinterest and waited. A second soldier appeared, an officer. Seán gently nuzzled the rifle-butt against his cheek. The officer edged his way forward and then stopped outside number 36.

'Move on,' hissed Seán, 'move on.' A half-panic started to flutter in his stomach. He breathed in as the officer reached the lamp-post, and held his breath as his finger tightened on the trigger. First pressure. He let his breath out almost in a sigh and whispered, 'Second pressure.' The heavy flat thud of the rifle exploded his words, sending the black and white cat scampering from the garden and the starlings from the dustbin.

Seán prised the piece of wood from between the slates, and closed his eyes as the lowered slate shut out the daylight and returned the attic to its usual gloominess. He scrambled from his perch.

The car whisked him away. Behind him the back gardens, crisscrossed by fluttering, flapping shirt- and nappy-laden clothes-lines, stretched between the back-to-back houses.

The twelve houses on one side and fourteen on the other side of the street remained silent and undisturbed. Against the solitary lamp-post the white rag cushioned the pale staring face of the officer. His patrol, scattered into gardens, lay hugging the ground. The starlings returned to the open dustbin and the cat, as stealthily as before, picked its way towards them.

Mrs O'Brien, oblivious to all this, bade her neighbour good morning, eased the coal bucket to her other hip and shuffled her way indoors.

The British officer's expression, staring unseeing at the clear Irish sky, was curious, surprised.

THE WITNESS TREE

The top floor of the convent, in the grounds of Saint Dorothy's Grammar School, was much higher than the little terraced houses which surrounded it. The large gothic windows in Sister Mary Ann's room looked down on and across the grey slated rooftops and the rows of narrow streets and up at the Black Mountain. It was a familiar view for Sister Mary Ann. She loved the way the mountain changed its colour from emerald green to black and all the shades in between, depending on the light. She loved how she could see rain forming on its upper ridge before it came sweeping down to lash the windows of her room and drench the streetscape, if that was the way the wind blew it. She loved how clouds scudding across a blue summer sky could throw shadows over heathery crevices or high gullies and little glens. Or how the mist could embrace the upper slopes. Or when the sun was out how it highlighted the white rocks on the mountain's lower reaches at the top of the Loney. She had a panoramic view of it all. This was the room she slept in. It was simply furnished in dark hardwood furniture. Her bed and locker. A large wardrobe and bookcase. A dresser.

And her favourite chair. A comfortable armchair. Beside the window so that she could sit there and enjoy the view. Or read. Or say her prayers. She used to kneel when she prayed. But that was when she was younger. She thought God would be content to let her sit now that she was eighty-three.

She prayed often. Well, it wasn't so much praying as quietly talking to God. And his mother. Or she reflected, sometimes for hours, sitting in silent contemplation, motionless and in silence. At times she was distracted by the skyscape or the mountain and its moods. Or by the flocks of racing pigeons tumbling and dipping in tight formation across her eyeline, their wings flashing in the light. Her gaze wandered also to the gardens of Saint Dorothy's. She watched little groups of schoolgirls sitting out in the sunshine on the lush green manicured lawns, flanked in part by trees. She would be particularly pleased if some of the girls were seated close to or below the branches of a tall and majestic oak tree. That was her special tree. The witness tree, she called it.

Sometimes she was so absorbed in her thoughts that it seemed her gaze turned inwards. But she was reassured, nonetheless, by the beauty of the scene set out before her. It helped her from being too introverted. It was a constant and a comfort to her. This afternoon she was deep in meditation. Dressed in her nun's dark blue habit, she had the appearance of serenity about her, almost dozing after her lunch. But this was not altogether so, for Sister Mary Ann carried something. She had carried it all her life. As her thoughts slipped back to childhood a slight frown transformed her expression. She sighed. That gentle sigh seemed to fill the silent room. Her gaze remained on the mountain but her eyes were filled with unshed tears.

Sadness enveloped her. She was a little girl again. In bed, listening to the sounds from the kitchen below her. She was Anna again. Long before she became a nun.

'Joe, you'll waken the children.'

That's what she remembered. Her mother sobbing. 'Joe, please. Please, Joe, don't waken the children.'

Her mother's pleas made Anna want to scream. She clenched her hands into fists until her fingernails cut into her palms. She pressed her hands to her ears. But still the menacing sounds rose from below to where she lay. She pulled the bedclothes over her head to drown out the scraping of a chair against the stone-tiled floor. She cringed at the crash of something being smashed. The slamming of a door. The suppressed shouts and sobs.

She wanted to leap from her bed. Especially when she heard her mother's muted but hysterical voice. Every fibre in her, every nerve, stretched as she resisted the urge to run downstairs to protect her mother from her father. She wanted to stand in front of her. To face her father. To get between him and the woman he was beating. She rarely heard her father's voice. After an initial angry outburst which heralded the beginning of the abuse, he said little. When he did speak it was in a brutally abrupt, threatening hiss. Or a drunken grunt. Her concern for her mother and hatred for her father was surpassed only by a panicked need to make sure her father did not hear her. That turmoil of emotion and, in particular, her own fear made her even more ashamed. She felt so powerless. Her father never did hear her. His drunken rages made him oblivious to everything. The drink seemed to trigger a sense of loathing that blinded and deafened him. The attacks lasted only for a few minutes. But it seemed like much longer to Anna. And to Kathleen, who tried to protect herself as she cowered away from him. Anna heard all this. She heard every drunken, intimidating, controlling expletive uttered by her father. But he never heard her terrified whimpering and sobbing. How could he?

'Don't you dare tell me what to do,' he would scream at her mother. 'You! You stuck-up little bitch! I work all the days God sends and you can't even have my dinner ready for me coming home. You! Don't you ever think you can tell me what to do in my own house!' he would roar, and Anna would hear the rush of feet or the crash of a falling object and her mother's cries again.

And she would feel guilty.

Deeply ashamed and guilty that she stayed where she was. The commotion in the kitchen would continue and her body become rigid and tense as she involuntarily stretched and then curled up and in on herself before dissolving into silent and near-hysterical keening. Body-wracking tears hot on her cheeks would dissolve in her mouth as she whimpered, 'Oh Mammy, Mammy, Mammy,' to herself.

As she got older she would whisper tearfully into her pillow, 'Jesus, Mary and Joseph, we give you our hearts and our souls. Please, Jesus, baby Jesus, please, Jesus, make him stop.' She repeated this over and over again until silence settled on the house. She would wait anxiously, rocking herself from side to side, until she heard her father's slow, heavy footsteps on the stairs and his hesitant, drunken entry into the front bedroom. It was then that Anna would drift off into a troubled sleep. Sometimes, if she wakened later, she would slip nervously downstairs to where her mother slept on the sofa. Her mother rarely stirred and Anna would return quietly to bed, careful not to disturb her, but more particularly out of fear of her father.

The next day and for days afterwards the atmosphere in the house would be brittle. That was bad enough if her father was sober. If he was on the tear everyone was a victim because there was so much tension in the house, even though Joe never mistreated the children, and he rarely abused their mother when they were in the room. Even the boys, younger though they were than Anna, seemed to have an instinctive sense that they could protect their mother by ensuring that she was not left alone with their father. But of course that could only be stretched out until bedtime came. Thankfully, sometimes their father would retire before them, and to everyone's relief peace, fragile but peace nonetheless, reigned. Until the next time.

It hadn't always been like that. Anna remembered when her father would laugh and sing to her and her siblings.

Ali Bali Ali Bali Bee.
Sitting on your daddy's knee.
Lookin' for a wee bobeen
To buy some Coulter's candy.

She was the firstborn. She remembered when her parents would take her and her brothers, Paddy, Seán and Michael, walking on summer evenings. Her father was a sales assistant in a big department store on High Street in the city centre. He eventually worked his way up to become manager of one of the floors. Men's Wear. He got discount. So he was usually smartly dressed. He was tall and sandy haired. She recalled he smiled a lot. Especially at her mother.

Their walks would take them up Iveagh Crescent and slowly up the Falls Road to the Falls Park. Seán and Michael were twins. Their mother pushed them in a high pram. Anna and Paddy would walk hand in hand. Their father would walk proudly alongside them, conversing pleasantly with neighbours who stopped to admire the twins.

Anna's mother, Kathleen, was pretty. Dark and slim. She was a few years younger than her husband. When Anna was small and things were still good in the family, her mother liked to tell her how she met Joe McLoughlin at a ceilí downtown at the Fiesta Ballroom. He was a big lad, not long up from the country, a hurling fanatic with an intense devotion to his local club back in Cushendall. He walked her home that night and they parted at the corner of Cavendish Street and the Falls Road with a commitment to meet the following week to go to the pictures in the Ritz cinema in the city centre. He had a steady job, unlike many in their part of the city. He was considered a good catch. Kathleen's parents were pleased when they started going out together.

It was a whirlwind romance. They were married at Saint Paul's church in a small wedding attended by family, Joe's clubmates from Cushendall and a few of Kathleen's girlfriends from the linen mill where she worked. After a weekend honeymoon over the border in Omeath, they settled in with Kathleen's parents in their overcrowded house in Harrogate Street, but soon had the good fortune to rent a house in Iveagh, just across from Beechmount on the Falls Road. Kathleen was in her element. Joe got his first promotion not long after Anna was born.

In those days, Joe didn't drink a lot. A few Guinness at the weekend or after a hurling game on a Sunday. Kathleen rarely drank at all. At a wedding or some family gathering she might sometimes pass herself with a Babycham or an Advocaat. But she didn't mind Joe having his weekend drink. He worked hard and he deserved his night out with his friends. Her mother, who didn't drink herself, had remarked once that a woman couldn't trust a man who couldn't drink a bottle of stout.

One day as a special treat, when her brothers were away for the day, Joe brought Anna and her mother into the Crow's Nest on High Street for soup and sandwiches. At one point Joe's boss came over to their little side table and praised Joe, congratulating Kathleen for what he knew would be Joe's future success at the store. Her pride and delight were obvious and Anna felt it too, even if she knew nothing then of what her father did. Afterwards, when they stepped out, he took her by the hand and showed her where Henry Joy McCracken was hanged in High Street. Henry Joy, a wealthy Presbyterian and a successful businessman, who loved the native harp music and was a great patriot, helped to found the United Irishmen. He was hanged for rising against the English. Anna was awed by the tragic story and the light in her father's eyes as he told it, but what came to have most significance to her later was his mention of Henry's Joy's sister Mary Ann, who hid him when he was on the run and walked with him to the scaffold. This was the day, Anna later said, when she became a feminist. She didn't know what a feminist was then. She'd never even heard the word and wouldn't for some years. But Mary Ann McCracken struck her as brave and independent and she never forgot the name.

Not long after that Joe was promoted. He started working longer hours. He told Kathleen he couldn't avoid it now that he was part of the management team. Sometimes, when he worked late, they would call into the Crow's Nest for a drink after locking up the store. There were times when he came home a little tipsy. This few drinks after work was also, he explained, something expected of him. Kathleen understood he needed to keep on the right side of the senior managers, but she also noticed he was becoming more tense, even at the weekends when he had the Sunday off. He was not as cheerful as he used to be. A little edgy sometimes. Kathleen put it down to the extra responsibilities he had in the store. She tried to keep his home life as relaxed as possible, but early mornings and late nights were taking their toll on Joe and the children had to be allowed their own space to grow as well. So Kathleen was always on the go. At times the kids would be in bed when their father got home. She rarely had notice when he would be working late. So the dinners which she prepared for him had to be kept warm in the oven or atop a pot of hot water at the back of the stove.

Soon Joe's Guinness was replaced by whiskey. At first it gave him a little buzz. Sometimes, much like the early days of their marriage, he would come home happy and clown around. A few half uns and he would be the best of good fun. He found it eased the tension. But somewhere beyond the few there was a crossing point and when he passed that point Joe disappeared and a darker, sinister, menacing person emerged. But only when he came home. Home where he began to find fault with everything. Home where his dinner was too dry or not warm enough. Home where his children were either angels or spoiled brats, depending on his mood. And on these occasions all of this was his wife's fault.

He confined himself to muttered or shouted insults before storming back out or staggering up to bed. But there came the day when he raised his hand to his wife. He'd had a particularly fraught time at work. Sales had been low for months. The cheaper multinational stores had enticed many of their customers away from the city centre and into the new shopping malls. He knew his job was under threat. His normal Saturday night after-work drinks with his workmates in the Crow's Nest had turned sour when his boss let that slip. Joe had had several drinks by then and his mood had turned dark. He'd lost his usual caution around his boss. He confronted him and sharp words were exchanged. Then he stormed out, consumed by resentment. He stopped for a few more half uns on the way home.

He arrived in a foul mood. The whiskey seemed to have triggered some new depth of darkness in him and a nasty, deeply troubled, self-absorbed bully emerged. When he hit Kathleen the first time, it shocked him as well as her. He didn't know what came over him. One minute he was giving off to her and then because she told him she'd had enough of him, he reached out, grabbed her by the hair and struck her across the back of her head. If she had not faced up to him, he reflected later, that would have been the end of it. But she defied him. He hit her again. His shock at his own actions was not enough to stop him. Instead he blamed her.

Kathleen was outraged, angry and deeply hurt. Though he was more belligerent than usual she couldn't believe it when he struck her. For a split second she was bewildered by what had happened. She faced up to him almost as a reflex to his aggression. He scoffed at her defiance. He hit her again and again. Short, sharp, cruel blows to her shoulders and arms. She fled from the room and later, as she examined the black and blue bruises, realised that he had avoided marking her anywhere that would be visible. He didn't come to bed that night. He lay on the sofa in the living room looking for justifications but in the end hating himself for what he had done. The next morning he apologised as he was leaving for work. Kathleen didn't talk to him for days and he was contrite and quiet around the house. After a while she relented a little. She didn't talk to Joe about what he had done to her. She couldn't bring herself to do that. But she was worried about the kids being affected by what had happened. She felt that there had to be some semblance of normality for their sake. So she started to talk to Joe again when the kids were about. He was obviously relieved. But even though calmness resumed, they both seemed to sense that a threshold had been crossed.

A month or so later Joe beat her again. Again it seemed to come out of the blue. As the drink provoked the beatings, so the drink relieved the self-loathing that followed. Kathleen began to see that these were her new circumstances. For the sake of the family she made adjustments. She distanced herself from her husband as she came to know the danger signs.

Not long afterwards Anna realised that something fundamental and shattering had occurred between her mother and father. This was when she heard the sounds of the assault in the kitchen, and she knew a line had been crossed by her father. Her mother's sobbing wakened her. Anna thought she was dreaming. But as she lay petrified in her bed she realised it wasn't a nightmare. It was real. She didn't sleep that night. In school the next day she was moody and lacklustre. Her mother, too, was subdued but as busy as usual around the house. She said nothing to Anna and Anna said nothing to her. But they both understood that each of them knew what had happened. Even if they did not acknowledge that. It was as if to give voice to it would make it even worse. So the two of them held their secret, unspoken, to themselves, and their lives reshaped around that awful undeclared obscenity and the sense of shame which it created for them both.

As she got older, Anna also came to sense each little mood

change and to know the triggers for her father's aggression. And as she grew out of childhood she came to fear and to hate him and the way he hollowed out her mother's sense of herself so that she became timid and wan in his presence. Anna herself felt inadequate. She willed her mother to make a stand but she could not bring herself to say this to her. She wanted to tell one of her grannies what was happening, but she drew back from this because she feared the consequences for them all.

And Anna particularly hated the pretence that all was well when others were in their home or when the family would sometimes be out for a social event. To the casual observer they were a happy wee family. Even if there was occasionally the hint of some domestic irritation, there was nothing to suggest how dysfunctional, fraught and soured their home life was. But Anna came to know when her father would be offended by some aspect, real or imagined, of her mother's behaviour. She knew he would store it up until they got home. She knew he would wait until the children were in bed before he would start on her. And she knew her mother knew this also. Nothing was said. Nothing needed to be said. Anna sensed the darkness, the shadow, the little cloud which flitted across her father's face and the nervous edge which entered her mother's eyes amidst the craic and the chat and the socialising.

She never discussed this with her brothers. They were

boys. She was a girl. Even though they were close they also lived in their own slightly separate, gender-defined worlds. She was also older than them. Truth to tell, Anna was never sure how much the boys absorbed the underlying menace that accompanied their father's bouts of drunkenness. While her own relationship with her father was now strained, especially in the wake of one of his drunken binges, it seemed to her that he and the boys continued as before. Maybe they too were trying to protect their mother by doing their best to retain a relationship with their father. Or perhaps they didn't realise the extent of his drunken excesses. None of this was ever spoken about, but at times Anna felt like her family was walking on ice which could shatter at any time. Her father still took the boys to hurling training on Sunday mornings. He occasionally played handball against the gable wall with them if he was home early. Or street soccer with them and their friends. When they were young the brothers slept together in the one room. Three of them in a double bed. Anna, the only sister, slept alone in the wee box room above the kitchen. So she heard everything. They were usually asleep long before her so they probably heard very little.

Although she was only a year older than Paddy, Anna was the only one who had chores to do around the house. It was expected that she would help her mother. So as she moved through primary school at Saint Kevin's she learned to make beds, to peel potatoes, to wash dishes and to mop floors. The boys were excused these duties. Anna didn't know why. The Mary Ann McCracken in her knew it was wrong. She never complained, but she resented it. Especially when Paddy lorded it over her if he was allowed out to play while she had her housework to do.

Anna was a good and diligent student. Her teacher informed her mother that there was a strong possibility that Anna could get a place in Saint Dorothy's Grammar School if she kept getting good results. So at her mother's insistence, most evenings, while her brothers kicked a football outside, Anna pored over her maths, geography and English.

'You have potential, young lady,' Kathleen told her. 'Be sure to use it, love. That's the only way you will get your independence.'

Anna took easily to studying even before she reached her teens. It allowed her to withdraw, even for a while, from the toxic atmosphere created by her father's presence or the nervous anticipation when he was late. Studying was an escape and a challenge. And she liked that. Her father, for all his faults, didn't discourage her. In fact, he held her efforts up as an example to her brothers. They didn't seem to resent that. They just continued to mess and play-act as soon as their father's interest waned.

Anna won the scholarship and was enrolled at Saint Doro-thy's. It had been established by Dominican nuns in 1870 for the 'educational training of the young ladies' of Belfast.

Its high-ceilinged, big-windowed rooms and long corridors were set back in enclosed grounds with fine trees and gardens fronting on to the Falls Road. When Anna started there she was the only pupil from Iveagh and one of only four from the Falls. Most of the other girls, who included boarders from the country, came from other parts of Belfast and were the daughters of publicans, solicitors, doctors and other better-off Catholic families.

But Anna fitted in well. She was a good pupil and soon made friends with her classmates. Each day she would make her way along the Falls, down past the Presbyterian church and across Broadway and the length of Children's Hospital before crossing the road below Mulholland Terrace. There she merged with the stream of other girls in their neat wine-coloured uniforms.

She took an active part in school life, joining the choir, the reading club and the school branch of the Legion of Mary, a Catholic lay society which did charitable work.

Her form teacher, Sister Benedict, took notice of this. She admired Anna's diligence and good heart. She was young, from Tyrone and had only recently taken her vows. She had a more than usual interest in the issues of the contemporary world, particularly those affecting the rights of women. One day when speaking about the history of Belfast she asked the class, 'Did anyone ever hear of Mary Ann McCracken?'

Eager, as always, to please Sister Benedict, Anna responded,

'She walked with her brother, Henry Joy, to the scaffold downtown when he was hanged. He was a leader of the United Irishmen in 1798.'

'That's true, Anna,' Sister Benedict agreed. 'But she was much more than that. She too was a member of the United Irish Society. The McCrackens were wealthy, but she campaigned all her long life for equality – for the poor, for the exploited races and for women. She was one of the great figures in our history, maybe not as known as she deserves to be, a republican and true friend to the poor of this city, particularly women and girls. At the age of eighty-eight she was on the Belfast docks handing out anti-slavery leaflets to emigrants heading for America.'

Anna remembered this and all the other stories Sister Benedict told her. She worked enthusiastically with her in the Legion of Mary. They visited old people and ran errands for them. At set times like Christmas they would fundraise to buy gifts for children whose parents could not afford them. Because her home was so close to the school, Anna was able to come back some evenings to join the boarders and other girls in these activities. Seeing how other people lived caused her to reflect a little on her own home life. On the face of it, her clann was better off than other people in their community. While they weren't rich they did have a steady income. Their father had a decent job. Their mother was a good housekeeper. She did wonder if all men behaved the way her father did. She sometimes wondered if their neighbours heard him when he was bullying her mother. At other times, when he was contrite and obviously making an effort to redeem himself, she longed for it to always be like that. But even then there was a deep-rooted dread that he would go on the drink again and back to his violent ways.

This dread was even worse for her mother. By this time, Kathleen was just going through the motions. More than anything else, she just wanted peace in her home. She wanted to protect and shield her children from their father's wickedness. She did think of leaving him, but where would they go? She talked to Fr Walker in confession once about the way her husband was treating her. She half-hoped that he would volunteer to intervene. But he didn't. Instead he told her that Joe was probably under a lot of pressure. He said he would pray for them both. He said this too would pass. He reminded Kathleen of her duties as a good wife. Kathleen never went back to confession again. Not to Fr Walker. Or any other priest. Instead she did her best to put on a brave face. She had given up on her relationship with her husband. He had destroyed that. She did not even want the old loving, happy, kind Joe back. As far as she was concerned that Joe was gone, never to return. The main focus of her life was her children and her little home in Iveagh. She was particularly protective of her only daughter. She had a real sense that life for Anna could be filled with great possibility and potential.

She also fervently and passionately believed that Saint Dorothy's was Anna's pathway to a better future.

Anna sensed all this. Occasionally when she passed the convent's small chapel she would pause at the melodious sound of the nuns' singing. She loved the wee chapel with its perfect acoustics and its Harry Clarke stained-glass window. Sometimes she would kneel there on her own and pray that her father would not hit her mother again. Other times she just sat silently and soaked up the quiet, comforting atmosphere of this peaceful, holy space. She loved the school grounds, the gardens and especially the tall trees. In her first week at Saint Dorothy's she sat under one tall and very grand oak tree to read her notes. It became her favourite spot and her favourite tree. In the summer she sat under it during class breaks. Sister Benedict told her the tree was as old as the school.

'Imagine all the things this tree has seen,' she said to Anna one day. 'The 1916 Rising, partition, two world wars and all the girls coming and going in Saint Dorothy's for almost a century. This tree has witnessed many remarkable events. Trees are sacred. Especially the oak. They are associated with holy places. The native oak was especially revered in pre-Christian days.'

Sister Benedict told Anna how the old saints had embraced and incorporated these cultural values into their teachings. Anna was very taken by that. The meshing of culture, spirituality, nature, history. A witness tree. She felt safe sitting with her back against its trunk. Gazing up at this wide-branched, great green giant put everything into perspective. Sometimes she went over her lessons there. Or said her prayers. Usually she was content to sit in silence beneath its branches. Once or twice she and Sister Benedict sat there and she almost told her about her father. But she didn't. It would be like admitting something shameful. Something she was guilty of. And anyway, she reasoned, what could Sister Benedict do? So she said nothing. Until one day, while sitting under the tree, she began to quietly talk to herself about what was happening at home. There was no one there to hear her, but the calm peace of the holy space formed by the tree's mighty trunk and its sheltering branches gave her the space to tell everything. She did it in a whisper. Slowly and thoughtfully. Afterwards she felt better in herself. As if giving voice to all that was wrong at home was in itself a public repudiation of the unfairness of it all. As if she was speaking out against the ill treatment of her mother. She felt that the tree space was blessed by holy spirits and that she was talking to them. Even though she was young, she knew that this was good for her. These contemplative moments brought her relief and solace. The oak became *her* witness tree, providing shelter and a sacred place to reflect, away from the anxieties of home and her father's malign presence.

Then he got the sack. It was a Thursday. Anna remem-

bered every moment of it. He hadn't arrived in from work
for his dinner, but that wasn't unusual. Her mother covered
the plate of potatoes, peas and meat and left it on the work
surface beside the stove. She had long ago given up trying
to keep it warm. Anna was clearing up the rest of the dinner
dishes before heading back to school for choir practice. She
noticed, as she had many times before, her mother's air of
quiet, passive resignation. And for reasons that her young
mind could not fully comprehend Anna felt annoyed at her.
Not angry. Just frustrated. Confused. Irritated. She was on the
point of saying so when her father arrived into the kitchen.

'Well, you'll be happy now, woman,' he said as he took
his usual seat. 'Here.' He pushed an envelope across towards
Kathleen. 'I got my cards.'

His wife turned, dinner plate in hand, and gasped. 'What?
What did you say?'

'You heard me. I got laid off.'

'Were you drinking?' Kathleen exclaimed.

'What I do in my own time is nothing to do with anyone.
They were just looking for an excuse.'

'And you gave it to them,' Kathleen said, putting his
dinner down abruptly on the table in front of him. 'What
are we going to do now? In God's name, what are we going
to do?' Then, as if she noticed Anna for the first time, 'What
about the boys? What about Anna's schooling? You think
you're a single man. You think you can just waltz in here and

announce that you threw away your job?'

Anna had never seen her mother like this. At last, she thought. At last she's taking a stand. Her father pushed his dinner plate away from him. Untouched. He put his elbows on the table and fixed his gaze on the wall opposite. Anna saw his eyes brimming full of tears and rage.

'I don't have to take this from you,' he exclaimed sullenly.

'So what are you going to do, Joe? Beat me? Beat me in front of our daughter? It takes a big man to beat a woman, Joe, doesn't it? Is that what you're going to do? That's your answer to everything.' Kathleen spat out the words with venom. 'I've had enough of you, Joe McLoughlin. I'm sick, sore and tired of you and your drunken antics. You were probably stuck in the Crow's Nest with your cronies during your lunch break. What do you expect? You think the world owes you a living. Get out!'

Joe looked up at her in surprise.

'Get out,' Kathleen repeated. 'Get out!' she screamed. 'Get out of my house. Get away out of here and back to your drinking buddies.'

Joe stood up slowly. Then with a speed that belied a man of his size, he grabbed Kathleen by her shoulder and pulled her round to him. Anna screamed and darted across the kitchen towards them as Joe roughly shoved her mother away from him.

'You will never talk to me like that again, woman.' He

glowered at his wife and their daughter as they clung to one another. 'You've turned that child against me. You think I don't know your game. You sleekit bitch. But you'll be sorry. What goes around comes around. You're nothing but a good-for-nothing useless hoor. You wait and see.'

And with that he made his way out of the room. As they sobbed in each other's arms, Kathleen and Anna heard the dull thud of the front door.

'Thank God,' Kathleen whispered, wiping her eyes with the back of her hand. 'Let's clear up before the boys get back.'

Anna remembered everything that happened next as if it was in slow motion. Not that she ever talked about it. But she relived it in her head again and again for years, as if it was an action replay. She relived the kitchen door flying open again. Her mother's startled expression as she pulled Anna behind her and turned to face her husband as he burst back into the room.

He laughed at them both. Then he snarled at Kathleen. 'You thought I would just walk out of here like that, did you? Well, you have another think coming! You're a good-for-nothing bitch. You neither worked nor wanted since you met me and now you think you can put me out! Me? Nobody puts Joe McLoughlin out of his own home. You hear me? You hear me? You bitch!'

Anna felt the rain of blows on her mother's head. The frenzied attack lasted only a few seconds before her mother collapsed on the kitchen floor. Anna fell with her and the two of them, half-entangled together, cowered below her father.

He leaned back against the kitchen sink, exhausted with his exertions. Kathleen and Anna struggled to their feet. Kathleen again pushed her daughter behind her. Her look of defiance rekindled the rage within him. He began to move towards them. Anna was sobbing wildly. She remembered her father's towering presence, the wildness in his eyes. The flecks of white spittle on his lips. His fists clenched like he was a boxer. She remembered his contempt. Her mother's bravery.

'You've gone too far this time,' he shouted. 'Turning my own daughter against me! You're dead. As sure as God's in heaven you are dead.' He lurched at them again.

'Get out, Anna, get out,' her mother sobbed.

The two of them fell back against the table as Joe struck out with a closed fist. Anna remembered pulling herself out of her mother's grip and slipping below her arm. She remembered her father losing his balance as she thrust upward with the knife. Anna didn't remember lifting the knife. She didn't remember taking it from the sink. She felt it enter his body below his rib cage. She remembered letting go as he made a sudden sharp, surprised intake of breath. Then, half-turning, he swiped at her before collapsing his full length on the kitchen tiles. There was a dull metallic twang as the knife broke off at the handle where it hit the floor. Her father gave a low grunt as his head hit the tiles.

The rest was pandemonium. By the time the ambulance arrived Joe McLoughlin was dead and the house was filled with neighbours trying to find out what had happened, to comfort Kathleen and look after the children. Kathleen was fully in control. Pale and tight lipped and dry eyed, she had pulled Anna into the small parlour before anyone else could talk to her.

'Listen, Anna.' She held her close, their faces almost touching. 'Listen, Anna, if you never do anything else for your whole life, please listen to me. Please?'

Anna nodded.

'Listen and remember this. You saw nothing. You were in your room and when you heard the commotion and came downstairs and into the kitchen your da was lying on the floor. That's all you know. Nothing else. You hear me, daughter? Promise me? That's what you tell anyone who asks you. The police, the priest, your brothers, your grannies and grandas. Everyone. You hear me? That's what you tell them. You were in your room. You saw nothing. You weren't there. You were in your room.' Kathleen hugged Anna gently. 'It's for the best,' she whispered. 'Okay, love?'

'Okay, Mammy,' Anna replied. 'I was in my room. I saw nothing.'

'That's right, love. You weren't there. It will be alright. It's for the best. It was the drink done it. He was a different man when he wasn't drinking. But he was a bastard when he was. And no woman should have to put up with that. I'm only sorry that I did.'

So was Anna. But she didn't say so. How could she? She had just killed her father. So she said nothing. Instead, she held her mother and her mother held her. They stood like that, gently rocking back and forth, clinging on to each other, while in the next room the body of their father and husband grew cold and stiff, stretched out on the kitchen floor.

That was probably the night that Anna began to think about becoming a nun. It came to her when she lay awake in bed in her granny's. Their own house was sealed off. Tall uniformed RUC officers stood guard at the front and back doors while plainclothes detectives gathered evidence inside and took a statement from her mother. They never questioned Anna at all. But they took her mother to the barracks where she was charged a few days later and then released on bail by the court. They took her father's body away to the morgue as dawn was breaking. Anna was off school. Her granny fussed around her and her brothers. Her granny and granda McLoughlin also came to see them. Granda McLoughlin identified his son's remains at the morgue. He was buried from the McLoughlins' house up in Cushendall. That's where the wake was. Those days went by slowly for Anna. The funeral was a tense, sad event, and although Joe's parents did their best, they couldn't look at Kathleen and her children without crying. Some whispered that Kathleen should not have gone there, in deference to Joe's parents, but they didn't object. They knew their grandchildren needed their mother with them. Anna stayed beside Kathleen through it all. Although she sat quietly in the chapel, she wanted to scream out, 'I did it! I did it! It wasn't my mammy! It was me! My daddy beat her all the time. He was no good. It was his fault. *I didn't mean to do it. But I'm not sorry. I'm only sorry my mammy is getting the blame.* She should never have put up with him beating her like that. But she did. And she didn't deserve it. And she doesn't deserve to get the blame. It was me not her who did it.'

But of course she said nothing. That's what she had promised her mother. But she also came to know instinctively, as days grew into weeks and she got back to school and family life settled back into a normality of sorts, that it was in her best interest to say nothing. And this niggled at her. And so the idea of entering the convent grew and grew over time. Sister Benedict was her role model. Mary Ann McCracken her hero. Her mother had instilled in her the importance of doing something positive with her life. That became even more compelling for her after her father's death. It wasn't that she thought she could assuage the guilt by going into the convent. But all these influences and events merged and guided her towards the Dominican Sisters.

Her mother stood trial for the manslaughter of her husband. Kathleen had made a statement to the RUC accepting responsibility for her husband's death. But an up-and-coming young solicitor, P.J. Mac Ruairí, who later came to prominence during the civil rights struggle and the war which followed it, won the landmark case when he argued mitigating circumstances and provided evidence of Joe McLoughlin's drunken and abusive behaviour. It seemed Joe and Kathleen hadn't been as successful as they'd thought at concealing the violence that had come into their marriage. The whole street knew about it, and several neighbours came forward with their testimonies. So Kathleen McLoughlin was found not guilty of manslaughter and returned, after months of tabloid notoriety, to a quiet and uneventful life with her children. They moved home and Joe's pension helped ease the poverty of widowhood. The relationship between the McLoughlins and Kathleen was never the same again, although the children spent summer break-time up in Cushendall.

Throughout all this Anna was making her way steadily through Saint Dorothy's. The nuns had welcomed her back after her father's death and her mother's trial. They were kind to her and the discipline and routine of their educational regime was what she needed at that fraught time in her life. Sister Benedict in particular kept a close watch on her. And her closest schoolmates embraced her unconditionally. But of course no one knew Anna's secret. They put her quietness and withdrawnness down to the terrible experience she had suffered without realising that the truth of the matter was it was she who had killed her father.

For her part, Anna was drawn more and more to the orderly life of the Dominican nuns. She had a sense of vocation. A sense of social justice. That was for sure. It seemed to her also, as a teenage girl, that there was a tranquillity and a spiritual simplicity and completeness to convent life. And fulfilment in their teaching vocation. So she formed an intention to go to college to become a teacher.

During those years she stayed close to the nuns in Saint Dorothy's, especially Sister Benedict. Anna spent many happy Saturday afternoons there, and frequently studied in the quiet after-school hours in the convent. She usually spent a while, if the weather was good, beneath the canopy of the witness tree. One day, without really thinking about it, she sat there and talked to her father. That first time she convulsed in streams of tears as she gave off to him. Later, much later, when she seemed to have exorcised her anger, she began to remind him in whispered confidences of the happy times they all had together before the drink destroyed his goodness. Decades later she reflected that her reconciliation with him came only when she became reconciled with herself. It was during this time that she decided to become a nun.

And so in the summer of 1969, as the Falls erupted when the northern state reacted against the civil rights demands,

Anna McLoughlin, fresh out of Queen's University, went off to Rome to study as a novice for the Dominican Order. Rome thrilled her. She had never been out of Ireland before. She had barely been out of West Belfast. Rome made her look forward in her life rather than back. She loved its history, the ancient ruins, the fine buildings, the good weather, and she loved Italian food. The discipline, security and ordered routine of convent life gave her stability. She got on well with her sister novitiates. Two of them were Irish, so they kept up with news from home. They had great fun slagging off each other and their respective county teams when the football championship kicked off. They were busy with their studies but on weekends one of the senior nuns took them walking in the city or in a minibus out into the countryside. Everyone looked forward to those outings.

An odd time Anna dressed in her own clothes, civilian clothes the older nuns called them, and wandered off on her own. She would pass for any other young visitor to the Holy City. She liked the exuberance of Italian café life, the cheerful excitability of the other diners or coffee sippers. There was an energy about it all and about the other strollers who, like her, were enjoying the Roman sunshine. She especially liked the freedom that brought her. She watched young couples – and some not so young – wandering hand in hand or in close, casual embrace. She was secure enough in her own vocation but that didn't stop her reflecting on how life may have been, or could be, if she wanted to take a different journey. She willed herself not to think too often like this. Just in case she aroused self-doubt. And she thought of her mother often. She deeply regretted what had happened, but she had got to know herself well enough not to dwell on what might have been. The past could not be changed, so she set her face and faith resolutely towards the future.

And so the years in Rome passed and at the end of her studies Anna McLoughlin became a Dominican Sister. She took the name Mary Ann after her hero Mary Ann McCracken and returned to Belfast in the midst of the conflict. She was delighted to get a teaching post in Saint Dorothy's. The witness tree continued to give her shelter and solace. When the weather was good it was her favourite place for contemplation. Her own little sanctuary. She quickly grew into her role as teacher and mentor to the girls and young women who escaped from the uncertainties and dangers of war on the streets into the relative safety of the walled grounds and the studious school routine within. Sister Mary Ann had an easygoing, non-judgemental but attentive affinity with all the students in her care, but she had an unerring instinct for the ones who were shy or awkward in the company of others.

She herself was a little reserved but she had a quiet confidence as well and a gentleness. She knew herself well by then. Reflection, a busy life and prayer did this for her. So she knew she was good at her job. She knew she had presence. She certainly had attitude. Understated. But there all the same. There in the confident way she held herself with her students and workmates. There in her sense of herself. She liked to think she got that from her mother. Truth is she got it from her father. From the way he treated her mother. Anna had long resolved that no one would ever treat her like that. And she would never treat anyone like that either. Never.

She resolved that when she was a small child as she lay awake in their house in Iveagh Crescent. She resolved that as she listened to the thumps and shouts from the kitchen below her. She resolved that as she buried her head in the pillow in a futile effort to block out the noise. And she sustained that slightly sad but gentle independence and decency for ever after that. That's how she lived her life.

Many years after she started teaching in Saint Dorothy's, at an event to mark her retirement, speakers paid tribute to her on behalf of generations of Belfast girls who came to love and to learn from the quiet, assertive sister teacher who guided them through turbulent decades into the more peaceful political dispensation that now enveloped Belfast, the North and the entire island of Ireland. The event was held outdoors in the garden, below the witness tree. Anna was delighted that a small bench had been erected below the tree as a retirement gift for her. She felt that she and the witness tree had grown older together. She had taken great comfort and healing over the decades from its shelter. She sat there contentedly as her friends and colleagues and some of the students spoke.

Some told of her sense of herself and of her great hope and confidence in the young girls who came into her care. One simply thanked her for keeping the faith. Anna spoke at the end. She told of her admiration for Mary Ann McCracken, a pioneer for rights for the Belfast poor and downtrodden as well as the African slaves and the dispossessed. She said she believed that young people should always get the best chance, especially young women, to realise their great potential and possibilities. She said she liked to think that she got that from all the brave and independent women she'd observed through her long life, from her readings about Mary Ann McCracken to some of the girls in her own school who knew where to draw the line where their rights were concerned, who understood that there were some things that nobody had to put up with, 'even if they were women', as her mother would have put it. Or, as Sister Mary Ann put it herself, 'especially if they were women'.

Of course she told none of them of her secret. She couldn't do that. How could she? She'd promised her mother she never would. There were only two still alive in the world who knew what she had done. That was herself. And the witness tree.

THE WRONG FOOT

Once upon a time Paddy was in prison. Truth to tell he was in prison a few times. That experience stays with you. Even now, Paddy occasionally has the sense of being a lapsed prisoner. He has a deep-rooted notion that he could end up back in prison again. Nothing to keep him up at night. Nothing more than a slight concern. He is an easygoing kind of an individual. He would also be the first one to acknowledge that prison never did him any harm. Paddy was an internee. That is, he was imprisoned without charge or trial. Indefinitely. In Long Kesh. Before that he was in a prison ship. Anchored in Belfast Lough. The *Maidstone,* it was called.

Long Kesh was better than the *Maidstone*, in Paddy's opinion. And in this case Paddy's opinion mattered. At least to Paddy. Not that he could do anything about it. His motto was easy come, easy go. He believed that all things in life are relative. He met many interesting people in Long Kesh. Not just other internees, though they were an intriguing bunch. Some prison officers were interesting as well. There were also other prisoners, mostly inside on relatively minor offences or in the last few months of their sentences. Some of these were known as trusties. ODCs. Ordinary Decent Criminals. Trevor was one of these. The ODCs emptied the rubbish. Worked in the kitchen. Or the hospital. The ODCs wouldn't have much truck with internees anyway. Especially ODCs from loyalist neighbourhoods. Trevor was a loyalist. Or at least that was his background. He told Paddy so himself.

Trevor worked with the prison doctor. He noted the details of all prisoners reporting in sick and scribbled a note of their complaint, which he gave to the doctor. He normally worked in a small cell disguised as a reception. Paddy was over one day chancing his arm looking for a milk ration. Getting a milk diet was a good way of avoiding some of the worst of the prison food. The doctor was stationed in a little facility within its own compound. It consisted of Trevor's little reception and a waiting-room cell plus a few big cells. There were four beds in each of them for prisoners who were sick or working their ticket – pretending to be sick in a usually futile attempt to get an early release. This facility was called the prison hospital. The prison officers or screws, apart from two medics, stayed out of the hospital but patrolled the compound and controlled the entrance.

Trevor was mopping the floor when Paddy arrived in for his appointment. He set aside the mop and noted Paddy's details in a file for the doctor. There was no one else in the waiting room. Trevor and Paddy were there together. Just the two of them. Paddy noticed that Trevor avoided looking directly at him.

'How are you doing?' Paddy asked him.

Trevor was a little bit surprised. He reddened slightly. He was taller than Paddy. A few years younger. Sandy hair cut very short. He was dressed in a prison uniform. Paddy wore his own clothes. Jeans and a T-shirt. It was summer. Paddy waited for Trevor to acknowledge his query. Trevor ignored him.

Paddy was persistent. 'How are you getting on?' he asked again.

Glancing up hesitantly from his folder – Paddy's folder – Trevor looked straight at Paddy for the first time. Then with a cheeky grin he asked, 'Who – me? You talking to me?'

Paddy grinned back at him. 'I don't see anybody else here. Do you see anyone else?'

'Nawh.' Trevor blushed again. And smiled. 'Just the two of us. I'm dead on. Just not used to one of youse talking to one of us.' He looked around anxiously. 'I'm not one of your sort. I dig with the other foot.'

'You mean you dig with the wrong foot,' Paddy joked. 'Good man yourself. What's your name?'

'Trevor,' he replied, 'and I know who you are.'

Paddy stuck his hand out. Trevor shook it firmly.

'You smoke?' asked Paddy.

'Yup,' he said, 'like a train. Nothing else to do in this kip.'

Paddy gave him a few cigarettes.

He smiled warmly. 'Thanks, mate. I appreciate that.'

'I'm giving them up,' Paddy said. 'Again.'

'Wait there,' said Trevor, ushering him into the bigger cell. Then he retrieved his mop and pushed the mop bucket along the floor as he finished washing it. Paddy noticed that he walked with a limp. Nothing too pronounced. Just a slight favouring of his left leg.

Trevor came back to tell Paddy the doctor was almost ready for him. As he did so, he slipped him a packet of Polo mints. 'Your breath is stinking.' He smiled. 'The doctor will call you in a minute.'

When Paddy finished with the doctor and returned to the small cell, Trevor was gone. But he saw him again the following week. The milk ration had to be prescribed on a weekly basis. Paddy didn't mind that. Getting a ration of milk every day was a big deal. And getting out to the doctor's was a break in the monotony of prison life.

He was glad to see Trevor again. He gave him a lump of tobacco and a packet of cigarette papers. 'These any use to you?'

'Just what the doctor ordered,' Trevor replied gratefully. 'I broke up the last fags you gave me. I got twelve roll-ups from them. They last longer like that.'

'I'm still trying to give them up,' Paddy told him again.

'I'm down to three a day. I love a smoke with a cup of tea.'

'Me too,' said Trevor. 'You want a Fig Roll?'

'I could never figure out how Jacob's get the figs into the Fig Rolls,' Paddy replied as he chewed thoughtfully on the biscuit.

'Jim Figgerty has a lot to answer for.' Trevor grinned. 'He's probably one of yours. Figgerty sounds like a Fenian name.'

Paddy laughed as he reached for another biscuit. 'Fig Rolls are non-sectarian. I read somewhere that Jacob's got a cross-community grant to fund Figgerty's efforts to get the figs into the Fig Rolls. Figgerty insisted on his method being kept secret.'

'Typical,' Trevor observed. 'Say nothing. That's Fenians for you.'

The two of them looked at each other for a few smiling, chewing seconds before they both burst out laughing.

That's how the two of them became friends. A couple of short conversations. But as the weeks went by those few stolen words, and an occasional little jibe, stitched together an understanding of each other's lives and their family backgrounds. Paddy would always bring Trevor a few fags. Even when he managed to give them up himself. Trevor would slip Paddy a magazine or a bar of chocolate. Or a few Polo mints. That might not sound like a big deal, but his breath did stink and when he was dying for a sugar hit a square of Cadbury's was a feast and getting a magazine was like a visit to the library.

Trevor was also taking a chance giving him this stuff. It could get him into trouble. The loss of his privileges. Maybe even loss of remission. Or worse. Other trusties or loyalist inmates could disapprove also.

Paddy? Paddy had no privileges. Or a release date. So it didn't really matter to him. Most of the time he was in with a bunch of other political prisoners. They looked after each other. They didn't have much contact on a daily basis with the prison system. Or with the trusties. That wouldn't be approved of by the prison regime. And maybe by their own ones as well.

But as luck would have it, Trevor and Paddy never got caught. These weekly encounters became part of their routine. They would only be together for a few minutes. Even less. But they liked chatting to each other. Trevor chatted a lot. So after six months Paddy knew he'd started his jail career for stealing drugs from a chemist he worked for. He said he was pressured into doing it. That's how he got his limp. He was shot in the leg for drug pushing.

'I wasn't actually drug pushing,' he told Paddy. 'I was forced to steal drugs, and when the people who did that found out I was giving some tablets to my mates, they shot me. Stupid, really! I got caught and that was their supply finished. That's how I got to work with the prison doctor. When I did my first stretch I was mostly in the prison hospital. On account of being kneecapped, I needed treatment for ages. And because I used to work for a chemist I got to help out here. Every time I've been back they bring me straight here.'

Trevor was married now with two kids. But since his first stint he was in and out of prison a good deal. Just for a few months or a year or so at a time. Nothing too severe. Mostly bits and pieces of fraud. Once for assaulting a peeler.

'What type of loyalty is that?' Paddy scolded him.

'I'm also fond of a wee drink,' he confessed.

'No harm in that,' Paddy said. 'You and me should go on the rip someday. I like a wee drink meself.'

One day they discussed Trevor's release. It was only a month off. 'Drink's a curse if it gets to you,' Trevor proclaimed. 'I'm gonna give it up.'

'Well,' Paddy said, 'you have a lot going for you. A wife. Two babies. You gotta think of them.'

'That's okay for you to say. Your side has everything going for you,' Trevor replied abruptly, his face reddening. 'The whingey child gets the ditty. Always gurning. Youse Fenians are always complaining about no jobs. No rights. No nothing. And the Brits always willing to bend over backwards to facilitate youse in case youse bomb the mainland.'

Paddy burst out laughing. 'Would you ever catch yourself on,' he exclaimed. 'I'm stuck in here. No charges. No trial. No release date. You're out next month. I'm sure there'll be a wee rehabilitation job waiting for you. There's no reason for you ever to be back in here again. If you mind yourself. Remember, if you can't do the time don't do the crime.'

'That's not what I mean!' Trevor retorted. 'You know that. I mean your side are getting everything that's going. All the oul' shite about discrimination is paying off. Always looking for your civil rights. What about my civil rights? You really think our side has all the good jobs and the nice houses? We have nothing. Not where I come from.'

'Well, do something about it,' Paddy said. 'Don't blame me. I don't blame you. Civil rights are for everybody. I don't believe in this two sides carry-on. Who does that suit? Me and you are the same, both working class, but they've divided us. Catholics versus Protestants. A load of oul' shite. But it works. Divide and conquer. The oldest game in the book and still some people fall for it!

'And by the way,' he added, 'this is the mainland.'

They left it at that. By then the two of them knew that they had both grown up in housing estates that looked very much the same. Both their fathers were unemployed a lot of the time. Their mothers kept their families going. And their grannies. Paddy could easily have slipped into a life of petty crime just like Trevor but, ironically, the conflict stopped that. In Trevor's case it might have accelerated it. They both had some understanding of how easy it was to end up on the wrong side of the law so it wasn't an issue between them. Certainly not a judgemental issue. On the odd occasion when they argued it passed quickly. Or one of them turned it into a joke and then they disguised argument as slagging. Banter. They always parted on good terms. On this occasion, as usual, Trevor slipped Paddy a packet of Polo mints when he was leaving.

'Your breath still stinks.' He smiled.

Trevor got out a few weeks later, out to East Belfast. When Paddy made his weekly excursion to the doctor's a few days later he missed Trevor. He missed their wee chats. Then eventually Paddy got out as well. Out to West Belfast. Internment was over but the war went on. Including a dreadful prison struggle which was worse than anything Paddy, or for that matter Trevor, experienced. Ten men died on hunger strike that summer not far from where they used to meet. Paddy used to think of Trevor every so often. He thought he was a decent sort who deserved another chance. He hoped he got it. He also hoped that he took it. He was sorry they never met again.

Paddy started up his own business, just off the Falls Road. He sold and repaired bikes. He was also active in the battle for prisoners' rights. The deaths of the hunger-strikers propelled him into full-time politics and he was one of the first Sinn Féin councillors to be elected to Belfast City Council. He enjoyed that work, though it was dangerous and difficult in the beginning. He was never attacked but some of his fellow councillors were shot and their office in the City Hall was bombed.

He never married and was contented enough living with his sister in the house they were born in. She often accused him of being married to Sinn Féin.

For his part, Trevor was as good as his word. When he was released he started work in a community scheme and slowly worked his way into a managerial position in a local redevelopment project, after spending some time going to night classes. He was blessed with a good wife and they got on well together, minding their own business, rearing their children. Trevor stayed out of trouble. And away from the drink. He often thought of Paddy. A few times he almost contacted him. In his role as a councillor, Paddy would be in the local papers and occasionally on TV. Trevor told his wife all about him and of their friendship behind the wire. She cautioned him about reaching out to Paddy. She was afraid that someone would find out. So he never did. And with daily bombings and shootings, he knew that was the prudent thing to do.

Slowly the years went by. Peace talks started, hesitantly and awkwardly. Eventually the fighting was brought to an end. Peace slowly replaced violence. Trevor watched all this unfold on his television screen. He was always delighted to see Paddy when every so often he was part of a delegation going in or out of some important meeting.

'He's starting to show his age, Agnes,' he would call out to his wife. 'Putting on the beef too. All them big feeds.'

Paddy was elected to the new political assembly after the Good Friday Agreement. One day in Parliament Buildings at Stormont he was on his way into Martin McGuinness's office when a man detached himself from a group of visitors. Limping slightly, he hailed Paddy. It was Trevor.

Paddy was delighted to see him. Trevor was delighted to see Paddy. They shook hands warmly.

'You've come up in the world,' Trevor exclaimed.

'So have you,' Paddy said, 'and lost your sandy hair.'

Trevor laughed. 'I'm a tour guide. I set up my own Belfast Tours business,' he replied, 'employing ten other people. Doing great. Today I'm showing these French visitors around the Belfast murals. Giving them the real history of our wee country. Will you get a photo with them?'

'Sure,' Paddy agreed, 'if you come in and say hullo to Martin.'

So they did. Martin was as gracious as ever. Paddy told him about Trevor and their jail soirées. Martin told Trevor that Paddy had written a speech for him about Trevor without telling anyone his real identity. It was a speech about building a society for everyone. About the need to reach out to loyalist and Unionist working-class communities. About all of them having the same rights.

Trevor was chuffed. 'I taught him everything he knows,'

he told Martin.

They all laughed at that.

'I'm serious,' Trevor insisted, with his wide grin mocking Paddy. 'Me and Paddy started the peace process. But I don't mind if you fellas get all the credit. That's the way I am. Isn't that right, Paddy?'

Paddy laughingly agreed.

Trevor insisted on getting a photo with them both. As he looked around the big office he turned to Paddy. 'Didn't I tell you your side is getting everything that's going?' He laughed.

'And didn't I tell you that I don't believe in this two sides nonsense,' Paddy reminded him. 'We disagree on things but we're all the one.'

'That's my position too,' Martin said, 'you won't be surprised to hear!'

'Ask my brother am I a liar?' Trevor smiled. 'Seriously, Martin, you're doing a great job.'

'You never said that to me,' Paddy chided him.

'I get the credit,' Martin laughed, 'he gets the blame. Now if you two oul' jailbirds get out of my office I'll get back to my work.'

So they left him and went back into the Great Hall where Trevor's group of visitors awaited him.

When they were parting they agreed to meet some evening.

'Come up here if it suits you,' Paddy said. 'We can reminisce about our time together in the clink.'

Trevor told Paddy he hoped he never would go back to jail again.

'I hope so too, Trevor,' said Paddy. 'You're a decent man. If you do end up in clink again that would be a disaster. Especially if I was there as well.'

'Too true,' Trevor agreed. 'Here.' He slipped Paddy another packet of Polo mints. 'Your breath is still stinking,' he told him.

That was Trevor.

Paddy meant to phone him many times after that. He often thought of it, but the work days were long as his party established itself at Stormont. He kept putting off calling Trevor to another time. Then one day after meeting a delegation of families of victims of joyriders, one of the women asked if she could see him on his own for a moment.

'Of course.'

'I'm Agnes,' she said.

'Pleased to meet you,' said Paddy.

'Agnes Nugent,' she said.

Paddy could see that she didn't find this easy. 'Do we know each other?' he asked.

'You knew my Trevor,' she said. 'From prison ... He talked about you a lot.'

'Agnes, of course!' Paddy beamed. 'He talked for hours

about you and your wee ones. I almost felt I'd met you. How is he?'

She looked at him with a hopelessness she'd grown accustomed to. 'He's dead,' she said.

Paddy was stunned. He felt he'd taken a punch in the face. 'Trevor, gone? I can't believe … He was just here a few months back, we were going to meet. How did this …?'

'He was run down by a joyrider, a young hood, high on drugs, in a stolen car. Trevor was just coming out of a local shop. He was on the way home. The boy who killed him made a run for it but they caught him.'

Paddy, like a lot of people from that city who'd lived through the times he had, had received the news of many deaths, had walked behind coffins into graveyards many times. But the death of Trevor hit him differently. His friendship with him had been special, unexpected. It seemed to exist within in its own wee private space. The news shook him more than he might have imagined it would. He felt tears come into his eyes, but they seemed so out of place there in Parliament Buildings. Agnes could see this and was touched.

'This is desperate,' he said. 'God help you. How are you managing? And your children, how are they?'

'It's a struggle,' she said. 'The two kids have their own children now. Trevor was devoted to them and to our grandkids and they adored their daddy and granda. It just isn't fair.'

Paddy had to resist the urge to hug her. Instead he put his hand on her arm. 'He was doing so well,' he comforted her. 'Full of craic and slagging as usual when he was here.'

'I know.' She smiled. 'He got such a nice picture with you and Martin. He was so delighted with that. He insisted on putting it on the fireplace for all to see. He said it was a cross-community photo. "Me and my two muckers who dig with the other foot, the wrong foot" is what he used to say to anyone who remarked on it. He told my da he was going to apply for an award for his reconciliation work. That was my Trevor, no harm in him.'

Paddy agreed. He was still shocked at what had happened. The unfairness of it. As he absorbed the sad news, he realised that Trevor meant more to him than he knew or realised until now. It was strange and good that they'd met again, just a few months ago, after all those years. He was genuinely angry for Mrs Nugent. It showed. And it gave her some comfort. That's what she told him.

'I was very unsure about coming to see you. You know the way things are in this place. I was afraid of what people might think. And to be honest, I wasn't sure myself. Me and Trevor used to keep ourselves to ourselves. We stayed away from politics. But I felt I had to join this campaign against death-riding for him. It was good to get meeting you. I'm glad I did. I believe you'll do what you can to help. I can see he was important to you. He used to talk about going down to see if he could meet you in the City Hall when you were a councillor. I put him off. I'm sorry I did. He always said you were good to him in Long Kesh.'

'He kept me up on Polo mints in there,' Paddy told her. They chatted on for a few minutes and agreed to meet again to review progress on their campaign.

'That's a funny thing,' she said to him as he was walking the group to the door. 'You said Trevor kept you supplied with Polo mints. He always had a half dozen tubes of them. I'm finding his Polo mints everywhere. In his coat pockets. In the car.' She smiled wanly as she rummaged in her handbag.

Paddy didn't know what to say.

'Here,' she told him, 'here's a packet for you.' She handed him the sweets.

'He used to say I had bad breath.' Paddy smiled.

'I know. He told me that. But it's not too bad.' She smiled back. She reached out to him and they embraced. 'I'm sorry you got the news of Trevor the way you did,' she told him.

Paddy was moved and comforted by her sympathy for him. She was the one who had lost the most but still she wanted to acknowledge his loss. Her sense of grace and compassion touched him deeply.

'I'm glad you and Trevor were friends in Long Kesh in the middle of all the madness of those days,' she said.

'So am I,' he agreed.

That's how they parted. Sharing their grief for Trevor and united in their resolve to tackle the scourge of death-riding. Mrs Nugent and the other campaigners went off out through the revolving door at Stormont. Paddy made his way back, through the Great Hall, to the Assembly Chamber.

As he passed the dark-uniformed security staff, for a second he was transported back to Long Kesh and his walk back from the prison hospital after his regular chats with Trevor. Then, as now, he had Trevor's Polo mints in his hand, his fingers closed around the packet to prevent the prison officers seeing it. As he took his seat in the chamber, he couldn't help smiling to himself. Once a prisoner always a prisoner. Old jail habits endure, he reflected. He opened his fist. Trevor's Polo mints were still in his hand.

THE BUS

All human life, thought Bobby, can be found on a country bus. People travelling to attend a funeral. Or a wedding. Or going to or from the hospital. As patients or visitors. Coming back home with bad news. Or good news. Harassed mothers with hyperactive children. Students home for the weekend with bags of dirty washing for their mothers to take care of. The occasional drunk. Lots of tourists during the summer. Backpackers. And exiles returning home. There were also the elderly regulars with their own routine, a free-travel pass and time to fill.

Bobby had been driving the bus for twenty-five years. In that time the roadscape had changed from uneven winding bog or mountain roads. Now there were stretches of motorway. They shortened the journey. The buses had changed too. When Bobby started work as a bus driver the buses were hard-seated straight-backed machines with limited suspension and little capacity for speed. In those days it was not unusual to have live chickens trussed up together in a sack hanging from the overhead rack, cackling and clucking in angry indignation at their undignified means of transportation. Nowadays there was a fleet of luxury air-conditioned Wi-Fi-enabled coaches. The chickens would have loved it but, as Bobby remarked to one of his regular passengers, 'There's not many people taking chickens to market these days.'

What hadn't changed, in Bobby's view, was that bus drivers, particularly bus drivers like himself who worked the long rural routes from village to village to the big market towns, got to know their regular passengers. They overheard secrets. Or possibilities of secrets. A misspoken word. A casual aside. A barely credible reason for travelling.

Bobby's daily route took him from Baile na Mona to the market town in the morning and back over the same twenty-five miles in the evening. There was plenty of time to talk. There were few people along the route he didn't know. Not only their faces and names and the names and ages and professions or school years of their children, but also their political opinions, their drinking habits, their sporting preferences, their ailments and remedies, romances and land disputes.

Bobby lived in Baile na Mona. He'd been born there and, he supposed, he'd die there. It was a sleepy little town of trimmed hedges, freshly painted houses and well-tended gardens. No one let the side down in Baile na Mona's quest for a prize in the Tidy Towns competition. There was a post office, a shop, a café and three pubs. There was a primary school too, though the old outnumbered the young these days. A high church steeple and a rural quietness presided over all. People were friendly, and there was no serious discord. It was a good place to live.

One of Bobby's regular passengers was a small woman in her late middle years who travelled to and from the market town on Thursdays, a widow by the name of Katie Gallagher. She was always neatly dressed, often in a tweed skirt and floral top, her hair carefully arranged. Though streaked with grey, it still had its natural auburn colour. Despite her age she retained a youthful vigour. Or maybe it was nervous energy. But if you looked at her closely or observed her for a while you would sense that she was just a little bit sad. Especially when her eyes looked into the distance as if she was studying something far away.

She sat in the front of the bus, the first seat to the left and a few feet behind the driver. This was where she always sat, arriving early every Thursday to make sure her place wasn't taken by someone else. A tourist maybe. Or teenagers on their way home from the Gaeltacht. She hated that. Noisy strangers gabbling away. Talking non-stop. In her seat. The last time it happened she was banished halfway up the bus.

That day two women were in her seat at the front. They looked like they might be a mother and daughter. Americans. They would have the wide windscreened view of the road that she loved once the bus got going. And the easy good-natured banter with Bobby. She had to clamber up the aisle with her bags of shopping awkwardly banging against everyone she passed. The bus was full that day. A young man helped put her bags in the overhead rack as she plopped herself down in the empty space beside him. She tried to pass herself with him when he engaged her in polite small talk, but as Bobby started the bus and eased it gently away from the pavement and on to the main road, she pretended she was sleeping. Later, when her usual seat became empty, Bobby sent one of the other passengers to tell her to come down. She did so quickly.

Then when it was her time to disembark she had to make her way back up the bus to get her shopping. The young man helped her again. But by now she was too flustered to thank him properly. 'I must be going mad,' she said, half to herself and half to Bobby.

'From now on, Katie,' he said as he helped her off the bus, 'you get here early before we start boarding and you'll have your seat before anyone else gets on.'

'Thank you, Bobby,' she told him gratefully. 'I never put in a bus journey like that before. I'm not fit for entertaining strangers. It stresses me out too much.'

'I know,' Bobby said with a good-natured laugh. 'You just can't abide being separated from me. See you next week, with the help of God.'

He watched her move along the road with her shopping and up the path to her house. He felt for her. She wasn't the same since her husband, Frank, had died. That was just over a year ago. She'd become fretful. Small things unnerved her. He'd known her in better times, for Frank had been one of his oldest friends. They'd known each other since their schooldays. They wound up teachers together, played football on the same team, chased the same girl, mitched school and got drunk for the first time together in the grave-yard from the same stash of cheap cider. They had a time on the building sites in London and then in Dublin together, but they came back to Baile na Mona, first Bobby and then Frank, just a couple of years later. Not long after that, Frank married Katie. They used to have Bobby around for a game of cards and a few bottles of stout on Friday nights. Bobby was grateful for that.

When Frank retired he used to take the bus with Katie into the town to shop. They always went on Thursdays and they always took the front seat. Frank didn't like the shopping but he liked yarning to Bobby about cars and tractors and the weekend's football games as the bus stopped and started on its journey, picking up and dropping off passengers along the road. And he liked the lunch in Maguire's Bar and Grill when Katie had done her shopping. And the decent pint of Guinness in Maguire's lounge. They never had any children, but if they minded they never let on. They always seemed well matched to each other.

Bobby thought to himself that was the reason she con-

tinued to make the weekly trip. She never missed a Thursday, even in winter. It was no longer for the shopping.
She rarely brought a lot home. Some bits and pieces that
she could have got in the village shop in Baile na Mona.
No, Bobby reasoned to himself, it was the loneliness. The
bus trip got her out of the house and the familiar journey
brought her a certain comfort. And a sense of Frank.

So when Katie didn't appear at the bus stop one Thursday
morning he was a little alarmed, and that evening he called
to see her. He found her bustling around with a bucket and
mop, wearing an apron and with her hair tied up in a scarf.
Her neighbour, Rosie, was watching her.

'She has a special guest coming tomorrow, Bobby,' she said.
'But she won't admit it. She won't say anything. She's been
going around like a devil all day dusting and clipping hedges
and swishing over the floors with thon mop. You'll have a
wee cup in your hand, Bobby, won't you?'

'I will, Rosie. Thank you.'

Rosie went into the kitchen and Katie moved close to
Bobby, speaking just above a whisper. 'Just the man I wanted
to see. I was half-expecting you. Are you working tomorrow?'

'I am.'

'I need a wee favour. I've a young man coming here to see
me. Will you look after him if I tell him to catch your bus?
And then show him to the house? Then you can take him

back in the evening.'

'I will surely. Is he your toyboy?'

'He is not,' she scolded him. Her face reddened.

He wished he hadn't said it. 'Sorry, Katie.'

'Not to worry.'

'So who is it?'

'It's my cousin's son. Seamus is his name. He'll be on the early bus from Dublin. That's where he lives. Not a word to Rosie now, Bobby. You know where that would lead.'

Rosie came in with the tea and a plate of buns and they sat around the table. She did her best to pry the information out of Katie about all the frantic housekeeping, but she didn't succeed.

Later that night Katie phoned Bobby to say that she'd confirmed with Seamus that he'd be on his bus. 'Sure you don't mind, Bobby?'

'Of course not.'

'You'll look after him, won't you?'

'Indeed I will.'

She was as fretful sounding as she'd been all year, but with a new excitement. He wondered why.

'Rosie's one of the best,' she said. 'But you know yourself how it is. I like to keep myself to myself.'

'I know that, Katie,' he said. 'When was the last time you saw Seamus?'

There was a slight pause. He sensed her getting flustered.

'Oh, when he was a wee lad,' Katie eventually said.

'Well, I'll deliver him safe and sound tomorrow. Good night now, Katie.'

'God bless. And thank you, Bobby.'

After she put the phone down Katie sat for an hour quietly on her own. She didn't like deceiving Bobby. They were old friends, but she was trying to come to terms with the way Seamus had come into her life. It was as if he'd landed from the sky. Unbelievable, she kept saying to herself. For a time she hadn't been able to get beyond that. They'd been speaking on the phone, but now he'd asked to visit her in her home. She couldn't very well refuse. And she was curious, among other things. Even excited. It was a long while since she'd had anything to be excited about. But still, it was unbelievable ...

The following day when Bobby pulled the bus up to the stop in the main square of the market town he saw a tall, dark-haired young man looking, it seemed, for the bus in the wrong direction. He stood out because of this and because he wore a suit, as if for a special occasion, and because he carried under his arm a large box of chocolates tied up in a red satin ribbon. This has to be Seamus, he thought. It was rare for someone to be waiting for his bus who wasn't either a tourist or known to him. Or at least someone dressed like this young man.

He let open the door with a whoosh. The young man

stepped in, with some relief, thought Bobby.

'Would you be Bobby?'

'I am,' he said, extending his hand. 'And you have to be Seamus.'

'Do I stand out that much?'

'I can spot a Dub at a hundred metres.' Bobby laughed. 'Take that seat there, if you like. That's where Katie always sits on her runs into town.'

'How's she doing?'

'Looking forward to seeing you. But old age doesn't come on its own. You'll notice a quare change in her.'

'Did something happen? I was only talking to her by Skype a week ago. She looked well.'

'No, no, she's grand. Just a bit stressed getting everything just right for your visit.'

The mystery deepens, thought Bobby, as he pulled out and made his way out of the town and into the countryside.

'You ever been this way before, Seamus?'

Seamus laughed. 'I don't think I've ever made it north of Dublin Airport.'

The bus rambled along through bogland and hills. Bobby noticed in his mirror that Seamus was trying to read but kept looking away. He couldn't seem to settle. The bus slowly emptied as people got off at the villages. Finally, Seamus leaned towards the driver's seat and quietly asked, 'Did you know Frank, Bobby?'

'Indeed I did. We were born just a week apart, me being the younger. We went to school together, got up to antics together. We were like brothers. When we had to start earning our keep we went off to London together and worked on the buildings. But we couldn't stick it, Baile na Mona bred and buttered, so we came home again. Though Frank did a couple more years in Dublin while I started on the buses. He always had in mind to build his own house. And he did. That's where you're going now. When he married I became their pet bachelor. So Frank and I weren't separated much until death did it. I miss him. He was a good man.'

'I'm glad to hear it.'

'Sure, you must have come across him yourself at one family gathering or another?'

'No, Bobby. He was gone before I could meet him. I regret that.'

They got into Baile na Mona and Bobby showed Seamus to the house. He had a few hours before he had to make the evening run back to the town. He went home to make himself lunch, but he was thinking all the while about what was going on at Katie's. He sensed it was a momentous day for her. He got a partial report from Rosie when he met her on the main road on his way to the bus.

'Thon young fellow,' she said, 'she took him all around the house, into every wee corner, around the garden and up the stairs, the whole lot, then they parked themselves in the front room and talked non-stop for near three hours. I could see them from my window. It was like they couldn't draw breath, they had that much to say to one another. I haven't seen her like that for years.' She stopped to consider. 'In fact, I've *never* seen her like that.' She stepped a little closer to Bobby and eyed him slyly. 'I didn't want to ask but I think he must be from Frank's side of the family. What do you think?'

'I don't know, Rosie,' Bobby said. 'What makes you think that?'

'Have you no eyes to see? He has Frank's way of looking at you. And his way of walking.'

Rosie was right, Bobby said to himself. He'd caught some aura of familiarity when he first saw Seamus, but had dismissed it. He readied the bus. No Seamus yet. He wondered should he call Katie, but he didn't want to intrude. Then he saw Seamus running up the path. The chocolates were gone, but now he was carrying a bulging envelope. He got onto the bus and took the front seat again. Bobby manoeuvred the bus out of the village and onto the open road. They were alone together. This was the run with the least passengers usually. He caught glimpses of Seamus in his mirror. He had a different look now. His eyes were bright.

'So what do you make of our wee Baile na Mona, Seamus?'

'It's lovely. I didn't see much of it, but it's ... just right.'

'Not too quiet for ya?'

'I've lived in London and Madrid for work, on top of Dublin. I've had enough clamour for a lifetime.'

'What age are you now, Seamus?'

'Thirty-four.'

'Married?'

'No.'

'Is there a woman in your life?'

'Not at the moment.'

'You want to mind that. You don't want to end up like me – an oul' lad living on your own up a long lane.'

'I'll bear that in mind, Bobby.'

'So did our Katie treat you well? Did she give you a good feed?'

'Fabulous.'

'She's a grand cook, so she is.'

Seamus looked sheepish. 'I'm afraid I didn't do her dinner justice. We were talking that much I just gobbled it up.'

'Looks like she gave you something to take away,' said Bobby, pointing to the envelope. He was aware how much like Rosie he suddenly sounded.

'Yes,' said Seamus, opening it with a noticeable eagerness. 'Pictures of Frank.'

He held a few up for Bobby to glimpse at as he drove. They went back to before Frank's birth, to his parents and grandparents and the way the village was in their time, then forward to Frank as a baby, schoolboy, first communicant, bridegroom and all the way through his life to his funeral and gravestone. There was even one of him and Bobby in suits and with slicked-back hair in front of the Galtymore dance-hall in Cricklewood in London. He went through them one by one when they made a stop in one of the villages.

'Seamus,' he said when they set off again, 'I don't mean to pry. But I suppose I can't help myself. Katie's such a dear old friend of mine. She said you were the son of a cousin of hers, but when I look at you and the pictures of Frank when he was your age I can see that you're the spit of him. Tell me to mind my own business if you like, but just what is your connection to Frank and Katie?'

He heard Seamus draw a long breath. 'I'm not supposed to say. You know Katie far better than I do. She's very private. But I know she trusts you. She says you know how to keep things to yourself. Frank was my father, Bobby.'

Bobby could hardly believe his ears. 'Jesus, Mary and Holy Saint Joseph,' he exclaimed. Then hastily, 'Sorry, Seamus ...'

'No, Bobby, don't worry. I know you weren't expecting that. I wasn't either when I found out just a few months ago and I'm sorry I never found a way of meeting him. Frank never knew he had a son ... that I was his son. He made my mother pregnant. She was married at the time so she never let on to me or anyone that her husband wasn't my da. When they split up she reared me on her own. My father, or the man I thought was my father, emigrated to America. We never saw him again.'

Seamus sat quietly for a minute, then he continued. 'On my mother's death bed she told me Frank was my real father. A big gentle culchie, she said he was. She was a true blue Dubliner. A proper Dub. From the Liberties. Anyone outside the city was a culchie. She told me that my real father was a very kind man she'd met long ago, from a little village way up the country called Baile na Mona. She'd never been there, she never knew what became of him, but she wanted me to know it wasn't Frank's fault we never knew each other because Frank never knew of my existence. She never let him know. She believed it was for the best, though she came to see that it wasn't. She was sorry. She asked me to forgive her. I tried to find Frank after my mother's funeral, but he was already dead.'

Bobby let out a long whistle. 'By the holy,' he said. He waited to let all this sink in. 'I thought I knew him, but it seems I didn't. What was your mother's name, Seamus?'

'Mary Fitzsimmons.'

'I don't recall him ever mentioning her,' he said. 'I'm sure she was lovely, poor woman.' That's Baile na Mona, he thought to himself. 'And then you found Katie,' he said.

'At first she didn't believe me. Then she was upset. For a while she didn't answer my calls. But then she came round to it. We talked often. Then she invited me to her home, and here we are.'

And there indeed they were, back at the stop where Bobby had first seen Seamus earlier on that eventful day. They stood up. Seamus reached out a hand, but after hearing all that, Bobby embraced him instead.

'Better not say to Katie I told you,' said Seamus. 'You know her way.'

Bobby agreed. They said goodbye, then Seamus ran off down the road with his envelope of photographs to catch the last bus home to Dublin.

All the way back to Baile na Mona, Bobby turned the story he had just heard around in his head.

When he arrived he called around to Katie. It was late. He'd never called on her at such an hour – he could see she was getting herself ready for bed – but he felt he had to do it. She let him in, a little surprised.

He apologised, he said he just couldn't go to sleep on the story he'd just heard, he had to speak to her. In twenty-five years of driving he'd never betrayed the confidence of a passenger. But Seamus wasn't just a passenger. Even if he'd only met him that day, he looked on him as family, for he was the son of his best and oldest friend. And, yes, it's true, he wasn't the only one guilty of betraying a promise to stay silent – Seamus had made this promise to her too. But hadn't they all by now had enough of silence? What good was it? Look at what it does to people. That poor boy's mother kept her silence only to see the folly of it on her deathbed. And what about Seamus himself? He'd been placed in a prison of silence at birth, and he was still in it.

'Let him out, Katie,' he said pleadingly. 'I'm sure that's what Frank would want. It's what Seamus wants. That's why he went looking for you.'

Katie fretted with her hands. 'It's Frank I'm thinking about. Sure, you know the way they are here.'

'Times have changed, Katie. Nobody minds about those things now. You'll see yourself if you try.'

'Frank never told me, Bobby.'

'He didn't know!'

'He never told me he'd been with a married woman. He kept that as his secret. Thirty years together and he never said. Whatever about the town, aren't married people supposed to tell each other everything? It makes me think I never knew him.'

'I won't try to speak for him, Katie. But maybe he thought it'd only upset you. It didn't mean anything to him once he'd met you. He loved you. And he was loyal. He never knew he had a son. He died not knowing. That's the problem with secrets, Katie.'

'I know that,' she said.

He watched to see if she'd say more, but she didn't. 'At least think about it.'

She sighed deeply. Finally she nodded. 'All right, Bobby. I'll think about it. But that's all I'll promise you.'

After that, life appeared to return to normal. Katie resumed her Thursday outings to the town. She sat up in the front seat and chatted to Bobby. She was in good form, telling him about her talks with Seamus and what she learned about his life. Once she described their visit to Enisgilligan Castle and their very nice dinner in the Enisgilligan Hotel.

'I linked Seamus by the arm on the way in. He looked so handsome and he was so nice to me, making sure my roast beef was done exactly the way I like it. He also told me that he has a girlfriend. He's going to bring her down to see me. Her name is Fionnuala. But she can't visit until her Christmas break. She's a nurse in the Mater in Dublin.'

Then that autumn Katie had a bad turn. It was during one of Seamus's visits. Bobby was on a day off and he was helping Seamus to cut the grass for Katie – the last cut of the year, he said – when she collapsed in the kitchen. Dr Magowan was sent for and he ordered Katie to stay in bed. Rosie took charge. Bobby and Seamus were confined to the front room. When Dr Magowan left, Rosie came down to tell them that Katie wanted to see them in her bedroom. They went in silence up the stairs. Rosie ushered them into where Katie was propped up in bed. She smiled at them.

'Don't worry,' she said. 'I'm not dead yet. And I don't intend dying for another while. But I have something to tell you. You too, Rosie,' she said, waving her hand to stop Rosie as she went to leave the room. 'Come here to me, Seamus.'

She took Seamus's hand as he stood beside her bed. 'Seamus and I discussed what I'm now going to tell you. He wanted you to know that he is my stepson, Frank's boy. I am very proud of him. It's taken me a wee while to come to my senses. Frank would be very proud of him also. Seamus is a good lad. And now that he and Fionnuala are going strong, I'm sure he won't be wanting to keep any secrets from her. Couples shouldn't have secrets. Me and Frank never had. Frank always tried to do the right thing.'

She looked directly at Rosie.

'Before we were married he told me he had a baby to another woman but her father sent her away once she fell pregnant. Frank could never track her down, or her baby either. He didn't even know if it was a boy or a girl. It was a cause of great sorrow to him. But as we all know now it is our wonderful Seamus. So there you are. I'm doing the right thing for Frank after all this time. And for myself too. And I don't care who knows. In fact, the more people who know the better.'

She smiled at the three of them.

'Oh, Katie,' Rosie exclaimed tearfully, 'I don't know what to say.'

You will, thought Bobby. That's precisely the point. He smiled at Seamus and shook his hand. Then he leaned over and gave Katie a hug. 'You did the right thing, missus. Well done.'

Bobby winked at Seamus. Seamus grinned back at him. Katie was still holding Seamus's hand.

'Well,' Rosie scolded, 'that's enough excitement for today. This wee woman has to rest.' She shooed the two men out of the room.

'That's some woman, that stepmother of yours,' Bobby said, as himself and Seamus made their way downstairs to the kitchen. 'I didn't see it coming. In one fell swoop she brought you into her family, she protected her husband from being seen as a latchico, dropping babies around the landscape that he didn't even know about, and then she made sure the news would spread without her saying a word.'

'How'd she manage the last part?' asked Seamus.

'Rosie. Everyone in the parish will know by tomorrow. Rosie can't help herself. And you're OK with what Katie said?'

Seamus paused for a minute before replying. 'I'm just glad she's happy,' he eventually said. 'She's protecting Frank's honour to the end. But she's also protecting herself, and at her age that's important too. It was hard for her to come to terms with me telling her Frank was my father. But she did. As we got to know each other, she relaxed with me but she was always in a quandary about how she would explain it all, so I suggested she say what she did. Frank never knew I was his son, so who's to know what he may have done if he had known. That's all in the past. I'm happy that Katie is in my life and she's happy that I'm in hers, and now she's content that everyone knows. It's not the full truth but that's OK. It's nobody's business anyway. We know the truth, and that's what's important. A wee white lie is better than a secret if that gives Katie piece of mind. You know, she could have sent me packing. She didn't. She welcomed me in and she's helping me to know my father. Some people aren't so lucky. So that's to the good.' He smiled. 'And I also got to meet you, Bobby.'

They parted for the night on that note. In the weeks after the news about Seamus spread throughout the town, Bobby would reflect to himself every so often as he manoeuvred the bus up and down the road. It was hard to believe that Frank lived out his full life with *his* secret, oblivious of the other secret, the one known only to Seamus's mother – that Frank was the father of their son. But that's the thing about secrets, Bobby thought. They don't always stay secret, even if the full truth doesn't emerge. And what is truth anyway, he thought. Maybe we all make our own truth.

And the thought of Frank, when they were both young men, in Dublin acting like the fly man in the love comics made Bobby smile. Not a word out of him on his visits home when he and Frank met up for a night out. Then Bobby would chuckle to himself. 'You'd think butter wouldn't melt in Frank's mouth. The sly dog, the sly dog.'

UP FOR THE MATCH

The Cube and Wee Root were great mates. They were born on the same day in the Royal Maternity Hospital on the Falls Road in Belfast so if ever the term lifelong friends applied to anyone it applied to these two. They went to Saint Aidan's primary, a very fine school which grounded them well in the three Rs before turning them loose into the wider world of wage earning and fiscal challenges. Probably on account of being thrust together at birth, the Cube and Wee Root were mired in each other's way of going. They never ever had a falling out. This is not to say that they didn't have differences of opinion. They did. Quite often. But any altercation between them rarely lasted more than a few minutes. This was mainly down to Wee Root's easy-going, quick-to-make-up disposition. The Cube would be the first to acknowledge that.

'What are you having, Wee Root?' the Cube asked. 'A pint?'

'Indeed and I will,' said Wee Root.

Billy the barman wiped the top of the bar counter and waited for the Cube to give him his orders. One time he had made the mistake of anticipating the Cube's requirements. His offering of two pints of Guinness had been summarily dismissed with great scorn by the Cube.

'It's nice to be asked,' the Cube had said, 'or to wait to be asked. Who ordered those pints, my good man?'

'That's what youse always drink,' said Billy.

The Cube had stared at him for a long minute. 'You should never anticipate the customer's wishes. I mean, if this was a barber's you wouldn't just hack away at the customer's hair, now, would you? Or if this was a restaurant you wouldn't just serve up the meal. No, my good man, you would wait to see what nature of haircut was required or what the customer wanted to eat. In a good restaurant you might give the customer a menu. You might even explain the culinary options. Or the specials if there were specials. But not here. Here you don't give the customer any option whatsoever. Here,' he had declared, warming to his theme, 'here you don't ever give the customer his, or indeed her, place. In this pub the customer gets no respect. So much for the customer is always right. Such a yarn.'

'What do you mean?' Wee Root interrupted him. 'What do you mean her place? Who is her?' he asked.

They were leaning against the bar. Wee Root was on the high stool. He had been there most of the afternoon.

'Why are you staring at me like that?' Billy the barman had challenged the Cube.

'I'm trying to get it through to you that you have to treat customers with respect.'

'So you don't want these two pints ...'

'I never said that. I said you should not anticipate the customer's wishes.'

So after that, Billy the barman always waited until he had very precise instructions on how he should proceed. Billy was like that. Contrary. But then Sullivan's Public House was like that as well. Its clientele seemed to like it that way. Although they would never admit it. Especially Wee Root and the Cube.

'Two pints of Guinness, please, Billy.'

'Coming up,' said Billy.

Wee Root smiled at the Cube. 'I got a few quid off the dole,' he said. 'Enough to take us to the hurling final tomorrow. What do you reckon? You up for that?'

'We've no tickets!'

'Don't worry about that. We'll get tickets in Dublin and if we can't we'll watch it in the pub. Are you up for that?' he repeated. 'I'll treat you. Okey-dokey?'

'How did you get money off the dole?'

'They gave me a grant to attend my uncle's funeral in Glasgow.'

The Cube took a long sip of the pint that Billy the barman had set before him. 'Ah, Billy,' he said with a smile, 'that's a great pint.'

'Thanks,' Billy replied. 'We aim to please.'

Wee Root put a twenty pound note on the counter. 'Get yourself a drink, Billy,' he suggested magnanimously, 'and another pint for me and the Cube. Will you have a second pint, Cube?'

The Cube downed his glass. 'As a wiser man than me said one time, "In for a penny, in for a pound."'

'I'm sorry about your uncle,' Billy the barman sympathised, wiping the top of the counter. 'Was he sick?'

'Aye,' said Wee Root. 'He was very poorly.'

The Cube waited until Billy the barman had returned, out of earshot, to his stand at the Guinness pumps. 'I didn't know you had a sick uncle in Glasgow. I didn't even know you had an uncle in Glasgow,' he said quietly to Wee Root. 'When's the funeral?'

'It was yesterday,' Wee Root replied, opening the local paper at the page of death notices. 'That's how I got the grant.' He tapped one of the notices with his finger before handing the newspaper to the Cube.

The Cube read the item closely. *Mickey Magee. Died at home after a short illness. In heaven now with Auntie Kay. Deeply missed by his loving nephew Aloysius Magee and family circle in Belfast.* He set the paper back on the bar counter, took another thoughtful sip of his pint and then turned slowly to Wee Root. 'Auntie Kay? Uncle Mickey? Loving nephew Aloysius? Are you having me on? You weren't in Glasgow yesterday. You were here with me except for the time you went out to the bookie's.'

'Keep your voice down,' Wee Root scolded him.

'Are you trying to tell me you put that death notice in the paper? That you made it up? What kind of man are you?' the Cube continued in a horrified whisper.

Wee Root looked at him for a long, slow minute. 'The kind of man who is buying you your second pint. The kind of man who will bring you to the All-Ireland tomorrow.'

'How much did you get?'

'That's for me to know and for you to find out. I got enough for a return ticket on the boat to be at Uncle Mickey's funeral –'

'You don't have an Uncle Mickey!' the Cube hissed at him.

'Do you want to put that in the paper? Is that what you want?' Wee Root retorted. 'I'm away off home before you tell everyone my business,' he snarled uncharacteristically at the Cube and, pushing back the high stool, he stormed out the door of Sullivan's.

Billy the barman looked at the Cube curiously as he set the two pints on the counter. 'Will he be back for this?' he asked.

'Nawh,' the Cube replied. 'I'll have it for him. Leave it there.' He raised the glass slowly to his lips. 'He's upset about the uncle. The two of them were very close.'

'I never heard him mention an uncle in Glasgow,' Billy the barman remarked, wiping the counter carefully.

'Aye,' said the Cube. 'His Uncle Mickey was in the 'Ra. He was on the run. Keep it to yourself. That's why Wee Root rarely mentioned him, God rest his soul, the poor man. He was one of the good guys.' He raised his glass in salute. 'Here's to Uncle Mickey. One of Ireland's finest sons,' he intoned.

'God rest him,' Billy the barman replied reverently. 'I'll not say a word,' he added. 'Tell Wee Root his secret's safe with me.'

'I know that, Billy. Uncle Mickey told Wee Root one time that you are a sound man. He told me that.'

'Well,' said Billy, reddening with pride, 'I did my wee bit. But whatever you say, say nothing. Walls have ears.'

The Cube reached across for Wee Root's pint and sipped it slowly. 'Sláinte,' he said. 'Whatever you say, say nothing.'

Billy the barman nodded, his face still slightly red. It's nice to be acknowledged, he thought to himself as he wiped the counter yet again before moving off to serve another customer.

Later, on the way home, the Cube called to Wee Root's house. Wee Root was sitting in the living room. 'Brrhhh!' The Cube saluted him cheerfully, anxious to make up after their slight misunderstanding. After all these years he'd learned from Wee Root the value of reconciliation, particularly when a day out in Dublin for the All-Ireland was at stake.

'It's bitter cold out there,' he volunteered, sitting down beside Wee Root. 'But it's cosy here.'

'Aye,' said Wee Root. He was seated in front of an electric fire. 'There's great heat from this yoke,' he acknowledged.

'Is that a new one?' the Cube asked, stretching his hands palms out towards the heat.

'Nawh, it's my brother's. Mine is broke so our Jimmy lent me his.'

'I'm round to see what time we're going to the final tomorrow.'

'Oh, you want to go now?'

'I never said I didn't want to go. Of course I want to go. Who wouldn't want to go to the hurling final? It's just I thought we had no money, or tickets for that matter.'

'Well, we'll let the tickets look after themselves,' Wee Root replied. 'We have the spondoolicks so it's you and me is for Dublin in the morning. An early rise is required, mo chara, so be off with you. I'm for bed now, so I am.'

The Cube stood up. 'Thanks, mate,' he said. 'It'll be a great game tomorrow. I fancy Cork. By the way, you'd need to turn that fire down. Them electric fires will run your bill through the roof. They're really expensive to run.'

'I fancy the Cats myself.' Wee Root smiled at the Cube as he left him to the door.

'And don't worry about the running costs of the fire,' Wee

Root called after him. 'I told you it's our Jimmy's. It's not mine.'

The Cube turned to reply. Then he stopped himself and bade Wee Root goodnight. 'See you tomorrow, mucker. Slán.'

'Slán a mhic,' said Wee Root, smiling to himself as he bolted the door. 'Up the Cats.'

They got the train to Dublin the next morning. No expense was spared. Two premium seats in first class. There was a big hurling contingent on the train. Gaels from the Glens. Tight wee hard hurlers from Dunloy, Cushendall and Loughgiel. Oul' boys from the Ards Peninsula. From Portaferry and Ballygallet as well as from Belfast, from the Falls Road and Ardoyne and Hannahstown.

The Cube and Wee Root fell in with Bungie and Big Bootsie, along with Wee Bootsie, his father. The son was taller, though when they were younger this wasn't the case and the father was Big Bootsie, but as his son outgrew him they exchanged nicknames. Head the Ball, Stinking Head, Duckser, Dark Cloud and Sambo were there also. Hurlers all. Back in the day. And the older they got and the more pints they scooped and the more spoofing they did, the better they were. Back in the day.

As the train sped through Antrim and Down and the green rolling countryside slipped past they feasted on big cooked breakfasts. By the time the train got to Newry all concerned had demolished black and white pudding, soft fried eggs and dipped soda bread. That, with bacon and sausages, was the very best companion for a slow swallow of Guinness. Nothing too intoxicating. No rush. These were men of a certain age. Lapsed athletes. Gaels. They knew how to pace themselves so that the drink enhanced what would be a long day. The big game was the main event, not the drink. So their journey southwards was shortened by the very best of banter and craic. And not a cross word between them. Wee Root was moved to confess that he could stay on that train and in their company forever. The hurling fraternity is like that. If you are in then you really are in. Hurlers stick by each other.

'I would never go to Croke Park by car again,' he said.

'Yup,' said the Cube. 'I remember the time Daithí A drove down for the football final. He had his wee dog with him. He was parking in a side street off Dorset Street and a wee lad came up to him as he was getting out of the car.

'"Mister," he said, "do you want me to mind your car for a tenner?"

'"No, son, thank you. I'm gonna leave my wee dog in the car. He'll bark his head off if anyone goes near it."

'"Is that so?" the wee buck said. "Can he put out a fire?"'

By the time they got to Drogheda all the talk was about tickets for Wee Root and the Cube. Everyone else had a ticket or the firm promise of one, but despite a few frenzied phone calls, by the time they reach the outskirts of Dublin Wee Root and the Cube were still ticketless. Not that they were too worried. Wee Root hadn't been in Dublin since Tipperary beat Antrim in the final. He reminded the company that on the day Antrim beat Kilkenny in the semi-final in Casement Park Gerry McGeown had dropped dead.

'It was the shock,' Wee Root declared. 'Wee Gerry McGeown worked the cloakroom in the Plaza dancehall and he wouldn't give you your coat if you didn't have a ticket. He used to drive fellas mad. They'd be rushing to try to leave a girl home and wee Gerry would keep them waiting. Many a young woman was saved on account of his diligence. He had a lisp and he would shout "No dicket! No doat!" That's all he was ever called. No Dicket, No Doat. Anyway, when we beat the Cats he collapsed and died on us. Under the stand in Casement. Despite Dr Pearse Donnelly's valiant efforts to save him. The shock was too much.'

'I remember that,' Bungie recalled. 'Poor No Dicket. And I remember during the final that Tipp destroyed us. Nicky English was on fire that day!'

'And Seanie A climbed up on the top of the old Nally Stand with an anti-extradition banner in protest at the Free-staters sending the lads back to the North and he had it upside down. We were all shouting at him to turn it the right side up and he thought we were cheering him on.'

'Aye,' said Stinking Head, 'that was Seanie A for you. If it was raining soup he'd be out with a fork, but not a bad lad for all that. A dreadful hurler, though. His cousin Gerry A was a lovely hurler. So was Gerry's older brother Paddy A. Paddy was small. He had a low centre of gravity. Could turn on a sixpence. Great stick work too. A mighty man for pulling on the sliothar on the ground.'

They all agreed that ground hurling was a neglected skill. Soon their train pulled into Connolly Station. Wee Root was glad to be back in the capital where all these adventures had happened. He and the Cube parted company with the rest of them at Summerhill. The Cube had arranged to see his cousin in a pub there on the chance that the cousin would have tickets. He didn't, or at least he only had one and that was his own, but they had a pint together anyway and caught up on all the family news. Then as the cousin, Brendie O'Hara, was leaving he caught sight of a man rushing through the public bar.

'Hiya, Sammy!' Brendie called after him.

Sammy turned and seeing Brendie he smiled broadly. 'Me old segotia. What's the story, Brendie?'

'Any tickets, Sammy? This is me cousin from Belfast and his mate. They're stuck for a ticket.'

Sammy eyed Wee Root and the Cube as he and Brendie embraced. 'From Belfast? I'd love to help ye, lads. I was to see two boys here to get them into the Hogan Stand, but I'm late. They must have left. That's why I'm rushing.'

'Russian? I thought you were Irish. A Dub!' Wee Root joked. 'Do you want a pint, comrade?'

Sammy smiled at him. 'A comedian,' he smirked.

'Don't heed him,' the Cube intervened hurriedly, 'he's only joking.'

'So am I,' smiled Sammy. 'That's a good one. I'll have a double wodka and coke. Comrade.'

'What's a wodka?' Wee Root whispered to the Cube.

'A wodka is Russian for vodka.'

'I thought he was a Dub. Why is he talking Russian?'

Brendie intervened before the conversation became too complicated. 'The two boys you were to meet?' he asked Sammy. 'You said you were to get them into Croker, into the Hogan Stand. Could you take our Cube and Wee Root instead?'

'It wouldn't work with them. Their accents is all wrong. And it'd cost them forty quid.'

'I'll give you fifty,' said Wee Root.

'Well …' Sammy hesitated. 'But ye'll have to keep your mouths shut. Let me do all the talking.'

Wee Root and the Cube nodded their assent.

'You can trust these two,' Brendie vouched. 'Ballymurphy men. Used to keeping their mouths shut.'

Wee Root sealed the deal by handing Sammy fifty quid. Sammy finished his wodka and signalled for them to follow him. Once outside, he handed Wee Root and the Cube two steward's bibs. He donned one himself. 'So just follow me and not a word outta your mouths.'

The Cube bade his cousin farewell. 'Thanks, our kid,' he whispered.

Wee Root gave him a thumbs up and together they fell in behind Sammy who was making his way authoritatively through the crowd which thronged towards Croke Park. The rest was easy. Sammy ushered them through various gates. Soon, to the Cube's delight, he was positioned close to the Ard Comhairle box in the Hogan Stand. Wee Root wasn't far away. The two best seats in the place, as the two of them told everyone afterwards. And the game was a humdinger. An epic display of hurling with the Cats triumphing in the end.

That night in Sullivan's Billy the barman greeted the two returning heroes with two pints and two glasses of Bushmills whiskey. For once the Cube didn't upbraid him for not waiting for their order. The truth was that Billy's warm welcome touched them both. It was a perfect end – well, nearly the end – to a perfect day. Wee Root and the Cube were in great form by this stage anyway. They climbed back on the high stools as Billy poured himself a large Jameson Ten Year Old. When he had that done he snapped to attention behind the bar.

'Here's to Uncle Mickey,' he said, raising his glass in salute. 'A true patriot.'

The Cube and Wee Root stood erect and raised their pints in unison. 'To Uncle Mickey,' they chorused.

'And to Billy,' the Cube added. 'A sound man, as Uncle Mickey put it.'

Billy the barman smiled proudly. The Cube clinked their glasses together with a flourish. Wee Root joined them. 'What a great day we had.'

'Sláinte,' they said.

In unison.

ACKNOWLEDGEMENTS

My thanks to Michael O'Brien for publishing these stories and for his great patience. He has waited for six years since first we agreed that I would write them. I am pleased that *Black Mountain* is published under the Brandon imprint. I have a huge grá for the now-defunct publishing house founded by the late Steve MacDonogh who published my first books. Michael O'Brien's kindness in sustaining the Brandon imprint in tribute to Steve is greatly appreciated.

My thanks to everyone in The O'Brien Press for their support, especially Ide Ní Laoghaire, who edited a few of my very first drafts. I hope she enjoys the final selection. If they meet her approval, Timothy O'Grady deserves a lot of the credit. So does Emma Dunne, who came in with her gentle editorial advice where Ide left off. Many thanks, Emma, and to Emma Byrne also for her cover design, and Mal McCann for his photo.

Timothy is one of our finest writers. His *I Could Read the Sky* is one of my favourite books. A classic. When he learned I was almost finished this book of short stories, Timothy offered to look at them for me. His advice has been invaluable and I enjoyed very much our long telephone conversations in the midst of the pandemic – he in Poland, me in Ireland – as he coaxed me to develop some of my characters or to speed up or slow down my narrative. I like writing but I do it only as a sideline and in stolen moments of occasional spare time. Timothy's tuition enriched the writing experience for me. I learned a lot from him. Thank you, my friend.

Mo buíochas, finally, to Colette, Drithle, Luisne and especially Anna and Ruadan for their ideas. And their mammy and daddy, Gearóid and Róisín.

I write a lot as part of my political activism. Speeches, blogs, orations, letters, articles, discussion documents and draft strategy papers, ably aided and abetted by my leader, friend and comrade Richard G. McAuley. I consider that to be work. This is my hobby. It is also one of the very few publications of mine that R.G. has had no involvement with. I dedicate it to him with thanks and in appreciation of his friendship and his activism, and the nine years we were exiled together in Dublin and Leinster House. We survived that. I think. Maybe someday he will write his own story.

USEFUL CONTACTS

A number of sensitive issues are discussed in this book. Below are contact details for organisations that can help if you are affected by any of these issues.

Domestic Abuse

Republic of Ireland

Safe Ireland has 38 domestic abuse centres across the 26 counties. Services are free and confidential and available to all women. You can find the service most convenient to you at www.safeireland.ie.

Safe Ireland freephone helpline: 1800 341 900.

Men's Aid Ireland confidential support line: 01 554 3811.

North of Ireland

Domestic and Sexual Abuse Helpline: 0808 802 1414; email help@dsahelpline.org.

Rape Crisis Northern Ireland information and support line: 0800 024 6991.

Women's Aid: go to www.womensaidni.org to find your local Women's Aid group.

Suicide Prevention

Republic of Ireland

Samaritans: confidential, non-judgemental support available twenty-four hours. Freephone: 116 123; email jo@samaritans. ie; www.samaritans.org.

Pieta provide a range of suicide and self-harm prevention services. Freephone 1800 247 247 anytime day or night; Text HELP to 51444; www.pieta.ie

Hospital and emergency services: if you, or someone you know is at immediate risk of harm, go to or call the emergency department of your local general hospital. You can also contact emergency services on 112 or 999 anytime, day or night.

Visit www.yourmentalhealth.ie for information on how to mind your mental health, support others or find a support service in your area. Information line: 1800 111 888, anytime day or night, for information on mental health services in your area.

Save Our Sons and Daughters (SOSAD): 041 984 8754; www.sosadireland.ie

North of Ireland

Lifeline, a crisis response helpline service for people who are experiencing distress or despair: 0808 808 8000.

Public Initiative for the Prevention of Suicide and Self-Harm (PIPS): support service for people who need intervention or for those who have survived suicide loss. Phone: 0800 088 6042 or 028 9080 5850; go to www.pipscharity.com; email info@pipscharity.com

Samaritans freephone: 116 123 or 0330 094 5717.

Extern Crisis helpline: 0800 085 4808; email CrisisTeam@ extern.org

Other books by

GERRY ADAMS

Before the Dawn

A unique, intimate account of Adams's childhood
in working-class Belfast and the turbulent years of
social activism that followed. This engaging and
revealing self-portrait is essential reading for anyone
wishing to understand modern Ireland.

'*A definitive history of the Irish struggles of the
1970s, from the nationalist point of view. Adams, a fine writer, presents a
straightforward, unapologetic memoir.*' Publishers Weekly

Cage Eleven

Along with hundreds of other men, Adams was
interned on the *Maidstone* prison ship and in Long
Kesh prison during the 1970s for his political
activities. *Cage Eleven* is his own account –
sometimes passionate, often humorous – of life in
Long Kesh. Written while he was a prisoner, the
pieces were smuggled out for publication.

'*Evocative and often witty cameos of prison life.*' The Times Literary
Supplement

The Street and Other Stories

Eighteen short stories that reveal the humanity and
indomitable spirit of ordinary people caught up
in extraordinary events. These moving accounts of
the fictional characters are set against the political
turmoil of Gerry Adams's native Belfast.

'He brings a wry humour and a detailed observation to small events …
If there is a unifying strand, it is compassion for people in difficult situations.'
The Sunday Times

Also available from

AN IMPRINT OF O'BRIEN

The Dead House by Billy O'Callaghan

Perched on an incline, with the land spilling down
to a glittering sea, sits a ruined cottage. It calls to
Maggie Turner, who is running from her own
demons. But this house has a long, grim history, and
has known hard living and far too much death. In
some places, some things are better left undisturbed.

'A moving work that builds to an elegiac climax and is a welcome voice to the
pantheon of new Irish writing.' Edna O'Brien

And by author Frank McGuinness:

The Woodcutter and His Family

In Zurich, a writer breathes his last, imagining his life till now from his childhood in Dublin. The voices of his family – wife, son, daughter – carry him to his end as he hears each separate chapter chronicling the power of their passion for their famous father, their love, their hate, their need, their sorrows and joys, their strangeness. And James Joyce has saved for them one last story: The Woodcutter and His Children ...

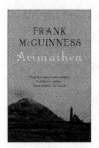

Arimathea

It is 1950. Donegal. A land apart. Into this community comes Gianni, a painter from Arezzo in Italy who has been commissioned to paint the Stations of the Cross. The young Italian comes with his dark skin, his unusual habits, but also his solitude and his own peculiar personal history. He is a major source of fascination for the entire community.

Paprika

In his first collection of stories, master storyteller Frank McGuinness writes above all about freedom: freedom to love, freedom from hate, freedom to speak, freedom to silence. In hypnotic, spellbinding prose, he hears the voices and sees the visions of his own troubled times.

'Prose that could be described as musical ... Elegant and thoughtful, often funny, never dull or repetitive.' The Irish Echo *on* Arimathea

At War with the Empire
by Gerry Hunt. Coloured by Matt Griffin

From the author of *Blood Upon the Rose* comes a graphic novel depicting the guerilla war against British rule in Ireland. *At War with the Empire* brings this turbulent era of Anglo-Irish relations to life with colourful artwork and lively text. It details the Declaration of Independence in 1919, the leaders involved in guerrilla warfare across the country, the groundbreaking signing of the Anglo-Irish Treaty of 1921 and the effects the Treaty had on Irish politics.

'Masterly. Will appeal to the younger generation ... but it is still a serious history of the war of independence.' Books Ireland

History's Daughter
by Máire MacSwiney Brugha

The amazing life story of Máire MacSwiney Brugha, daughter of Terence MacSwiney. Taken by her mother to Germany after her father's death on hunger strike, she was reared as a German girl for years before returning home to Ireland to live in the Gaeltacht with her aunt. In 1945, she married Ruairi Brugha, the son of another famous republican, Cathal Brugha, thus uniting two of Ireland's most prominent and revered nationalist families.

'A beautiful book with captivating pictures telling an extraordinary life story. A moving and highly unusual memoir.' Irish Independent

Sinn Féin by Brian Feeney

The fascinating story of a political party which has repeatedly reshaped its identity over a hundred years. From Arthur Griffith to Gerry Adams, Sinn Féin boasts a roll-call of major personalities from 20th-century Irish history including de Valera, Markievicz, Collins, Ó Brádaigh, Goulding, MacGiolla, and McGuinness. Brian Feeney traces Sinn Féin's zigzag path towards constitutional politics and presents a critical analysis of the party's personalities and policies over the century.

'Diligently traces the party through its various incarnations from the loose grouping launched by Arthur Griffith in 1905 to the slick machine of today. Feeney's work is clear, thorough and fluently written.' The Sunday Business Post